Bambina

Francesca Piredda
Bambina

The Porcupine's Quill

Library and Archives Canada Cataloguing in Publication

Piredda, Francesca, 1956 –
    Bambina / Francesca Piredda.

ISBN 978-0-88984-295-3

    I. Title.

PS8631.I77B35 2007   C811'.6   C2007-904138-8

Published by The Porcupine's Quill, 68 Main St, Erin, Ontario NOB 1T0.
http://www.sentex.net/~pql

Readied for the press by John Metcalf.

Represented in Canada by the Literary Press Group.
Trade orders are available from University of Toronto Press.

We acknowledge the support of the Ontario Arts Council and the Canada
Council for the Arts for our publishing program. The financial support of
the Government of Canada through the Book Publishing Industry
Development Program is also gratefully acknowledged. Thanks, also, to
the Government of Ontario through the Ontario Media Development
Corporation's Ontario Book Initiative.

ONTARIO ARTS COUNCIL
CONSEIL DES ARTS DE L'ONTARIO

Canada Council   Conseil des Arts
for the Arts   du Canada

To Gil

To Giulio

To my friend Eugenio

1. June 23, 1970

Aboard *Chanteclair*. Flying the Panama flag, on dock at
Civitavecchia, one hour north of Rome. Place where somebody,
Stendhal or Chateaubriand, went to be vice-consul or something
like that. It's the Martellis' boat, or yacht, as they would say in
Paris Match, I'd die before calling it a yacht, knife please, I will
explain another t. I liked the idea when Dad suggested it, no, *told
me*. But reality is different, reality is many disagreeable real details
put together, in one bundle.
      Why me here. Two weeks ago, my parents were invited for a
weekend sailing by our semi-neighbours Martelli. Drove to the
marina, here, in Civitavecchia, but weather is bad so they try to
pass time, go visit something, go to the restaurant (they had fish)
and finally spend the night at anchor, in hopes the weather would
improve.
      They were: Maria Sol and Claudio Martelli, Marie and Jacques
Laliberté, and my parents. Rain next day, melancholy, drive back to
Rome discontented, and Claudio still has this invitation dangling.
He wants to show off his boat, he wants to have my parents. By
then, it's the end of June, the invitation has been renewed. Daddy,
rather than having to endure the lugubrious shilly-shallying in case
of bad weather again, has made up his mind that he actually
dislikes boats. But what to say? Idea. Who needs to learn the ways
of the world, no shoes on board, civility at close quarters, what to
wear and all the rest? Eugenia. Daddy says he unfortunately has
urgent business matters and suggests they take *me* over to Ponza, etc.
      The only reason I accepted is that Tommy, my boyfriend, said to
Phil, friend of mine, that he may go there, 'this summer', *Pownzza*,
in that accent he has. He did not tell *me* directly, we don't keep close
communications, this is my first more grownup boyfriend (we are
both fifteen) and I am a provincial, I am not an expert, I make of
necessity a virtue, do you say that in English? Not for us the family-
like atmosphere of fifty mopeds and motorbikes outside the school
gates of the Lycée, where, to listen to Andrée's reports, everybody
notices everything, shifts in *bise*-giving, and moped rides. Tommy

and I go to different schools, boys-only and girls-only, and until now we have met only at two parties and another time. I tell myself it's all right, some unhappiness is fine if you think of that crazy heartbeat that lifts you to the stars when you look at the sky at night. Here it goes again. It's a good thing that hearts are not visible. It's not official that he is my boyfriend. Fine too, better.

The adults are the top tormentors. *'Eugenia, ce l'hai il ragazzo?'* the question you will hear a hundred times, from the day you are eight till about twenty-five. It's asked by all servants and familiar people, and by casual (uncouth) acquaintances, who want to appear modern. 'Do you have a boyfriend?' Actually, if you are a girl, they'll stop earlier, it's for boys that the rude intrusion continues forever. It's mean because suppose you don't have one, you are likely not to have had too many, therefore you are shy about it, you think you are a zero. It's mostly the servants, joking among themselves, when you go by, capturing you. After all, they clean our clothes, wash our bathrooms, make our beds, we irritate them so much, they don't mind taking a small revenge. Ah, kill them, strangle them, they are so annoying. And, when summer comes, *every summer:* 'Did you pass?' (not the servants – they know very well, they've heard the recriminations and the admonishments), it's generalized, *anyone* will ask, the grocer handing you a paper bag, the janitor's wife. This is a strictly Italian mania, this nosiness about school results, again, suppose you didn't pass, how are you going to say that, I flunked? Yes, I passed. My school is not Italian, but French, in Italy. I'll be in *première*. Be prepared to answer this a hundred times for the next weeks. Not that it was easy, there was a lot of debate about it, my marks were not that bad, but there was concern about my maturity (something to do with one of my brilliant ideas). Suspense to say the least. Did I suffer, did I hide in the shade, away from the telephone! A merciful veil, please. And of course it was too late to *do* anything. On one side, the summer and all the rays of the sun, on the other the embarrassment, the curved shoulders of the immature not admitted to *première*. All the while hoping that Daddy would come up with something.

It's partially in exchange for the trouble I gave him that he said I must go on this *irresistible* holiday. Also there was a bit of uncertainty, at home, a hiatus as Aunt Valentina would say. Instead of the familiar transshipment to Capri. I only know my family and the Chéniers are all coming together on the Côte d'Azur, near St. Tropez but better. We are specialists of the better. And I'm going two weeks to England, in August, to a new riding school, with Elsa, and Vanna of course, she sticks to me like glue. Otherwise, we'll be at the new house, at the farm, we have a swimming pool and horses, it's practically a resort, said that idiot the other day – ha ha. Daddy has rented the house in Capri, he says we have so many other things to do now we are older.

So I'm here on *Chanteclair*. I have brought my diary, flapping its little sails in the wind. It has monstrous gaps. I wonder how Simone de Beauvoir wrote her book. She looks like one of those women who wake up early and work hard. With something *more*. Carlo Martelli too has his log to keep, as captain. I wonder how much poetic licence he has. 'June 22, 1970. I am on the bloody expensive boat with Maria Sol and the kids, and sulky Eugenia, and Carlo Silva, my new lawyer. At least I have Pablo, bless him, thank God for good skippers, at least I don't need to keep him happy and he'll take care of the boat and perhaps catch something interesting for dinner.'

I hope nobody's going to use my swing, under the trellis, in Capri. There, I can talk to myself, weave and unravel. Dream, fantasize, talking to yourself – all ridiculous or forbidden. I knew it – the skipper turned to look this way, he must have overheard me. I'm going below deck.

Nobody has invented a way to record thought. Ginestra's father works in something rather secret called electronic brains, but it's not the same, I think. The transcription of thought. Kilometres of transparent tapes, swirling in a closed room. 'That's where I keep my thoughts.' Think of the photographs of cars that pass fast in the night, slowed down, captured in one filament. Tracks of movement. Compressed statements of the unimportant, the common. A car passing, then another. Just wonderful. *Rêverie* – everyone is your enemy.

OK. The program is: Ponza – home. Then, Sainte Maxence – home. England. Home.

Reveries (1)

2. Inside the shoe closet –
With Mummy at the couturier's

We are going to look at dresses. It's delectable. I'll have a whole
morning with Mummy, and she'll be swishing in and out of lovely
boutiques, with a faint perfume of hairspray, the eyeliner precisely
above the curve of her eyelids, and she will take bills and bills out
of her purse as if nothing was more natural. I run up and down the
hall to her door and back, with little embellished steps I have
learned in my ballet days (but I don't go to ballet any more).
Mummy is not ready yet, so I'll go and explore the shoe closet. You
almost need a guide, like for the Pyramids in Egypt, to take you by
the hand. A guide, a guide, I'll find one for you, ladies and
gentlemen, he is a famous professor, Monsieur Radisson, of La
Sorbonne, in Paris. Here he comes, in his black gown:
*'It's a small chamber, windowless (we are well inside the
Pyramid), with a sloping ceiling. As you walk in you can stand,
but as we proceed you will have to stoop ... Note the numerous
shelves on two sides, painted white. Women's shoes are kept on
display, for use in the various occasions of daily life, and
ceremonies. Pumps, booties, sandals, slippers, espadrilles
(typical of the* bassin de la Méditérranée, *classic colour, dark blue).
This is a stiletto slingback in mother-of-pearl pink kid leather, a
classic afternoon shoe dated 1965, from Grilli (Rome, Italy), a well-
known maker situated on Via del Corso, employing Venetian
artisans.'*
  My favourites are made of grey lizard ('Iguana,' says my
brother Piero, he is one year younger than me, 'or *possibly*, young
armadillo'). But the clerk said lizard, without blinking. (A foreign
lizard, unlike ours, a lizard who didn't mind to be made into shoes
and matching handbag.) Tennis shoes too, well scrubbed by
Nannina. Sandals from Capri, suede booties too, with a little bow
at the side for tying, not buttons, 'Summer boots!'
  All our shoes are here. Here, we are a family. My father's shoes,
black or brown, with laces, and perforated little designs, some
smoother, some more rigid. There is one pair of light moccasins
(which are worn without socks, at the seaside), and riding boots,
brown, quite new. Sand shoes ('For the desert', he says, smiling)

and a special pair, triple-reinforced, yellowish, bought in Berlin, which makes a special creaking sound, squeak-squeak. He wears them when we go to the countryside, or when visiting building sites, and if it's cold he'll also have his loden coat on, green outside, yellow inside. In some pictures, next to engineers in business suits and blue coats, he has an air of 'I know you don't know, this is the exact proper attire for this occasion. I have a pure conscience.' Daddy.

He's always saying things like that. 'At the beach, one wears primary colours; no sleeveless dresses in town, in the daytime.... When you go to a horse show ... at a wedding ... when you ... the proper shoes ... Moss Bros in London ... Magli`... Old Scotland ... Emilia Bellini for embroidered linen ... Leri for school uniforms ... Zingone alla Maddalena ... Giolitti ... Berardo ... plum cakes ... ties at Borsalino ... marrons glacés, candied violets ... salt almonds....'

Mummy's name is Marie-Hélène Ceccomori, and she is dressed by Luciani, no no, it's not her nanny, it's her couturier. Although sometimes she buys things at Randy Bennison's, and here and there. Wait wait wait. I mean, for town clothes. When summer comes, there are others, who really belong to the summertime, they use great dashing colours and lighter fabrics, and prints, which they call *fantasie*, but also, we go to Capri, a place that has its own fashion, and – I'll explain. This is the city and now, at the end of winter, Mummy is shopping for spring clothes.

Tonino dropped us off near the Hotel Hassler-Villa Medici, at the top of Via Gregoriana, a little out of the way from the crowds. Here, shops are supremely elegant, and we are conspirators, the habitués who know that this afternoon, above the Luciani boutique, on the second floor ... Mummy is greeted with smiles and I make myself invisible behind her, I worry because my name was not on the invitation but I know I shouldn't. We sit with other ladies (and one man) on upholstered chairs on the sides of a parquet path. There is a sort of Madame la Directrice, in a black long-sleeved dress, serious, with little tortoiseshell glasses. Perfumed with art. Models appear at a special door, then walk through the room, with that rhythmical step, almost a dance, opening the tailleur's top with one hand, showing off a stole, showing their shoulders under a coat. They behave like in a ballet for men, although this is not a men's place. The Directrice reads from a little note.

'For our spring collection, we have created a playful yet classic style with contrasting materials *ton sur ton*. "Mimosa", a morning tailleur in coral pink, silk wool shantung, on a sleeveless blouse in printed muslin, appliqué pockets, gold woven buttons. "Vanessa", ivory crepe, sleeveless cocktail dress, with oversized bow above the shoulder blades. "Anne-Marie", afternoon suit in lightweight wool, Prince of Wales check, three-quarter sleeves, straight skirt, shawl collar.'

The models walk, stop, turn, walk, coldly looking ahead, coldly appraised by the clients. I hear the language of their legs, crss-crss, a friction between their knees, the embroidered trims of their petticoats rustling, the fine grain of their stockings connecting, trembling like the wings of bees.

Over. The ladies open their handbags, pull out their enamel compacts. Make funny faces as they dab their powder puffs on their noses, furtively. Apply lipstick tilting their heads – cowboys interrogating the barman, with cold empty eyes.

3. Waiting in the car – The snack bar –
   The ladies and the guide

Another summer has begun, whether we pay attention or not, weeks in advance. This is Rome, and Rome, if you have eyes, is on offer all the time, with nuances of weather and light that combine with the architecture, the fountains, the piazzas. The Eternal Tourist, so often from a colder climate, walks the streets, cheeks pinkened, yes, pinkened. You are an Englishman at dawn, in the early morning you are a Pole, in the afternoon you are French. At dusk, looking from a bridge, you are longing for love. You walk, and if you have eyes, a naiad beckons among splashes of water. By a portico, you reach out to touch a column, the grain and the curve, and it's cold but alive.

School is not out yet. In the morning, we look into our drawer for a cooler pair of socks, Pure Scotia thread and hope for the safe return of our old white cotton shirts, long-sleeved, yes, but cooler than the fake 'DuPont percale' which so torments our necks, I would not have thought it of the nuns to modernize the uniform, but the shape of the new skirts has changed, too, from pleats to kilt. A kilt, never. There are short-sleeved uniform shirts, Vanna got one, once, by mistake. My mother thinks they are unbecoming. Our cool shirts must be at the bottom of the wrong trunk. Hearing of this, my grandmother pleaded for more *attention*, care, love of things, attention to durability, preservation. She was trying to explain how satisfying it was to have order in all things. 'Marri-Élenn, the personnel cannot be relied upon to do these things. They must be shown how to …' and arranged to come the next day.

* * *

I was left waiting in the car. 'Just twenty minutes, Gengia, you have all your schoolbooks to read …' and she walked away. Twenty minutes, it will be an hour. Twenty is close to thirty and a big half hour is close to an hour. 'I'm going to the naturopath.' Not the herbalist, it's near San Luigi dei Francesi, and we are behind Santa Maria Maggiore, I think. My mother is a believer of beauty promises, not so different from the maids, who believe in Leocrema, Felce Azzurra and Cera di Cupra, the funny beauty products sold in tobacco shops and advertised in some gossip magazines. Only hers are spelled out in more elegant names.

The car was getting hot, and double-parked.

If the *vigile* in his white summer uniform and safari hat comes dangling his whistle, I'll die.

I'll tidy up the traffic tickets and the mess in the glove compartment.

She did not go in that little bar, did she?

I'm dying of thirst.

* * *

It's not a pretty bar. You go in through a sticky curtain of plastic beads. Sitting at wooden tables there are a few clients, bricklayers and market sellers in their work clothes, who have come for wine and a game of cards before heading back to the suburbs. By waves, imprecations erupt, greasy cards are slammed and an espresso machine wheezes. The ferocious bar owner – let's call him Cat-eater – draws damp bottles from a refrigerated box and holds them by the neck, uncapping them in slow movements.

From the back room, the ladies can hear only the loudest roars of the players and the familiar noise of small motorcycles darting forward.

Under a small baldachin of shimmering material, the fattened little prophet, the baby-adult sits on three ascending silk pillows. She wears muslin, pink knickerbockers and white-rimmed sunglasses. Her voice comes from the nose, circling from the sky, surveying the world and its fate from unfathomable altitudes high above.

'It was a day when all soufflés would burn, and stockings get large rents....' The ladies in little black dresses sitting on chairs around her nervously touch their pearl necklaces. 'Nobody would be spared. Chauffeurs could not find an open gas station, cooks would quit just before dinner. Poodles would get bad trims. Coffee shops ran out of almond croissants. Shoe whiteners everywhere dried up in their bottles.'

'But where was She?' asks a pretty young woman with dark bobbed hair, anxiously leaning forward, her legs crossed. 'Why wasn't She...?'

But here, answers are sought, not always found. The guide has retreated inside her bubble. The ladies get up, calmly click open their lustrous pocketbooks, take thousand-lire notes and put them in a basket held by a stout woman in black, round-faced (how do you say donnone facciatonda, femme omasse, she-man?). They leave the room from a side door. The guide remains in her bubble, eyelids closed.

* * *

Sometimes I scare myself! Mère Marie Léon says that if I take the trouble to check my facts I will be able – she said I could be a journalist. This was about a very bad written test on Napoleon. She said it with reluctance. Maybe she had to confess afterwards. I blushed, but how could I accommodate more time for lessons? All I cared for was the compliment (as opposed to the expected reproach). Compliments are odd.

4. Menu for a spring luncheon

Jellied eggs Juliette
Lobster salad
Galantine of chicken
Bavarois à l'orange

'*Maria madre santissima!* ... What is this?'

Rosalina reads the menu Madam wrote for tomorrow and fidgets. She objects, first, from a philosophical point of view, because this stuff is not good, hearty family food, and also she is worried at having to do some difficult manoeuvres, making jelly, finding lobster (Madam, would some nice scampi do as well?). As for strawberries, to decorate the dessert, there are none to be found, except, counted as rubies, and just as small, in tiny baskets of nothing at all, and so expensive. And for that she'll have to send the chauffeur all the way to the deluxe shops of Via della Croce.

Here he comes, Alfredo the chauffeur, with sleek hair, greasy or dirty, it is not known. 'When I went to Canada, over the sea, in those *supermarkets*' – giving the word a personal flavour, he saw the really authentic ones – 'they have the biggest red strawberries, in large baskets, super-baskets, all the time.' 'And now you're going downtown, not to Canada, right away,' says Rosalina, flourishing *downtown*, the overseas of the maids and cooks, a place of prestige. She pushes towards him a coffee, as she is expected to. And Alfredo, as he is expected to, although affecting not to hurry, puts on his blue raincoat, meticulously tying the belt, checking the breast pocket where he keeps the car's papers. On the landing of the service elevator, he can be heard whistling to himself – what a malfeasant bantam cock! (Rosalina) In the garage, he smokes with abandon one of his Astor super-filters, then continues his protest by speeding all the way through Ponte Flaminio, the Olympic Village viaduct and Viale Tiziano, windows rolled down – another victim of Madam's lunch.

'Eugenia, come here, you promised ...'

Put my book face down, slowly follow Cook. I agreed to help deciphering the recipes for Rosalina, who reads slowly. This is the price to pay for building up my prestige, telling all those stories of

restaurants and wedding lunches, and having given Rosalina
fabulous accounts of white gowns and buffets. So I am an expert.

First, the apron! I have my own, green with a white trim, with
a white and yellow embroidered little donkey with his cart. Aunt
Valentina brought it back from Portugal.

Then solemnly washing hands at the big marble sink.

'Eugenia, will you stop all your ceremonies?'

'Repeat after me, Rosalina: "Vacherin" ...'

'What is this, a lesson in the tongues? You think I have time to
waste? Va-sce-rré,' she sighs.

'Bavarois?'

'Ba-varuah.'

'*Va bene, allora*, it says: you need two large, fine oranges; two
large sugar lumps. We begin. "Wash and dry the oranges. Rub the
sugar lumps until they are *impreg, impreg*, im-preg-nated with
orange oil." Mash the lumps in the bowl. Grate the orange rind
into the bowl. Squeeze the juice. Now the gelatin and set aside.
That's it.' The bowl goes in a corner of the grey marble table.

'Now the *crème anglaise* – Rosalina?' I lift a finger like a
singing teacher, waiting for a note.

'Cremm anglé.'

'It's just a custard really, Rosalí, you know it, with seven
yolks.'

Rosalina is gathering speed. It's true, she can make a lovely
custard. She cracks the eggs cleanly, catching the whites in an old
enamel cup. She puts up a bain-marie, and airily turns the custard
with a wooden spoon.

'"Mix the custard with the gelatin mixture. Beat egg whites
until soft peaks are formed." *Dai*, Rosalí, go.' Rosalina has got into
her stride; the whisk going in long and luscious strokes.

'"Fold with the custard," it says ——. Now make a Chantilly.
What is a Chantilly?'

Rosalina has given up all resistance. She has the air of a
bulldog captured by children and submitting to being dressed with
an apron and a hair bow. The cream turns into a cloud.

'Now, Rosalina, what you should really do is add a bit of
orange liqueur, but please, please, can you not put it in? It gives
me the goosebumps.'

'You want the death of me, child! You know your mother ...'

'Oh, Rosalina ... can I have some, tomorrow? And some cookies...?'

Rosalina sends me away with bread, butter and sugar.

Then she takes a little bowl, pours some of the custard in it, covers it with a saucer, puts it at the bottom of the Frigidaire. She pours liqueur on the rest of the *bavarois*. And a little glass for herself.

5. At home, bored – Geneviève –
Catalogue of the school's girls

A grey afternoon. For nine more days I have to stay home in case I caught Piero and Vanna's measles. In Italian, it sounds fun: *morbillo*. '*Moor-bill-oo, moor-bill-oo,*' Piero hisses like a ghost when he walks about in his slippers and dressing gown, his face very pink, looking like a small grandfather.

They have come down with spots and I must not go near them. I am not sick. I think I am immune.

The house is inanimate. I feel convalescing from something. Maybe I am not immune. I think of all the school I am missing, and how, after all, I would prefer to be there. I have been told, vaguely, 'Of course, you must keep studying,' but how? Why? Would now be the time to start studying properly, to catch up on dozens of important matters such as the composition of the soil and the affluents of the Rhône? Where would I start? The weight of all my derelictions chokes me up.

It's half past ten, recess, right now, and my friend Geneviève must be walking alone, with that calm expression, thinking, contented with her thoughts, or maybe talking to Mademoiselle Danois, who supervises us, recess bell sticking out of her knitting-bag.

We became friends imperceptibly. Maybe she remembers exactly the first time we said hello, as things tend to be clear in her head, she is *première de classe*, in absolutely everything except English. She arrived from Vienna one September, with one of the waves of new girls, because her father had been posted at the French embassy.

Wed Mar 26-08 1:30pm

Acct: 3790 Inv: 452921 T 00

Qty	Price	Disc	Total Tax

808898842953 Bambina

| 22.95 | 1 | | 22.95 1 |

Subtotal   22.95
Tax GST   1.15

Items   1 Total   24.10
Cash   24.10

===== Frequent Buyer Status ==========
edit earned with this purchase $ 2.30
tal credit on your account... $ 4.63
nimum required for redemption.. $ 10.00

GST# 867714131

I must have told you, my school is French, but a French school in Rome, which makes it an international school, a large aviary where many species are gathered, the the French, the foreigners, the Latin Americans, the cheerful ones, the aloof, the quiet, the silent, the complicated.

The main reason foreign girls come to Sainte-Marguerite is that their fathers have been posted to Rome; otherwise, they are sent from abroad, by parents who are half French, or belong to a *zone d'influence française*, or are Catholic. French girls whose parents live in Rome usually come to Sainte-Marge because their parents tend to be strict, or very Catholic, or worried. After all, they could be going to the Lycée Delacroix, the French public school; or, even to l'École Belge, but that would be rather unFrench. But if your parents, French, strict Catholic or *comme-ci comme-ça*, absolutely insist that you go to a French *boarding* school, then ours is the only choice.

Those were the French. If you are Italian, parents and all, the main reason is languages. As a boarder, you'll be surrounded by French, and learn a second language (English, your third), and maybe Latin. *Le lingue*, the languages. They are key to the World, the Future, it is not clear how, since being an air hostess is not what they have in mind, you can see it from the way they let the subject drop. They look away, don't pursue it. To be a hostess: tall, beautiful, smiling, to speak three languages, to be travelling all the time, what could be better? Unattainable, yes, if the daughter is not growing tall and beautiful. Maybe that's what it is, too wonderful to hope for.

So both your parents are Italian, and wealthy, because money is necessary to pay the 'outrageous tuition', as Santabarbara puts it, she knows all these things, and makes a fuss when the classroom is not warm enough. Behind all those names in 'a', Elena, Nicoletta, Giovannella and Marina, you can be assured, there are fathers who are industrialists, doctors, in the liberal professions, princes, or just naturally wealthy, *and* have given consideration to the matter of their daughters' studies and future. Which means they are fairly intelligent, or snobs. Except that my father always jokes about *jeunesse dorée* 'who know languages and nothing else' (but he doesn't mean us).

Last October, we had a spiritual retreat to prepare for Advent, a small one, not like going to Assisi for three days, visiting monasteries etc. So even we non-boarders slept overnight at school, sharing a few large rooms. It was a very exalted evening, we were supposed to think and pray, whereas we were eating shredded coconut, brought by me, and chatting away, with my friend Alberta, and her sister Maria Laura and other big girls.

We decided to straighten up the subject with a detailed list. 'A reasoned catalogue to the girls of Sainte-Marguerite', Maria Laura, with her little gold glasses at the tip of her nose, found the name for it. We wrote it down (I was writing).

100% reason for studying here:
French or French-speaking girls, Catholic, whose parents live abroad, can't take care of them, no local boarding schools or war, civil war.

0% reason:

('We have a tie, Honourable Members of the Academy,' said Maria Laura, strangling herself with laughter.) Foreign (neither French nor Italian) girls who are sent to a foreign land and a thirdly-foreign language, AND the one-hundred-percent Italians, who are just coming here to learn French.
'No, no!' interrupted Émilienne. 'It's those whose parents speak absolutely not one language in the world!' (She meant not a language apart from their own, which was true, but I mean, we could not give them less that 0% reasons to be here.)

0.5% reason:
The French who have been sent away from France to study in French!

(Émilienne: 'Absolutely no-o-thing strange here?...')

50%:
The French girls living in Rome, the half-French, the quarters-French, the French colonies, the French-influenced.

(Fifty percent because they had a chance out of two of attending the other French school, the Lycée.)

Émilienne said we could have done it much more simply, with a tableau, and I gasped with admiration. Everything, I thought, could be put in a tableau.

In my bed afterwards, throwing back little pinches of coconut, I thought after all I was in a category of my own, since both my parents speak French and my mother is French Canadian. And I also live as an Italian.

Afterwards, we always joked among ourselves about 'the catalogue'. But after taking it home, the next day, I never brought it back because the nuns would not be amused if it was found – as that kind of thing always ends up being *'confisqué'*, you understand, right, confiscated, falling *tac*, like a guillotine, and that would be just the beginning.

But there is a reason for even the zero percents. For instance, Emily Rauchembach got sent here because she needs a warmer climate. Her parents are English, and don't speak a word of French; she knows absolutely nobody in Rome, except for the school, and a friend of her mother, who dresses in funny colours and sometimes picks her up for weekends. Or Corinne Petitpas, she does live in France but her father is a lyrical tenor (not famous like Di Stefano, but very good, says Daddy, even better) and travels all the time, with her mother, so maybe they thought that being in Italy would be a sort of nice travelling for Corinne, too. And Milena Moranti, who arrived from Sweden in fourth grade without speaking one word of French, who was not actually a foreigner, since she was returning to the original country of her (Italian, non-French-speaking) father. He is an engineer, of a travelling kind, and there are many more French schools than Italian, in the world. It's funny, no, why?

Couldn't all these people stay home or nearby and stop making all this confusion about where they live and where they'll go next? No, they all like to *go*, and to come back.

In addition. If your parents live in Rome, you can be either *externe* (and, like Vanna and me, go home at four thirty), or *demi-pensionnaire*, a five-days-a-week boarder, who goes home on Fridays. The others are full-fledged *pensionnaires*. They go home only at Christmas and Easter, like Myriam Bernatchez, her parents live in Teheran, or Catherine, who normally lives in Ibiza, she's been a boarder here for ages. Or Leila Melançon, she comes from Lebanon, her parents have sent her here with her little sister Mercedes because there is a war.

They all come here. I find it hard to believe, but Sainte-Marge is one of the most attractive schools. It has a good reputation and good, old-fashioned, prudently modernized nuns. Cultured, well-informed. Pious, of course. The grounds, the lawns, the rose-bushes, the well-maintained buildings in a mix of brick and travertine stone. Last year, two medium-sized swimming pools were built, and a second (hard) tennis court. From my desk I can see the two gardeners eternally fishing out leaves from the water, and tending to the roses. For many girls, especially the hardened boarders, this is a very nice place. The constraints, the uniform, good behaviour in class and politeness, studying, attending church, are to be expected. Many girls are – happy, or not unhappy.

I can't compare, I've never been anywhere else for school (after at least two jardins d'enfants – where they made experiments on children's education.) Then my mother chatted with one of her French-Canadian priests at some party and heard of this burgeoning school. At the same time, Ginestra's mother was having tea with one of her old friends, whose husband works at the Holy See, and ... Did I tell you mine was the first name on the register *here*, and Ginestra's was second, which makes her my oldest school friend. A school that not even *existed!*

On dull days, when Ginestra and I drag our feet about in the courtyard, laughing hollowly about our destiny, the absence of freedom, of pleasures, of variety, we excogitate ways to obtain some consideration 'as explorers, discoverers and founders'. Something eatable at lunch, that would be a start.

6. Matilde – Tales of Sardinia – Easter – Rosalina in charge – Intimations of the supernatural – Cicerone

Matilde is the new chambermaid, before, it was Assunta. She sleeps in a room by the side of the kitchen, her bed hides away in the wall, and there is a gilt grille to let air go in the hidden space, as if the bed was a prisoner needing air. The room is also the ironing room, with an ironing table, a counter, baskets, but everything goes back to bed, hidden away, in the evening, when Matilde's bed comes down.

'In Sardinia, *anima bella*, there are tiny fairies, beautiful, some are kind, some mischievous and disgraceful. They keep large treasures, boxes full of jewels, gold coins, rooms and rooms of precious fabrics, brocades, silk of all colours and patterns. They live among ruins, *nuraghe* – you know *nuraghe*, your grandfather surely has told you ...'

'Those round towers.'

'To be protected, you carry coral beads like mine,' a little branch on her gold chain.

'In our town, we have feast days, Nostra Signora del Rimedio, Easter, we all walk over to the convent, up on a hill, and we talk and eat – we bring some food, then there are food vendors bringing milk and sweets, and we dance ... Oh, the women dance in a circle, you know the *costume sardo*, with their skirts whirling, and nice black bodices, and their embroidered blouses ... And if you climb up to the top, far away, there is the sea.'

But if all is so beautiful down there, why did Matilde come here? Maybe she heard about the fine shops in Rome? Or someone told her to come here and take care of us? Maybe she heard we needed her?

Dear Donna Anna,

I received your letter, only twelve days it took. Rome is big and beautiful, tramways and cars everywhere. The master yesterday took me to the Social Security and had all my papers done. Tell Zia Monina I will send the money order we agreed on the first of the month. The position is good. Please remind me kindly to Don Armando, Maria Flores and Antonio Salvi.

My best salutations.
Matilde Sunna

In her spare time, Matilde embroiders my parents' bed linen. She has already finished a top sheet and two pillowcases of byssus, most people don't know what it is, it's a very fine flax fabric. She made little garlands of pale yellow flowers. It's funny because I don't think my parents know how difficult it is to embroider and to make the reverse look smooth. My grandmother (the Italian one), she knows, and how she said that Matilde was *brava*, the 'r' trembling with emotion. It's because my grandmother is a hard-working woman herself, and brava to her means, hard-working, skillful and good-hearted, it all goes together.

Now Matilde is gone to Sardinia for Easter. She told me she'd take the train to Civitavecchia, then the ferry to Dorgali, then a coach to get through the mountains to Sassoli. She wore a blue coat, her hair in a white foulard. She looked like one of the big girls at school, who looks like Heidi, with dark curly hair in a thick braid, just arrived in town from the Swiss Alps.

* * *

And I was left with only Rosalina for an audience. My parents had gone to Paris for five days, and my brother and sister were with the *zii*. Rosalina, finding herself in charge, was full of prohibitions and rules about Easter, and made me want to be horrible and wriggle away in utter revolt. She said, it was forbidden to eat nice things until Sunday (when I can open the big Easter egg I know is hidden somewhere); I couldn't play any modern music on the big record-player, as for herself, she would not listen to any *canzonetta* on her transistor; I probably should not read any pleasant book, just catechism and prayer books, or do my homework.

I stomped away to my room, with dignity, but soon found I was bored. *I did not*, like Sophie (of *Les Malheurs de S.*), start cutting up the goldfish or shaving my eyebrows. I only worked a little on my bangs, with uneven results. *I did not*, like Sophie, capture lost flies to put them on pins (for which she was made to wear a collar of dead flies). Poor Sophie, her stepmother (No. 2), whom she fears, is a horrible selfish woman, and her adoptive mother (No. 3), whom she loves, is a firm educator, rewarding meanness with meanness. I did not either, like Vanna when she was four, climb over the terrace railing and promenade on the catwalk while the concierge Ovildo paced below, half fainting, half kneeling, yelling to alert the household but trying not to scare her into jumping from the fifth floor. Forever people of the palazzo will pinch her cheek (softly, that's how you do it in Italy to say you love someone) and say, You are a proper holy terror, which she quite enjoys.

I cried from behind my closed door: 'You don't know anything!' and picked up *The Sheik of Alexandria* ('for 13 and up' but it's easy). Rosalina says the Madonna will be displeased, so will God, and so will the curate.

'Which curate?' I asked, knowing there is ambiguity there. 'The one at school, the French abbé, or the Italian one?'

'Why, the Italian one!'

'Ah? The one of Via Cassia Nuova or the one of Ponte Milvio?' Since my parents take us to both, uncertain about their allegiance, unenthusiastic. 'Or the one at the farm?' triumphantly.

She would have liked to run after me and do I don't know what, but *I had paralyzed her.* She was so upset that she had to check herself. She made gasping sounds and I retreated.

But I was uneasy. Big names had been invoked, and I felt the menace of them. It felt like watching on TV, on tiptoe, immobile, behind my father's armchair, *Belfagor the Dark Master.* My parents say I am impressionable. The scary music, the Egyptian statues lit from behind, the steps in the night, it scares me. There is nothing on TV, nothing, just words, sounds, fogs, lights, darkness, used by some puppet-master to make us fearful. So if Rosalina says the curate won't like what I do, I fear him, but only because I am impressionable. Not because he knows. What he says is like music hall, TV, *The Count of Monte Cristo,* the theatre.

The Madonna, too, has never been seen to scold someone. She is, on the contrary, always interceding, wherever you go, whatever her name: Santa Vergine del Rosario, Santa Maria d'Aracoeli, Santa Maria di Loreto (all Italian parrots are called Loreto – surely she rescued one, or did the parrot rescue her?), Santa Maria Antiqua, Santa Maria in Cosmedin, of the lovely incomprehensible name, S. Maria in Trastevere (the one old Romans love), Santa Maria dell'Anima, S. Maria della Pace, della Vittoria, S. Maria Maggiore, S. Maria degli Angeli. I go to churches all the time because my parents like to be helpful to foreign visitors. Though they don't invite them to sleep at home. *Chez nous.* Where we sleep. Or perhaps the hospitality could not be elaborate enough, since we have no proper guest room. 'Things must be done right, or not at all.' But there will be cocktail parties, dinners, summer suppers on the terrace. My mother will meet them at the airport, at the station, flowers are sent to their hotel rooms, they are taken for dinner at picturesque restaurants with serenading guitarists, photographers, flower girls. Semi-private audiences in the Vatican are obtained. And when it comes to sightseeing, my father has a ready reply: Eugenia is an old Roman, Alfredo will drive you and she will be your guide.

They want to see the fine churches, the fountains they set their hearts on as they read travel guides on rainy afternoons in Baltimore or Toronto. I try to keep them away from San Pietro, which everybody wants to see. I hate bigness, I hate San Pietro. Visitors *want* San Pietro, either because of the religion or because of the architecture. My brother Piero was christened there. The nannies all write home about it. It's supposed to be very majestic. Christened in San Pietro, even named Piero! He's the top, and what a family to work for!

So off I go with Zia Filomena and Uncle Fred ('Filo and Fred from Philly!' as they say – famous for calling together on two telephones), Yvonne Laledit, the Bonneterres, the Plaxtons (my favourites). 'Eugenia speaks very good French and very bad English,' as Daddy says, but I manage. And I know the language of Italian manners. Convince the taxi driver to wait for us, order things at the snack bar, take shortcuts through the city, sometimes guided by the sound of a fountain, or the memory of an ice-cream parlour. I know where to find lavatories (called *toilettes* to make it sound refined), mostly at cafés, or at some of the best hotels. Just imitate my mother who walks in as if she was a client. Nobody ever asks a thing.

'If you are in Rome for only two days,' says the guide *(Rome in 2/3/4 Days)*, menacingly. Better wear good shoes, although the ladies will always complain of sore feet. Take a lot of snapshots, otherwise you will not be able to remember, in the speed of the conquest. *Dear Nicole, do you remember when we had an ice-cream cone?* We sat on a little wall, under the Gianicolo, there was a drinking fountain, and the steps of the horses slowly drawing carriages on the cobblestones, and ruins, little terraces, wild greenery growing here and there, pink and red geraniums on some balconies, the greens and browns of the shops' shutters, closed at the height of the heat till four thirty.

7. Walking with Dorly – The Swiss guards –
   Madame Ceccomori gets her driving licence – In St. Peter's –
   The ordeal of the parables – Interrogation – Holy images

My mother takes me everywhere. I am an accessory. 'Little girl of the lady.' 'Lady with her little girl.' She prefers that to 'Lady on her own'. I heard her say 'Men are annoying, in Italy.' The foreign nannies (called *signorine*, to differentiate them from the maids, who only have a first name) say that, too. The men on our side of the fence make serious faces and agree.

My daddy has given plenty of instructions to Dorly when she first arrived from Berne. Not to go near Termini, the train station, when she crosses the town to visit *la zia suora*, her aunt nun near the Vatican. Not to speak 'if men make comments'. For goodness sake, NOT to answer, which would be difficult anyway since she only speaks Swiss German and a little Swiss French. But she is nice. Dorly looked puzzled, you can see that a girl from Berne is on the contrary told to be very friendly and hospitable, the Swiss are the champions of tourism and hotel courtesy and always will answer if asked for directions. Dorly too used to take me with her, I seemed to be a shield, the glances of men would bounce back, they would just say a little something, a compliment, they would not insist, insist.... It does not matter that we don't know them, or that they are dusty, white with chalk and wear paper hats, they have this privilege, of saying things to women who go by, and never to be caught. They are eating their sandwiches on some old stone, and murmur,''a bbbella', like they were sheiks or pashas. It's a kind of teasing, the kind you can't respond to otherwise you'd look ridiculous, and you could not anyway, since you don't know them, and what would you say, it's unfair, that's what it is, like mocking someone who can't fight back.

One day Vanna was playing with her new wooden telephone. She said, 'Alloo, vant to speak viss Hans Linter, Svviss Gaard.' The Swiss German accent was just right. Vanna looked up to the adults, for the usual compliments. Instead, they were silent, thinking, concluding but still hesitating at the conclusion. *It was not the aunt, it was a Swiss Guard.* My little parrot of a sister had revealed the true aim of Dorly's errands to the Vatican.

I don't remember when Dorly, like all others, went away, but at least once, in a dream, I saw her again, in front of her pretty chalet, happily waving to her Swiss Guard, coming home from work in St Peter's, climbing the mountain in his uniform, long thick stripes of yellow and black, using his halberd as a walking stick.

* * *

As Mummy's accessory, I've been to the concert, and to the charity bazaar, and to ballet auditions. She knows when all sorts of things happen, the address and all. She has a little white book for ladies just like her, it's sold at a special charity tea, with all sorts of special addresses, and dates of other teas. She does not need an interpreter, as Daddy says with a tone of absolute objectivity, 'Ellie learned Italian within six months,' and she knows Rome very well, that is how she first came, she was a student of history of art visiting from Canada. But she does not understand everything.

At the petrol station, she calls the attendant 'tu', as if he was her friend, or a little boy, instead of the necessary distant 'lei', and it's not that she doesn't know the difference, it's the same in French, *tu* and *vous*. And she mixes up the imperative and the infinitive. So she will have a way of being both imperious and familiar. 'Boy, *senti*, listen, you do the fill-it-up. *Super, niente normale*, OK?' And I look afar, in embers of embarrassment. My dad does not know this thing of the petrol station, because of course she does not drive, if he is in the car. He drives, shoulders bulging above the backrest, his glasses on. I sit directly behind him, my nose on the grey velveteen of the upholstery, looking at his gestures, careful and precise. The same way he lights a cigarette or closes a door. I hear his shoulders click, at times, the rubbing of his jacket against the lining of his coat.

Ellie tried many times for her driver's licence. So much so, that the news of her final passing was greeted with considerable enthusiasm. Rosalina came to the terrace to hear, too, warned by Alfredo who, driving my father home, had been told. It was a nice spring day, when the sunlight feels like sea water in your eyes. Daddy was very pleased, Mummy made her Sphinx face, with a touch of 'You see?'

Now that she has her licence, she can do things her own way. She drives as if she was alone in the city. She parks anywhere, often disengaging the fenders from something. She does not see traffic lights particularly, neither green nor red. She will stop, then start again, resolutely, often with a hard-handed shifting of gears. So often that even in the intricate traffic of Rome, she gets caught.

The police carry a special tool in Rome, a disc attached to a handle, painted red and black like a bull's eye. It prolongs their arm, and saves them from being chopped off. It's called *paletta*, and gets waved in front of the car they want to stop, with a terrific whistle-blowing. From the back of the car comes the anguished cry of the children: '*PALETTATA!...*' She had been pinched.

'*Documenti!*' is the curt request. She'll start by pulling out some old Canadian pale green paper (as an initial statement that she is a foreigner, to show that *in my country...* wanting to sound freshly arrived, and road regulations don't really apply to her). The policeman does not read or speak English. He is from a small village. He is intimidated by this elegant blond foreigner, in a large Lancia, carrying two respectable children. '*No, no, ma senti...*' ('Boy, *senti*, listen!') More searching of papers in her crocodile bag ... in the gloves compartment.... The policeman is now dizzy, confused. She shows splendid bad faith, we at the back also are getting confused, mothers cannot lie, she is saying the truth, she did not see the light, a truck was ahead of us, she did not notice her *abbaglianti*, the blinding high beams were on – she starts fumbling, tries all the buttons on the dashboard, in distress, do *you* know how to turn them off? – she did not hear the police following us and did not see the *paletta*. (When she did stop, abruptly – and the car sighed, she extended her right arm to keep the child in the passenger's seat from hitting the dashboard. It's very kind, and she does it even if the seat is empty.)

We shrink behind the seats, feeling a sense of reverse

orphanship, we want no such mother, she's dangerous, maybe she should be taken away, we feel bad, we feel sorry for the policeman.

ALMOST KIDNAPPED

As I said, Mummy and I often go out together. Without Daddy, without the others. We went to a ceremony in St. Peter's. Such a distance to go from the point Tonino dropped us off, behind the barriers, through the square, over the cobblestones that repeat over and over the pattern of a fan. By the entrance on the right, walking behind a crowd, slowly, in the shadow. I was carrying Mummy's bag, very proudly, and she was holding the invitations and her thick black prayer book, almost as large as a Bible.

We were progressing very slowly towards the main altar, among hundreds of faithful. People were silent, or would murmur if necessary: it's a church first and foremost. On my right, a man in a black suit insinuated his hand into mine, caressing, lifting my fingers one by one, finding the handle of Mummy's handbag, trying again, wordlessly, caressing my hand, as in a game well-known by both. It was an old hand, very soft, like my grandfather's, and I felt a sense of familiarity. I thought for ten seconds maybe he was a friend of my parents, someone I should know. Then I thought he wanted to steal the handbag, or maybe steal me. The problem of this ambivalence preoccupied me. I felt stupid. I did not *understand* him. Then my position became clearer. I felt the indecision was on his part, and he was being *impolite*. I felt resentment at this. But could it be possible that a thief or child thief would have been allowed inside St. Peter's? No, of course. The clerics in their marvellous embroidered white tunics (*rocchetto*, rochet, ratchet) had looked severe when they had verified our invitation at the door. So maybe he was a visitor. He had seen me in my little coat: a little girl he thought was sweet. Not knowing how to talk to her, because he was very shy, he thought that caressing her hand was going to win her over. But the way he tickled, touched lightly did not connect with joy. For a few more steps along the nave, I felt the man's loneliness, and leaned closer. Then I broke away, swinging a little ahead of Mummy, who protested I was in her way.

We finally reached our seats, on the top row of a fairly high wooden structure, facing a corner of the famous bronze baldachin that protects the main altar. Mummy took back her handbag, I opened the prayer book. The words of the celebrants did not connect with any recognizable feast or mass, and oppressed by boredom I decided to follow a parallel ceremony of my own, reading the Annunciation, Latin on the recto, French facing. Then turning the pages to find something new. Smoothing the thin cool pages, and their red edge. Moving the blue ribbons, trying to look knowledgeable. Looking for the few holy images Mummy keeps. And a sturdy, thorny variegated leaf, which I think comes from the Holy Land.

A clumsy movement, and the book went falling down with a sort of scream, through the scaffolding and into the tenebrae, into the catacombs probably, a fall without end. Maybe somebody found it one day, but in Rome, even in St. Peter's, what do you expect.

UNFAIRLY ACCUSED OF CHEATING

I find that God does not pay attention to many things. The thief in St. Peter's. Then the Catechism *composition*, where he should certainly have been alert and ready to save me.

This was in third grade, the year Cristina arrived. Mère Maria Amor, as our *maîtresse de classe*, was also in charge of Catechism. We were waiting for her to throw the subject of the test at us. She balanced herself a little on her soles, on the edge of the platform. 'Tell in your own words the story of a parable of Our Lord Jesus Christ.'

Now that was a wonderful *composition*. 'In your own words', what sweetness, what generosity. I was beside myself with joy, this was easy, I knew many, many parables in detail, it was going to be a wonderful composition. The dazzle dazzled me. I sparkled.

'Which one? Which story can I tell the best, in the most detail?' There were not going to be enough marks for me, I would have a mark to break all scales.

Nothing. My pen stayed up. I could not remember one story, one title. '*The fisherman and –* ' '*Jesus talks to –* ' It was terrible. Although I don't study very much, there are things I know *normally*, things that are part of my other life, at home. I *know* many parables. I like parables. But nothing came. All tracks got more blurred as I kept trying. I was slipping as on ice, my mind was empty. And MM Amor would pick up my copybook, see the empty pages, send me a wave of blame, immediately, then the scathing commentary when corrected work would be returned, then the mark on the report card.... At least four reverberations. And it was unfair, horribly unfair, I knew the stories but they did not want to come to me.

I thought I would have a quick look at the index of my prayer book, inside my desk. I only needed to remember one title and I would get started. I was not cheating, but I knew it should be done secretly. I found the book, and slowly opened it at the end, pulling it out, tilting it very cautiously, casting lightning glances to the text. Nothing. The text was blurred, the page was blank, it was not even the right page. I was desperate. I shifted. Amor must have been suspicious of my lack of diligence, and patiently waited. She now caught my sideways flashing glances, and was upon me in two elastic steps. She snatched my copybook. She was a guard, who had caught a trespasser, a thief.

There would be no possibility to explain. And, like the titles of the parables – oh! my explanation was spinning in my head, irretrievable. I could not find the words. And, now I saw, nobody would believe me. Until the bell rang, all was lost.

* * *

From my account, it may appear there is considerable illicit activity – tremendous undercurrents behind our brick walls and classroom windows, racking our modest, small-scale life (and we are still small, with the exception of Milena, who is tall and strong). Things do happen, but they are disposed of in a flash. The nuns apply a sort of DDT spray, neutralizing misbehaviour, without much commentary. They have clear, unwritten laws, and no occasion for appeal. I have never seen the Regulations. Discussing the school is much discouraged. Criticism of the ways of the school is called *faire du mauvais esprit*, creating bad spirit, a notion that nobody ever spelled out for me (and Ginestra doesn't know either) and we obscurely understand is shameful – therefore not to be talked about. To create, foment, entertain, perhaps in a viscous state – like a bacteria, a germ – a right to oppose.

Obscurely, too, most of us understand what behaviour the nuns would prefer we adopt. Obedient, polite, studious. But we keep bumping into unforeseen misbehaviours. For instance, why, by just *being there*, in front of her, does Catherine make MM de la Conciliation become pale and angry? Is it her sullenness? Her wounded meanness? Her shame? Shame of being. Why does it reverberate? What about when Stella and I hid in a lavatory, to avoid going to our *italien spécial* class? It was a substitute Mademoiselle, not our adored Anna-Maria. It was going to be boring. We would hide. Of course, we were looked for and found (Stella even kept pushing the lavatory door closed against muscular MM de la Paix). We knew that we should not have strayed from the stairs, nor resisted arrest. But what about the question: '*Avez-vous joué avec le corps?*' I said no, unconvincingly, unconvinced, not knowing what it meant: 'played with the body'. A corpse? I could see it was something very bad.

A NARROW ESCAPE

After all this anguish, these unfair accusations and condemnations, I witnessed a tremendous reversal of fortune, as unfair as anything.

I love holy images. I covet them. My throat feels tight when I see a new one I like. If possible, I steal them.

We each have a green-and-gold missal and a few images. We used to each have our little book, with prayers in Latin, and it did not matter what edition. Mine had etched illustrations. But last year, we all had to buy the same new book, all French and no Latin.

Holy images make the book's originality and value. Like charms on a bracelet. For instance, the parents of Italian girls have a First Communion card printed, which is given to girls and family as a memento. There will be a religious image, a line like 'Oh God, here I am, your little lamb....' The French girls soon started imitating. '*Souvenir de la première communion de Patricia Elizabeth Prouilly*', and the date. So we exchange those. Then there are images given by the nuns, at Easter, or at year's end. They may carry a religious thought, with an embellished first letter. The nun will inscribe it with your name, and a few words of her own. The nun hands it out to you gravely, and you are very serious. The nuns personally have no money and it's a big gift, I know they must save and plan who should get what months ahead.

Then we can buy our own, at the *boutique*, a weekly shop where the Mère Econome, and the Gym Mother, terribly business-like, briskly sell stationery, copybooks, French-ruled loose-leafs for *grandes* to do homework and exams on, pen nibs and religious trinkets: rosaries, crosses, images. It's held in the library every Wednesday at morning break, the nuns walk in quickly, dangling keys, open up drawers and take some of the goods out of cupboards. It's meant to be for boarders, but if you are an Externe they won't mind.

At one time, I had for months a fever to buy a small crucifix painted copper with a glued-on inset of plastic mother-of-pearl, the size of a child's hand, till I found the courage to ask for it. I would have paid double the price. I felt it was incomparably beautiful and that I was not worthy of it. Maybe it was the Christ's expression. Anyway I also *knew* others would declare it ugly (even Aunt Valentina) and that my father would doubt my 'eye', so I never took it out of my night table.

And the images.

There were just a few, at the boutique. A Sainte-Marguerite, austere in very contrasting black and white, unsmiling, in a sort of painted photograph of at least a hundred years ago. Then a few of the modern ones, with just the drawing of a fish (for Jesus being a fisherman of men) or a lamb, and inscriptions like the ones in the Catacombs, in beige, grey, orangey with a little white, like the decorations on Aunt Valentina's new Danish breakfast set. A lovely one in stained-glass with a cross and St. Francis of Assisi. But, although I had the money, I would not buy many images at a time – I felt each had to have its own moment.

I needed more variety. I started stealing images from the other girls. I would stay behind in the classroom when lunchtime came, or go back inside earlier than the others. The classroom was still. The prayer books were easy to spot, smaller than the rest. You only needed to slip your hand under one of the desks. There, resting among the pages, exploded the images. There would be Madonnas, Holy Lambs, Sacred Hearts, Little Communicants, scary black

Marys – mummies or statues, you did not know, Saints with their
Attributes and special flowers, and Christs. Without words, they
exposed their pure souls, then charged for the heart of the youngest
the simplest the most good with everything they had: Mary
Magdalene in her long hair and deepest repentance; St. Vincent
protecting a bare-footed child under his cape, holding a newborn;
Le Curé d'Ars (only the French know this one, I don't know the
translation) with a stern face glaring at a fire (that is, the Devil) …
Concentrated, precious. Colours! Gilt, and knife-cut lace-like
borders, sometimes embossed, ruffled and gilt-edged. Thick with
good-quality Bristol board, evanescent in see-through host-paper,
troubling to the touch, or glistening with photographic paper, *well
made* …

I would pluck them from their nests, immediately re-
acclimatizing them into my own prayer book, without trauma.
Mine became the image of Ste Bernadette in her azure cape, mine
the bleeding heart inside a palm tree, by a Caribbean seaside. Mine
the dark Madonna di Tindari, swathed choked bedecked in pearls
and jewels and silver hearts.

Apparently, no one else had such a passion for the images. No
querulous exclamations, not even from the most orderly of the
girls, the kind that made a fuss if you picked up their ink rubber
by mistake, no dramatic announcement was made by Mère Maria
Amor, about an abject epidemic, where the name of the Daemon
would be hinted at.

I was embalmed in my impunity. I thought nothing could
happen to me.

Nothing could happen to me. One warm, sunny afternoon, as
we walked from the classroom to the courtyard, with our prayer
books, to go to a special prayer in the chapel, I stumbled on the
door step, and fell. My book, by now fattened to porcine levels,
spilled its riches on the ground. I was caught red-handed, as bad as
Ravaillac murdering Henri IV in full view of everyone. Could I say
I had borrowed them to copy them? Could I cry that nobody ever
bought me any? Could I say that I dreamed of them, that I could
not live without them? No, I couldn't. I stopped breathing.

Some girls helped me get up and fussed over my grazed knee,
others (some of the very girls, I observed in a dark cloud that

clogged my brain, I had dispossessed) helped me pick up a myriad images, and in perfect good humour gave them back to me, without noticing. Only one comment, and calls of shrill recrimination would have turned into a chorus of infamy, which the nun would have interrupted with an almost wordless escorting to the director.

Nothing was said, nothing happened. The sun stopped blinding me and went on shining and encouraging, my saint protectors, Saint Affrique, Saint Gervais, Sainte Marthe reine, Saint Louis de Gonzague, Saint Stanislas, from their crypts, their ossuaries, from their little clouds, with a sigh, returned to their silent exhortations to be a good girl.

8. June 27, 1970

Back from my reverie.

Oh what a joy to be on *Chanteclair*, pale, un-tanned and lonely *and* crowded on all sides, impossible to stay in my cabin, too hot and sickening, impossible to lie quietly in the sun because of that sickening Carlo Silva, humming things like 'This Fine New Skin'. He runs his finger over my back while I am reading. I was pretending not to notice, I managed well, but I did shiver and he said, 'That was arousal, my dear,' things like that. He is monstrous. Pronouncedly wormish. With the kids, we agreed to throw him in the water, dressed and in the harbour, preferably, but he is suspicious and switches from blasé intellectual to watchful reptilian, and all of a sudden does not seem to like jokes.

* * *

We did get to Ponza, with the auxiliary engine, having wrecked the propeller. Claudio at the helm insisted on crossing between two rocks, the skipper kept begging, *'Por favor, capitán, por favor,'* and Maria Sol too. The more she tried to distract him, the more he kept going, a gleam in his eyes, his white cap on, looking quite beatific. So she put on a lovely smile and went to the bow, chatting with us guests, joking and offering mineral water. With the kids we had fun with the book of flags, wondering whether we should fly the Require a Tug flag, the I Need a Doctor (to check Claudio's head) or Require a Helicopter (to remove Carlo Silva).

So now we are in Ponza, more or less disabled, and Claudio is busy supervising mechanics. He asked me to help him choose a necklace for Maria Sol, something for a summer evening.

* * *

It's crazy how difficult it is to find someone without an address. Seen from afar, Ponza was 'the place where Tommy is'. Here, everything is *not* Tommy. I walked from bar to bar, daytime bars, not the bars in *Chocolates for Breakfast*. There were clusters of boys and girls our age dangling their feet sitting on their mopeds, trying to decide on something that would not be too dull. He could have been with them, but he never was. I almost felt he was hiding, doing it on purpose. I imagined the surprise, the awkwardness (for both) quickly replaced by happiness. I have never seen him in the daytime. How could it be that we would not meet?

The strain from trying to look relaxed and ready for a surprise was terrible. My white canvas trousers were too 'covered', too city-like. My espadrilles rubbed against my feet. *Why did I not have his phone number?*

Maria Sol rang up some friends who have a villa and we walked up there. I walked and compared with Capri. I kept rehearsing some easy greeting to the hostess, and now I cannot remember whether I did say hello or not. Drinks, sparkling fluids, coloured glasses on the terrace. The odious Carlo S. chatting with a female reptilian.

* * *

The water close by, with a sublime *discesa a mare*, a descent to the water, a proper 'place', an in-between arch-private place, with a little terrace, a platform for lounge chair, tall agave and rocks. My sea, warm, lapping, healing. I went in.

Apparition, by Stéphane Mallarmé was written for you. '*... quand, dans le soleil et dans le soir, /Tu m'es en riant apparue ...*' It was written for a woman, but it's the same. It's for everyone. Everyone wrote it for everyone. I wrote it for you.

You did appear, one afternoon, laughing, your hair glowing, your eyes cut, cast elsewhere, in the land of turquoises – beautiful, consuming. Happy to see me.

Fluttering, roaring, I'm beating a determined crawl. If anyone comes in the water he will be confused and deafened by my wake. The kids will warn me, they said.

We only write LOVE in noncommittal places, margins of Cicerone version, psychedelic drawings during math. Others say it for us, songs, T-shirts. You could be here, where are you, have you found another girl?

Reveries (2)

9. In conference with Mère Marie de la Conciliation –
   Promises, and how they are kept

The parlour of the convent is clear and serene like a soul after confession. Outside the large windows, the garden is retreating into the shadow of the late afternoon. Sitting on one of the visitors' chairs, I am following the pattern of the marble floor, delicately veined grey and white tones, mostly white. Inside her glass office, the porter nun, small and fierce, is working with vigour on the switchboard.

Inside a small salon, Mère Marie de la Conciliation has been talking to my mother. Now they call me in. 'Eugenia, madame, is well-behaved, polite (compliments suppressed). I have her marks here: *dictée, rédaction, poésie....* In the science subjects – *un sérieux manque d'effort'* (no need to translate, I don't study, but it's quite understood that in fact a pupil who succeeds at French is excused for not knowing much beyond additions and multiplications.) 'Overall our concern is mainly in areas of conduct. Eugenia – with another classmate, it must be said, whose parents I am corresponding with, has been seen at recess mostly with older girls, *on the hill* ...' (Not saying smoking is going on, afraid of being scolded for her deficient surveillance system, and what would the Bishop think?) 'She is eleven, and we can grant her a certain maturity ... youngest in her class ... classmates *are* older, but she keeps company with *grandes* of fifteen, sixteen! It is strictly forbidden that the sections mingle ——'

'... so you understand, Eugenia, you can have all the good marks you want, the nuns are not happy at all, it's a bad example to the other *moyennes*, you should play with your classmates and not go after the big girls like a poodle. Another thing, you know the rule about books, they must all be authorized by La Directrice des études and signed, before you bring them in. That is very strict and you will possibly get a *"Médiocre"* next time, you know ...'

'They like my books! There are too few in the library! Myriam, her parents are in Teheran and she never gets to go out and buy any!' making a huge fuss – thinking what shall I do about the *Tom Jones* already smuggled in and all the orders I still have to fulfill.

I needed to restore my reputation. A few days later, using all the organizing skills I had, I was at the door of La Directrice des études and shyly showed a great big book left behind by the Larivière girls. 'Oh, what a beautiful book: *Jeannette de Domrémy*! About our beloved Jeanne d'Arc! With a foreword by Charles Péguy!' The nun pensively turns the pages, charmed by the modern illustrations. She would like to borrow it herself. But she has a strict timetable, she renounces this pleasure. 'Very good, Eugenia,' and she writes a few words on the front page, with her little pencil. The nuns are bébés really. When it comes to their affections, the saints and their power over nice pupils. I am devious and deceptive, although still nice and noble-hearted, and yes, older than my age, or something like that.

10. Capri – Encounter with the painter –
    The piazza – Three things –
    Definitions – Cristina and her parents at La Pergola

The island of Capri is perfume, colour, breeze, fruit, water. Sometimes, when I am away, I feel hungry for Capri, the air, the salt water, the plankton. My grandmother says that the seaside is good for you. There, I am just a small fish nobody notices, part of the coastal waters. I am a girl, dressed for Capri, blending in.

How did it happen? It's been arranged, through a chance meeting at the café, and subsequent telephonic communications, that I will walk alone to visit Cristina, who is spending all summer here, at her parents', the owners of l'Hotel La Pergola. If it had been left to Cristina or me, who knows? Perhaps we would not have known how. We would have resumed our friendship back in school. Nobody realized that this is the first time ever I am alone. My parents have made no special recommendation. I am to go there, spend the afternoon, then come back.

It's three in the afternoon and everybody is asleep. I walk, half running, downhill; our house is on one of the small mountains, the town itself more or less in the valley, the sea all around. I stay in the shade, I don't want to sweat. I make my sandals clap. A group of tourists, German, are coming upstream, strong-boned, red from too much sun, wearing big brown leather sandals, monk-style, and brown leather cases for cameras. They are going to collapse on their beds at la Pensione Castello.

I go down a stretch of very wide steps, one two steps, skip, one-two-skip. Those are snapdragons. On the right, there is a rounded waist-high wall; on the left, the façade of white houses with their ornamental gates guarding courtyards. Ripe aromatic carob pods, but now is not the time. 'Ca' dell'Alba' says a ceramic nameplate painted in blue and yellow – House of Dawn. 'La Dragoncella' with a smiling she-dragon blowing wind. Glazed tiles gleam in the penumbra, in patterns of sunbursts, cool, precious. There are pots of green plants in a corner, the door proper, with a large black iron key plate, and a ground-floor window with wrought iron rounded bars, decorating more than protecting. An opulent espalier of purple bougainvilleas reaches to a balcony.

In this house, I decide, lives a small, lively, precise woman, in white trousers and a hand-painted *chemisier* tunic in tones of royal blue and pale green. She is dark-haired, she flashes her gold cigarette lighter quickly. She has a way of picking up her straw beach bag and getting up from a director's chair, saying, 'Goodbye then, I'll see you at eight for drinks.' She knows how to handle life. When she walks into the coolness of her living room, she'll find her place set with yellow dishes and bamboo-handled cutlery, breadsticks and Ferrarelle water. Her maid will bring her a platter with fresh mozzarella and tomatoes, sprinkled with oregano. She – she always knows what her next step will be.

* * *

From above, I can see him, like in a bad dream, turning from Via Caruso, and slowly beginning to walk up. He wears a long flowing bonnet in bright stripes. He leans on a large curved stick, his head enormous with his too-human brown eyes, large nose and chin. His head sinks inside his shoulders.

Le Génie de la Montagne. Maybe you know the tale, Good Little Henri has to ask the Genie of the Mountain for his help, to save his dying mother, and the Genie is a little man, hunched, and very demanding, *malgracieux*, boorish. He just does not give his help freely, he asks Le Bon Petit Henri to plough his fields, and harvest them, and to make the wheat into flour, and to bake the flour into at least thirty-six thousand loaves. To make himself useful, *quoi*. Of this man here, Rosalina would say, '*un po' disgraziato*', lacking in luck – feeling compassion for the cripple. What I see first is his intelligence, the way his eyes see everything, and maybe also the desire to be *malgracieux* and vindictive.

His costume is extraordinary. The bonnet, the large rings on his fingers, the bag, woven in black picked out in red and green, a shawl draped around his shoulders. He walks like that, as if on a stage. I would never dare to walk outside in my special costumes. I have heard him called 'the painter', with respect, did Daddy say Reiner, but this is not a painter's costume, like Rembrandt, with a béret and cape.

He always smiles when we meet, with envy, perhaps, at my quick legs. Maybe: 'Stupid, ignorant little girl.' Maybe suffering, because he can see he makes me ill at ease. I don't know what my face tells him: go away, disappear, or, I am a nice girl and know I must be nice to unfortunate men like you. Because I don't know how to be kind, simple, natural, go beyond my nervousness. I feel a limitation. He is too old, too different. He has strength equal to the powers of a fairytale magician, he dares to dress like a pirate, a woman, a gipsy. A fool. Chooses to be one of those glistening green and gold beetles, admirable to some, scary to others.

Afraid that he will talk to me, and I will fall short. Maybe he smiles because he understands. I walk fast past him, looking ahead.

I have almost reached the passage framed with pale blue campanulas. He is talking to me! '*Bonne promenade, mademoiselle!*' No diabolical laughter. I turn and wave. '*Au revoir, monsieur!*'

* * *

I call out my favourites, and keep silent for the smelly passages. Villa Fiorella, Il Muretto, Villa Sant'Anna. Sleepy shops, a shop window with sandals on display – 'Sandali Capresi'. Behind some louvred blinds there is a faint clinking, a coffee cup hitting a saucer, the sugar pot being refilled. On the right, Il Pipistrello nightclub, with a bat on the sign, and a poster announcing Peppino di Capri e i Rockers, with Peppino wearing dark glasses. We have his records, in Rome. He opened the shows of the pop group the Beatles when they came to Italy, says Daddy, and is becoming very well-known. He has a villa, white, large, just like us, three doors up our road.

Under another underpass, past the vendor of prickly pears sitting on his heels, dozing. Past the Big Church where every Sunday there is some fuss about the tourists wearing shorts, here is the main square, La Piazzetta. My father says La Piazza. It's vaguely round, and small.

I am at the top of the large steps, on the side of the church. Here you can stop, and admire. Ahead is City Hall, a toy one, at left the tower with the telephone sign and the large clock made of coloured tiles. Buildings are two stories at most, in sandy yellow stucco. There are some shops, some down-to-earth, others selling jewels for happy times. The piazza is dotted with café tables and brightly coloured umbrellas, yellow at Caffé Cuomo, green bordered with white at Tontani, and orange at Vuotto. When you sit at one of those little tables, you are the luckiest in the world.

But the steps to the Piazza – they are very important. They are part of the three things never to be forgotten. 'The beautiful blond girl running down the steps at La Piazza'; 'Carolina the donkey'; 'the rooster on the stamps of the letters from France'. Never am I to forget these three things. To forget them would mean I forgot too much, I lost my way, my power oozed out from Aladdin's lamp.

The big T of the tobacco store, where you buy post stamps and salt (coarse and fine). Then right, past the pastry shop where the cakes for Vanna and Guillaume are purchased (10th and 15th of August), always the same, hazelnut and chocolate, and we always expect them with pleasure, and they are always a very warm mixture for a summer afternoon, but we drink lemonade with it. This is Via Camerina, where most food comes from. Fruit, vegetables, wine, meat, fish, poultry, eggs, dry goods. Here and there, the K of Kodak, and Ferrania, and Agfa-Gevaert. Postcard racks, hanging from the open shutters of some small coffee bars (with maybe only two tables outside), with humming iceboxes for ready-to-eat ice creams. We are allowed only Motta or Algida brands although once Lello absent-mindedly bought us Camillino ice-cream sandwiches. They were *so* good, and very bad for you.

So I go up a flight of stairs, not remembering exactly where Cristina's place is. It's somewhere not far. I keep walking. Capri's streets always come to a solution. You cannot be lost. To me both a dream and my normal place. To a child's scale. To the scale of dreams. But I don't call myself a child. They still say bambina, but it's ragazzina, more and more. Some even say ragazza. I am 1-2-3, first, second, family name, born a day, a month, eleven years ago. I have a father, Italian, dark hair Italian eyes, a mother, blond pink pale blue, one from here and one from far away. They are contraries, my parents and my places, I am the one who chooses. I want to become the heart-stopping blond young girl skipping the large steps on her way to La Piazza in Capri.

I have taken the wrong turn, I am now above Tragara. I am not lost but I don't know where to go. There is a silence. I lean on the low wall with its familiar roundness, covered with a sort of grey cement with little sparks in it. From behind the gates of this part of the island, cold, indifferent people could appear, say 'Who is this child, what is she doing here? what right? does she have money? what parents would let her wander? where is her au pair?' But I almost fall asleep on the warm *muretto* and it left a print on my cheek.

I see the terraces of Cristina's hotel and some sheets flapping in the breeze. I went too high up to the left. I start running down again.

They are Capresi. Imagine somebody asking: where are you from? And you: Capri. People would think you are lying. There is Cristina's father, the Cavalier Enrico Colli, her mother, *la signora* Gianna, her brother Tanino, and Cristina. Mister Colli greets me, '*Come sta*, Donna Eugenia?' not joking, he gives me the title of important women. And Madam Colli, sitting very small behind the reception desk, says Cristina is downstairs.

Cristina is in the laundry room, turning the crank of two rolls that smooth over folded sheets. It works like grandmother's pasta-making machine, only gigantic. Cristina does little jobs when she is home for the holidays. She starts removing her apron, but I say I'd like to try.

I help her sprinkle water on a thick wad of towels, the thin damask type, white, with 'Hotel La Pergola' in pale blue. She shows me how they fold them here, in three, vertically, then pouf, she presses them with a large steam iron bouncing from a suspended coil, then I fold them in two and make piles. Cristina chats, a lovely little budgie. She's gone to the open-air cinema, and do I like Tony Dallara? I'd like to ask her to use the iron, but at home, they say I always hurt myself.

I am happy, things are tidy and machines are suited to the work. Cristina and I are making the world run.

Madam Colli has prepared a lemon custard for us, and cookies, under the vines of green grapes. I feel ill at ease, eating there, not really entitled to it, not being a client – even if this is Cristina's home. She has a hotel for a home. She shows me her room, a real hotel room, except it's her own. The family rooms are grouped at the end of one corridor, with a fourth one set as a sitting room, with sofas, a television set and an upright piano, and their bathroom.

I have lived in a hotel too, once, that is, in my own town, in Rome. My aunt and uncle from Ottawa were there for something international, how much fun, they stayed four months at the Excelsior on Via Veneto, their apartment had many rooms, all beige and white, and we took turns, Vanna, Piero and I, sleeping there for a few days with our cousin Guillaume. Having a holiday in our own town. I loved the sound of the traffic humming inside the room, the live city, leaning on the balcony, and the leaves from the tall trees, and breakfast on a tray.

Oh, it was marvellous, thick little pots of everything, hot chocolate, and brioches. Brioches with two puffs of dough, a glistening crust, and plenty of soft, yellowish *mie* inside. When I grow up, I'll have an apartment with a balcony, and brioches for breakfast, every Saturday.

II. Capri – Valentina's fiancé – Her recent producer – Americans – Daddy's work – Stories of the war

Here comes Lello, suntanned, teeth sparkling. He is Aunt Valentina's fiancé. He was here last summer, too. Everybody loves him, children, dogs, grown-ups. He knows magic tricks, woof, a coin disappears, a cigarette appears behind his ear. He is beautiful (but he says 'sono Lello il Bello' with a clown's face), he laughs beautifully. This morning when we went to ask him to play, he said from behind his door, 'I am working, kids, don't disturb me.' Now we have our recompense. We have moved sofas and ottomans, like a theatre, and wait, all dressed to go to the beach, me, Piero, Vanna, Guillaume and Lilliana Otti.

The sliding doors of the living room open a crack, and Lello puts his face through, like Pulcinella. 'C'est magique!' he cries, and closes the doors. We yell at the top of our lungs, he is such fun. Then he reappears, humming a little air, tum ti dum ti dum tum ... He walks in with a bathing-cap like a huge yellow cauliflower and a white terry bathrobe ... He waddles along like a chicken with nice feathers, two steps down, two steps to the left ... He sings, 'C'est magik, c'est fantastik ... ce dentifrik ...,' flashing a big, square smile and fluttering of eyelids. 'DEN-TI-FRI-CE!' we yell. Lello, horror-struck, starts backing down, singing: 'Oh la li, oh la la, ça ne va pas!!!' And he is gone behind the door, leaving us to laugh and scream.

Lello works for an advertising agency, and he has to work when he is on holidays, but not very much. Sometimes he'll say, 'I have to meet a client,' and goes to one of the cafés, on the Piazza, and once I saw him there, he looks different, serious, even in his sunglasses and his vacation clothes. Sometimes when he is lying on a deck chair at Marina Piccola, he'll jump up like a madman and ask the barman for some paper coasters, and write something hurriedly. Then he calms down and goes for a swim, or he sits with Vanna on the pebbled beach and plays with her.

This year, Aunt Valentina too has brought work to do here in Capri. She is writing a book. She usually writes film scenarios, but now she is trying for a novel. She was very excited on the day she arrived.

'Enough of those awful producers! And film people – augh!'

'Valentina is going to enter the holy orders,' announced Lello.

'I had this grand finale, ambiguous, very, with the whole cast' – she smoked one puff – 'retreating to this hermitage, and they walk around in those long flowing robes, contemplating nature, final redemption, catharsis – well! That swine, bloody Pollardoni, he decides the film needs a lighter touch, he has them all go to a nightclub, the girls dressed I don't tell you how … no no no no nooo, enough, *basta*, to hell with Pollardoni *rompicoglioni.*'

'Auntie Valentina swears like a fish wife,' says Lello. But it doesn't matter. Even if she seems mad, she really is quite happy to be swearing, *telling the truth about the swine*, delivering him his supreme, definitive label, 'Il Porcello'. This language is made by Valentina, only for Valentina, we would never, swearwords are absolutely forbidden, although once or twice I did say '*brutto stronzo*', alone in my bedroom, against Daddy who had caught me watching TV after a quarter to nine. Then there are more normal swearwords, 'ugly words' in Italian, *stupido*, or *cretino*, or the worst, *stupido cretino*, arch-forbidden. To protect us against bad language or swearwords, we are very seldom given comics, Paperino and Topolino (Donald Duck and Mickey Mouse). Not that we really like them, but we know we could be entitled to them, we don't want to be taken for granted, they are a terrain where discussion is possible, like for Coca-Cola or chewing gum.

America comes to us in many ways. Blue jeans and basketball shoes. 'American Bar.' American means modern, clean, comfortable, must-have. Italians say gomma americana for chewing gum and noccioline americane for peanuts. Toothpaste, and comics, also sound American. 'Could I have my American toothpaste, please? Can I borrow your American Mickey Mouse?' that's how it would sound. Americans are perfect advertisements of those things. They walk up our road (although there is a big Private sign) wearing jeans, sneakers, chewing gum, unbelievably casual, relaxed, smiling, parents and children alike, bouncing on those chewing gum shoes, laughing those flashy laughs, their jerseys flapping tied around their waists – and nobody tells them a thing! They would not understand anyway.

* * *

My dad works in a different way than Lello. When he works, he wears a suit and shoes, and goes to his office, rather, to his studio – in Rome, that's the way you call an engineer's office. He has a studio with another engineer, and a secretary, Lisetta, who lets me play with her typewriter and sends me sweets on my birthday.

It happens too that he'll be working at lunchtime. The telephone will be on the dining table, when he is expecting an important call, and he'll pick up the phone himself. There is a big difference between expecting a call and having to make a call, you won't call if you are meant to be called, at least not right away. He always knows what to say. Sometimes he'll say 'ahan, aha aha', and I'll be around, not far, trying to understand what it's about. I hear it so often, your dad's work is so important, your dad is so clever, and I'd like to understand, to be able to talk to my friends about what he does. But one time, instead of merely getting confused with names, appointments, undefined business, appointments in places unknown, I followed the whole conversation from A to Z.

Dad was on the telephone with the man who takes care of our farm. He said, 'Really, he is born?' really happy, and I immediately understood: our donkey Carolina had had a foal! Oh happiness, a baby donkey, all mine, I would take care of him and ride him and he would love me above everyone else. It was immense happiness. Behind Daddy's shoulders, I did a little jig. Then, he asked for the name of the hospital. I did not quite understand. He put the phone down and said, smiling, 'You know, Giovanni's wife has had a baby boy!' Bang, my lovely donkey gone, an ugly little boy on the farm, oh misery. From explosive joy to nothing, ashes. I hurt so much, I did not cry.

Daddy's work. One day, I had left the soap bar in the water of my bath. He saw it. He talked very seriously to me. 'Soap must not be wasted, you know, your dad needs to work to buy things, I have to work' (he hesitated) '– half an hour to buy it.' I was astonished. Then I understood. One day my dad would work to buy soap bars, another day to buy spaghetti, another to buy a car, another to buy books – every day was hard and long, and all we had came from his work. His work made my life possible. That's how things stood. I felt his infinite love for us.

* * *

Valentina has stayed up at the villa – she has work to do. I know what she is doing, I know exactly. Right now (eleven fifteen), she is sitting on the kitchen table, in her short white kimono, dangling her feet and clapping her mules, a coffee bowl in her hands, chatting with Assuntina, the wife of the caretaker, she has her transistor radio on, she is crazy for Mina, and she makes me dance the twist, *Tintarella di luna*, you laugh all the time, it's even funnier because Mina has a funny accent.

'The Salvalaggios have rented this summer – to some Milanese, he is a doctor, with two daughters, young girls, about seventeen, eighteen. The Marchesa is away to Ischia for two days.'

The Marchesa has a caravan of troubles, except that she has a fabulous villa – what a shame to leave it empty in the middle of summer. I have been there once, smuggled in by Assuntina's son Antonello, who had to go and shut down the windows against the rain.... I was so nervous about being there without an invitation, I hardly remember a thing, except a very grand sweeping staircase, and a black piano. It all seemed very beautiful.

I know what happened to her: during the war, there was Fascism and Italy was with the Germans; the Germans had Nazism and swastikas and Italians had brown shirts (actually, black, based on some sartorial dictum). Her husband ordered her father killed. Then was killed himself. 'This is what happens when the dogs of war are unleashed' would say my uncle Elio, he is a pacifist, although he looks like a furious Viking when discussions turn political.

* * *

I heard something about Assuntina's husband – Daddy was pouring drinks, one evening, and someone said, 'Did you see the colour of that fellow's shirt?'

I know. When he's off work, Anselmo dresses almost like the well-off Capresi, with good loafers, and trousers, and an open-necked shirt, smoking, leaning on a wall, waiting to go for dinner.

Except that he tries too hard, because his shirts are silk, and they are very odd, dark, black. But then, many vacationers wear dark, or coloured, Provençal patterns – they are like paisleys, but much livelier, I have a pair of Bermuda shorts just like that, in navy blue.

12. The Club Vesta – The buffet – Mayonnaise –
Careers for women – The guide falls asleep

Arianna Gardelli awaited at the top of the stairs. Her own little
palace, a Liberty villa, highly consonant with this part of Rome,
outside Porta Pinciana, pallid yellow things of charm, palm trees
and, in season, wisteria. She was wearing one of her signature silk
ensembles, and matching silk-covered shoes. 'Dearest!' she greeted
the ladies, 'isn't it wonderful you were able to come!' Wonderful,
wonderful. 'So happy you have brought Dear Eugenia.' All that
garnet shantung, broken only by the diamanté buckles of the
shoes – fascinating.

Now that I was there, I wondered what took me to torment my
mother into bringing me. She had to call first the vice-president,
then the president of the club, Madame Moscardìn. Mme
Moscardìn let herself be persuaded and promptly counter-
suggested that her own daughter, Maria Maurizia, would come,
'and we'd keep each other company during the *in camera proceedings*.'
They were not telling us their little secrets. Bah. And here was
Maria Maurizia, an eager girl guide who within five minutes told
me how much she likes parish meetings and her school and her
professors, everything. She probably also likes the bus ride to
school and Greek interrogations, with all her soap-washed heart.

The ladies sat and stood in the living room, luminous in the
one o'clock sun, white and gleaming with crystal and mirrors
framed by the warm amber of the parquet and the furniture. Tray
of *spumante* going by, pick up a glass, sip, it's Asti, not to be
touched even in the Gobi Desert according to Marchese Isola, he
knows everything. The buffet was of the very sumptuous kind, and
the ladies daintily helped themselves and ate while chatting of I
don't know what. Nothing *real* could ever happen in front of those
white tablecloths. 'I met him at the buffet table and madly fell in
love.' 'While helping myself to a mountain of Russian salad, I met
her eyes and felt a stab at my heart.' 'The eggs mimosa inspired
me to modify my schedule and unplug the bomb I was going to
throw on the assembled diplomats.' 'Mimì, *I hate you*.' 'Have some
salmon in aspic, Rodolfo, and, I hate *you*.' Maybe it's the
mayonnaise. Mayonnaise is a treacherous food.

I used to have a mayonnaise adoration. It was the most attractive food in the world, connected with sandwiches for picnics and downtown *tramezzini*, the soft triangles of pleasure, the marvellous, irregular half-meals. I would wake up in the middle of the night, and walk to the kitchen, tremulously. It was the dark night after all and I was eight or nine. I distinctly remember my legs feeling weak. Could I have been starving? I opened the Frigidaire and in its perpetual light there was almost nothing, milk, butter in a small packet, a small tin of tomato paste (Arlecchino brand) and eggs. How could the fridge of a family of five, plus servants, be so void, so scrubbed? A small grove of *déracinés*, lugubrious, incomprehensible, Angostura, Tabasco, Lea and Perrins. But always, always a tube of Maionese Kraft. My prey. I would twist the top off and suck it in big long gulps. I think the spout was serrated, to make a pretty effect when decorating a dish. I swallowed the serrated mayonnaise. Then, although nobody took the trouble to forbid stealing mayonnaise, I'd try to cover my tracks, plump the tube up, and feverishly twist the top back on the wrong way. I closed the door, which made an infernal racket, and returned, *le coeur barbouillé*, with a smeared heart, queasy, to bed, where I dreamt such dreams as I could.

The ladies of the Club Vesta are not all frivolous, but *together....* Our hostess Arianna, for instance, a specialist of protocol. She gets a call from the Quirinal and La Farnesina to 'do a ceremony' when a royal family, or government officials, come on official visits. It *might* sound frivolous, but it's very hard! You need to know the Italian and the Spanish ceremonial, for instance, and the order of precedence, and just to set a dinner table is fraught with dangers. (My Marxist-Leninist friends at Lycée Delacroix would launch into biting diatribes, especially Luis whose father is in exile, *in exile*, in Rome from the Franco regime – can it still be him? Didn't he die?) Spain has a special place in her heart, she says, her mother was from Madrid (well connected, says Daddy, her family into sherry) and she just loves to 'do things right'. And Louli Peroni, who is a film agent, always on the telephone and at parties, but she earns real money, having such a great time. Once, my parents were at one of her cocktails. Daddy was introduced to an English actor he adores. They shook hands – and stared. They were both wearing a suit cut in the same cloth, a grey with a special coloured reverse, the same suit actually. They both burst out, 'But the tailor told me it was exclusive!' 'Exclusive, that's what he told me too!' They had been betrayed. 'You understand,' said Dad, 'afterwards, things were not the same.'

The Club Vesta is a women's club. There is a reading committee, a social committee and a cultural committee (and that's where the power is, says my father). What power? I thought that clubs are where you meet with people exactly like you, and you wallow in comfort. (Not the Club des Jacobins, that was different.) We did a psychology test in English, in *quatrième*, non-scientific said MM Andrew, but for thirteen-year-olds what an improvement on the horoscope. Pisces: Beware of ambiguous situations. Good news in the afternoon. So this test put us under six great categories, and it said I am under 'Phlegmatic'. I think of it all the time, it must have had a grain of truth – maybe that's what it means: I'd prefer spending my time in a made-to-suit club, 'Les Flegmatiques', with my books, my newspapers, my favourite everything.

They speak English here. The agenda, typed by a virtuoso.

CLUB VESTA

- Report of the social committee
    - Inclusion of a Valentine's Dance
      (C.ttee Pres. Melina Panayotides)

- Report of Cultural C.ttee
    - Report of Reading sub-committee
    - Upcoming Activities
      (C.ttee V. Pres. Eliane Babinger)

- Report of the Treasurer
      (Miss Ann Brunswick)

- Committee of the Whole (in camera)
      (Pres. Elmira Moscardin)

It was boring. Maurilla was taking notes, she is going to make a school project out of it, I thought. They spoke with great civility but there were a lot of pinched looks and biting of lips. Oh la la. Mme Moscardin would get everything done the way she wanted. Help!

At a nod from the Presidentess, we got up from our chairs in unison. The well-behaved *jeunes filles!* Maria M.: 'Did you bring anything to go over?'

We were supposed to go and admire the winter garden on the ground floor (they stopped themselves from saying we were to *play*). We went through the hall, found our coats and opened the door to the stairs. A pestilential perfume of tuberose was floating. I picture them as begonias, fleshy and tortuous. It was fresh, *not from when we all arrived.* Pestilential, I detest it. I once took a taxi with Valentina and we were almost sick, some woman had doused herself with this killer tuberose, possibly in the cab (besides, it's very impolite). The cabbie was pale and answered by monosyllables. 'It's Fracas!' cried Valentina. 'Lethal! That infernal French film editor almost poisoned us with it when she was visiting the set!'

'I'll join you in a moment,' I told Maria-Maurilla. 'I'm going to the bathroom.' She went like a good girl.

I went to look for the bathroom, always a momentous task, hopeful to catch a little of what was going on *in camera.* What very elegant corridors she has, Arianna. The scent was more and more Fracas and something else.

* * *

'Come, come, young one,' she cooed.

I knew it. A Prophetess. Of course. She was sitting in a sort of anteroom to the bathroom. I did not want to talk to her, just see who was there! Now I was glued in the web.

'I will see the ladies shortly … I am preparing. I am re-centring my soul in this *fine* room. *Mmmh....*' She was cross-legged on a fluffy little armchair in front of a coiffeuse. Her voice was somnolent. The wisdom she imparts comes from long and patient contemplation of a fog that at times clears up, and it's tiring. She was wearing a sort of chasuble of heavy purple silk, in the hyper-eccentric category. A vertiginous topknot and no eyebrows. Colossal amber balls on her earlobes. The white-rimmed sunglasses, I saw, had thick lenses, the eyes bobbing as at the bottom of a well. At her side, a thin long iridescent strip she seemed to be knitting, like any grandmother.

She leaned forward and thoughtfully sprayed herself with one perfume, another, another. 'I am always *so* pleased to see the ladies, their heart is pure and *see*king.' Her voice went to a nasal acute with every emphasis. '... looking for the inner self ... mmmh ... and you, young one, are you in the dream or are you wakeful?' As I feared, I was being questioned about my political opinions and what I meant to do about everything. I did not know what to say, really, but she kept nodding, nodding (nodding as a camel would, to be perfectly frank) – and she fell asleep.

From the living room, a well-behaved expectant applause could be heard. I gave her arm a great big shake and leaped out.

13. How to be happy in a cave – Capturing happiness –
    Books – The most charming girl in the school –
    Dream of the red spider – Sonny B.

To want, to have. It. To want something you know, to hope for something you don't know yet. To expect. To wish. To say, May I please.

There are ways not to depend on others, to create your own happiness. If you are lost, all alone in the mountains and find a cave. If you arrive in a new country without your coverlet and your bedroom decorations. Your dressing gown becomes all the decoration you have and you must take extra care about washing it so that it doesn't get ruined. Then, slowly, you have a tiny bit more. An old chocolate box to keep your stamps in, your images, your ribbons. In a cave, you must think first of all of keeping warm, that is why I would like to have my own dog, who would follow me everywhere, but I must improve my marks, says Daddy. Then to find food, hoping it is the season of nuts and wild asparagus, and a source of water (you follow the sound). Maybe make flat packets of hay, string them together and make a warm waistcoat. Then, to show the cave is yours, you would make boughs of wheat, garlands of pretty vines, and add fresh flowers, you always get new ideas when you go walking.

Today, the greatest happiness is mine. I have the apartment to myself while Germana, the washlady, her wash pinned outside on the terrace, has gone downstairs to have a chat with Ermilla (who is from the same village). I can be the lady of the house, just do everything I want. Be happy. I am never left in peace. Piero and my sisters are always disturbing me.

But do you know how it is when you want to be happy and it doesn't come?

Such fine boredom. Great lovely nothing. 'Torture of the thin broth with overcooked vermicelli, with sniffing of gratin macaroni and chocolate pudding.' 'Falling asleep in your bath and waking up in cold water. Somebody has walked on your pyjamas with wet feet. Your new adored pair of slippers have been found by a passing dog. They lie gnawed, and dampish.'

There is nothing special coming up. The nuns at school are making a big fuss about it being the Second Trimester and your last chance before the Third. 'The All-Important Second Trimester.' Only to think of it, so long, so packed with lessons, so important, I feel discouraged. And nobody is coming, no trumpets are being blown. Aunt Valentina, who always walks in with armloads of excitement, or a new handbag with silky interior compartments, and matching comb and mirror compartment, with closures that zip and snap, she is shooting in Spain, she said the set is 'far from everything', in some desert, nothing grandiose, nothing pleasant. Poor Zia.

I could read, but isn't reading on this magnificent afternoon, a waste of other, more rare, fun?

When I was given Les Malheurs de Sophie, I wrote my name on it. I was so small that I thought you could draw in books, and I drew a little girl's face on one of the empty pages. So small I could not imagine there would be enough time in my life to read them all, the Comtesse de Ségurs. And of course I did, even the one I kept for last because it was a fake – fairytales, not stories, some copied from Perrault, told in other words, the first one only was original, how can that have happened, didn't anybody notice? And I have read all the Tintins and never again will there be a new one, Hergé has stopped writing, said Daddy, it's over forever, the happiness of reading a new Tintin. All I can do now is re-read them very slowly, and try and not think of them, forget them a little, then read them again, sometimes find *Tintin au Congo*, and *Tintin au Tibet*, the early ones, which we don't have, forgotten at the bottom of a pile in somebody's playroom, and read them while the others are playing board games. I have calculated that by the time I am seventeen I will only be able to read them, at most, every three years, because the more you read them, the less you forget them. I now look at each frame slowly, carefully, trying to decipher every detail, every allusion, make them fresh again. It hurts to read, like removing a Band-aid, you destroy the book as you read it, the more you read the less you'll be able to forget in order to read again; it's terrible. You must not put your heart in earthly possessions, but Tintin and Haddock are so lovable, like bread, like Dad, the stories are so good, to wrench it all out, you would need a scalpel, or want to renounce the world, like the nuns. Do the nuns not love us?

'Comtesse de Ségur, née Rostopchine', that's how she signed, to keep the terribleness in her name, her father burned down Moscow under Napoleon's nose, but, while rather upset, Napoleon showed his moral superiority by calmly writing down the statutes of the Comédie Française that night, looking at the flames, not at all nervous that they could burn him, thinking how best to make France's comedians and theatre triumph – so finally la Comtesse decided to put a stop to all this nonsense and anyway Russia was an ally most of the time, so she married a Frenchman and became a famous writer. You can see she is a woman of character, she knows right and wrong, and what is proper and what is just ridiculous. The French say it all the time, 'C'est ridicule,' and it's very hard to reply. What can be done if you are ridiculous?

She would be able to tell me, why do I feel discontented when I read my old books? Monsieur de Réan (nice papa) will say to his children: 'No, children, I cannot play, I have to work with my books.' Then he retreats to his den. Our schoolbooks, *those* we have to work with, but how could one *work* with one's own books? Daddy's studio too has a nice Scandinavian desk, to work on, and the bookcases are populated with books, but he read them *before* this apartment. 'There is not much time for reading when you grow up. Daddy adores books but he is too busy.'

Maybe working with books would mean reading books I don't really like, like Piero's *The Children of Captain Grant*, *Treasure Island* and *Moby-Dick* and *White Fang*.

I am lazy. Here and there, I'll learn a poem by heart, and it keeps them happy. And they don't ask if I have any homework. Daddy is pleased I read all sorts of books, like *Taras Bul'ba*, *Oliver Twist*, and *The Paul Street Boys*. And *Misunderstood*. But I won't reread those, they are too close to real things and it's too horrible when people are mean. If you have no escape and really believe the book. In *Ragazzi della Via Pál*, the boy really dies, even if he's only a character. You cannot erase that.

Even Elsa thinks I am a good student, because I tell her only about my good marks. When she answers my letter, she'll say, congratulations on your marks, and sometimes I cannot remember what she's talking about.

I could study more English, I was already beginning on my own before we started in school, and I felt ashamed, for the first time, really ashamed, that some of the girls knew quite a lot already, and I was the one not understanding. I was angry too, that neither Daddy nor Mummy had taught me any. That way they still have a secret language. Anyway, they are not in a hurry that I learn English. Daddy says he is worried our Italian is too influenced by French. And by all means, I should not even think of learning Spanish, much too close. I worry, too, I am extra careful, weighing words carefully before I speak, is this a Gallicism, is that an Italianism. Sometimes I hang on to words and Daddy gets impatient.

I could do more. '*Peut faire mieux.*' It's impossible, because you would need to be studying immediately after school, and you would not be able to breathe ever. Enjoy yourself on your own. The best, the rarest. The most fail-proof.

I knew it. If you wait a little, the zing will zing. The zest will return. The appetite. I must review Mummy's things, tidy up her drawers a little. Her drawer of foulards. They are never arranged properly, by colours and by seasons. Solid colours, blue, red, cream, all together, showing their luscious folds on top of each other; the one with dolphins dancing, turquoise, with golden ropes and the sea in pink, signed Emilio, he has changed since, on the labels it is now Pucci, we saw him on television, because his shop in Florence got flooded, and Dad asked if I recognized him, and I was sorry that all those lovely things got ruined, but there were no floods in Capri, his boutique is safe, that's the most important. There are others, with bridles and horse bits, in *camaïeu* of brown, it means matching shades, that's a word Mr Audibert taught me, he told me the etymology and was surprised we don't do any at school, it comes from cameo, and that used to be an Arab word. Then the absolute best, with a large dark pink butterfly on a light beige background, in a navy blue frame, it's by Christian Dior. That one is certainly for the city, somehow butterflies are not for the sea-side. If you don't want to wear it on your head, you can knot it around your neck. Or on the handle of your handbag. If you are someone like Mummy.

Next to my parents' room, there is a bathroom, clearly my mother's, in white and pink-beige mosaic, and a marvellous three-sided mirror, with little glass shelves everywhere. It's perfect for playing shop, a *profumeria* with all sorts of jars and bottles. That's where I spend a lot of time, talking, pretending I am a salesgirl, or a client, saying things they would say, or re-doing conversations that have happened, changing my own answers, trying on the face that goes with my answer. Face, profile, three-quarter. I am never very happy with myself, after I've said something. But I don't know what I *should* have said. I am as soft as Plasticine. I think I should be very serious, then some girl will mock me and say I look like a statue. I think I should laugh and be happy, and the nun will scold me. I want to be like a butterfly and make a costume with two knotted foulards, and my ballet *collants*, but Daddy will say go put your pyjamas on.

Do you know *rotolini*, the game you play around a table, and each player draws a head on a long piece of paper (it doesn't matter if you can't draw well), and folds the paper to cover all but the neck, then passes it on to the next player, who adds the abdomen of his own character, you do about four parts, then you unfold the paper, it's so funny, you laugh till it hurts, the characters have four mismatched parts, and sometimes some ambiance, a skull, a crow, clouds of dust. I would like to be harmonious, and very interesting. Long hair. Run very fast. Dance the ballet and also with boys.

There was a *grande*, one everyone knew, she always walked with two or three friends, Ottavia Limorani, I never talked to her, of course, but sometimes we were asked to run errands for them, or we just followed in their wake, little birds after rhinos, catching a few words, happy to be tolerated. She was always smiling, or making her friends laugh. She had a limp, but walked joyfully. One day – I was quite small, I was struck by the thought: if I behave like Ottavia, maybe I'll become like her. Her smile, her radiance. And I transformed myself, and forgot all about it. Then one day, as I was passing Ottavia's group, she stopped and said to her friends, '*Questa bambina é tanto simpatica, sorride sempre,*' this girl is so charming, she is always smiling. I was stunned. I had succeeded. I ran away to a corner where I could keep the spark alive.

At school, the nuns say of course nothing beats making sacrifices if there is something you really want. Skip eating desert, that is, fruit, because at home we don't eat cake, crème caramel or pastries like the French. Only on special occasions. It would be nice. At school, if you are a boarder, you get a tablet of chocolate for the four-thirty snack, and there is always dessert in the evening, well, sometimes it's only a bit of jam, girls eat it with a little spoon, or an ugly apple, but that's an exception. But it's not enough to make you want to be a boarder. If I really wanted something, what could I sacrifice? What do I really like? Warm baths, particularly on Sunday evening when we are all at home. Going to the bookstore. My gold chain. My holy images. Receiving letters. Going to my grandmother's. My future dog. Playing with my mother's things. Do friends count? You could not sacrifice having a friend, could you? The more you think, the more you find things you don't want to sacrifice.

I knew it, now I've thought an inconvenient thought. If I

sacrifice my time running down from the hill, and doing flips, and do my homework, there are good chances the sacrifice will work.

* * *

When Ottavia said 'simpatica', I heard it over and over. It meant that happiness exists. Burrows in hiding, and one day comes laughing, in its best clothes, towards you. The one you love can love you.

It's not so far away.

When we were small, Sonny Bonocore took us for a ride in his red cabriolet. Piero in the front, I in the middle at the back. I wore a white scarf, although it was Piero who had just had an earache. This car was amazing, it had a record player, and a small fridge with Coca-Colas we drank from the bottle. And the wind! We put our faces out like dogs do, Sonny didn't mind. It was the end of the day, in the early fall, and I see us at a precise point on the Flaminia, zooming by the restaurant at Saxa Rubra. We were going at a hundred an hour! Almost sick with happiness. Piero, for the red car, and the horsepower, and the tires, listening to Quando Calienta El Sol and Sonny talking to us about surfing, American cars and the fine life.

Because Sonny is wonderful. He lives in Florida, he is a friend of Daddy's cousins down there. He comes to visit his mother near Caserta.

From the day of the red spider, I have dreamed.

In the dream, Sonny is in the passenger seat and Piero is driving, maniacally, hunched on the steering wheel like in his red pedal bolide on the terrace. Piero nearly misses many cars and trees and he is not stopping. I am afraid but Piero doesn't hear me. When I have become too afraid, I wake up.

Once again, Sonny had come back. He was chatting and laughing in the living room, my parents and the Chéniers. I had already told my aunt, as a sort of secret, I would have liked to go to the restaurant with them, but she said it was not possible. Then, in despair, I tore off my shyness, I told them all, I said I was eleven, and, Daddy you had promised I could go, someday. I saw

Daddy making a decision, and it was no, bellina, it's too late, look, almost bedtime. I said goodnight properly, and went to my room, and cried. It was horrible, they were going to have a lovely evening, and I was excluded. Oh the chiffon, the shining cars, the perfect hairdos, the scents; the restaurant, sitting outside on the piazza if Mummy is not cold. I threw myself in the worst despair, I fuelled it, I stoked it, I was crying desperately, stretching the pain, wearing it out. Then I stopped and kept quiet. Immobile. I was not sad any more. I recoiled. I thought 'If I behave properly, there will be a recompense; if I don't cause problems, they will be grateful.' I held my breath. Then I heard little cautious steps on the marble of the hall, on the wood closer to the bedrooms. Someone was coming to see if I was all right. My aunt and Sonny.

'Gengia, Gengia?' *sotto voce*, to wake me only if I was just barely sleeping, but laughing. I opened my eyes. 'Your parents say you can come, if you want.' I jumped out and Aunt Simone helped me dress in two minutes, and I took my knitted vest. Outside the main door, Sonny said, 'We'll meet you at Cecchino's,' and we went inside a white car. We went across the bridge lit by enormous faceted lamps, passing other cars in the night. We drove through Villa Borghese, then the side street that gets above Trinità dei Monti. The night felt good, healing, with a faint aroma of good wood.

Sonny had a sigh in his breast, under his smile, his tan. He was dressed like an American in Rome, in a tan suit, the belt too tight, one side, assured, but nervous, on the other, because of all the things he doesn't know, since he's not Italian any more. He was thinking of someone, a girl, the divine girl who would be Sonny's girlfriend, where was she, this stupid girl, clearly not the right girl, or maybe she was travelling on a tall ship to India, her white palazzo pyjamas flowing in the wind, but she wasn't there. He stopped the car and pulled the handbrake.

We were above the Spanish Steps, above Piazza di Spagna and the fountain. From there, you see a cascade of piazzas, scattered with balconies and banisters, beige-rose and white, connected by staircases, fluid, the train of a dress in movement. Even if the girl wasn't there, we were taking the most beautiful route. If the girl had appeared, she would be very surprised that he was going down the Spanish Steps with me, like that. 'Oh, yes, this is my friend

Gengia,' and it would sting her. Because I was his friend, and she wasn't. And he had rescued me from staying home. I had stood very still and happiness had taken consistence. We were together in the night, the lovely night, and I was walking with Sonny, and we were going to the restaurant, and we were not hurrying. I sat on a banister and he sat too. 'Wow,' he said, '*bello qui.*'

14. At the movies

With an air of 'It's really not possible to avoid this any more, what may be may be,' our parents said goodbye and went for their siesta, while we very slowly and silently began assembling our outside clothes. Piero and I were going to see *Snow White* with Uncle Elio and Aunt Costantina, at the Cinema Cola di Rienzo.

We arrived early and waited on a bench, the street was asleep between opening hours, the merchants and salespeople all gone, sleeping or eating, and thinking that they have to return to work one more time and find the right size of shoes at the back of the shop and ask the owner for a rebate and the manager not so pleased as if it were not for the client and all that. The only pleasure would be doing the package, although now it's more and more plastic bags with a drawstring.

This is the street where we do Carnival, something we get talked into – evidently, Carnival is made for children, therefore.... Our handler will be giving us constant instructions about throwing our confetti and streamers to the children coming the other way – to blow our horns, to have fun! And we do, as much as possible, trying to move normally with the mandatory thick sweater under our Columbines, our Antoinettes, some with a fake mole, repulsive, made with a little piece of black silk. They are all having fun. Older boys run through our crowd, wearing bizarre hats like beaks and hit you on the head with plastic orangy and yellow clubs and hammers – it's all for fun.

My parents go to the movies, with other people, after dinner, and they never tell me what went on. But Daddy tells me scenes from long-ago movies, bit by bit, such as *Stagecoach*, and recognizes every actor on TV, with relish, jumping out of his seat. I can recognize Myrna Loy, James Cagney, Tony Curtis. He knows all the Italian comedians who are on TV. He knows them as if he had been to all the shows, before the war, before TV, before. Nobody knows them outside, they are for Italians only. They have nicknames, Peppino, Tino, Nino, Lina Volonghi. Totò, who makes you laugh and you love him so much that it hurts.

Snow White. The images were lacquered, coloured. Large and perfect. Wonderful. From the beginning though, you knew it couldn't last. The stepmother was envious and would stop at nothing, not with that expression of rage. When the mean stepmother reappeared for the third time, her cruel long fingers with pointed red nails, an alarm rang in me. The protectress is your enemy, there is no safe haven – escape, escape, Snow White! I was really scared and Piero, smaller, was squirming and actually began to cry. My aunt said we had to leave, as if it was an emergency. We came outside to the opaque afternoon, both scared and filled with dismay.

What a catastrophe. What an ignominious exit. Our first film! Piero was crying a little, and I was shaken, and awfully disappointed. What a shipwreck. My aunt and uncle tried to save the day by hustling us to the car and once inside, pretended nothing had happened and we were on one of our regular outings. That meant going to the park on the Gianicolo to look at the statue of Garibaldi on horseback, run on the pebbles, look through the paying binoculars, look at the cannon that is fired every day at noon. I know that Piero would like a job like that. Then drive home with the sacrosanct stop at the pastry shop.

Things got better when we got to the song of Salome,

> *Mustafà, il nobile pascià,*
> *tranquillamente sta,*
> *seduto sul sofà,*
> *e con solennità, intanto fa ...'*

which is so funny, and even funnier is Uncle Elio's face as he seriously beats the tempo on the dashboard.

By the time we arrived at the pastry shop, all melancholy was gone. The ever-renewed trays glittered and the freshly painted pastries seemed to want to pop out of the displays and jump at you, there was Uncle Elio calmly ordering without errors, the cardboard tray picked to suit exactly twelve, fifteen pieces, *cannoni*, éclairs of two kinds, beignets white, pink, brown, and beige, and those with coarse sugar and the caramelized bottom, and always one square *diplomatico*, the one my uncle prefers, always his favourite, he will always like it, not like me, not knowing which one will be my first one, my second and maybe my third – and when he'll bite into his well-deserved diplomatic cake, Zia Costantina will call him Elio il Diplomatico, and he just smiles.

15. Cine-club

Zia Valentina had to say yes this time, she took me to a beautiful film, *Le Joli Mai*. It was playing in a ciné-club, which is for those who really like cinema. She was wearing a trench coat, and she gave me her golf umbrella to carry. I have been to the movies twice now, *Snow White*, but that was a long time ago, and *Misunderstood*, with Mummy, which made me cry and cry, and she did not know what to say. Zia Valentina knows the film-maker, I must remember his name, Chris Marker, he decided to go about with a cameraman in Paris and ask Parisians what they remembered as an important event, something that would have been in the newspapers, a recent one. Also to say what they thought is happiness.

The camera was on the roofs. Paris, all those wonderful grey buildings knit together, a white light, and the Seine and the bridges and La Tour Eiffel. And you went walking along, in Paris, seeing all sorts of French things, cars, Citroens, Peugeots, Simcas, Renaults, and people, inside shops, working, walking about in the avenues. He was very clever because he found people who would stop, tell him about their life, and answer him. It was the month of May.

(What he knew and they had all forgotten, was that there had been a war in Algeria, where the French were fighting, and that peace had just been made. He was wondering if they would remember.)

He found a mechanic who had started painting canvases, just like that, and he explained how he thought of his colours as he did his regular work, and showed some paintings with stars, and flying characters. He found two fiancés, just like drawings from Peynet, giggling, he in a uniform, she pale and shy, they said that life was wonderful, and that they only hoped to be married soon and to be happy together. There was no way they were going to say anything about sad things or anybody else. A woman, with her hair pulled tight, on the door of her poor dwelling, very very happy because she was finally moving with her eight children to a bigger apartment. She explained how the postman, who knew she had been waiting for years, stayed to see her open the letter from the City, and how she just put the letter in her husband's bowl when he came at lunchtime. Then there was a pied-noir young man, an Algerian, in a suit and tie, who explained he did good work in a factory, and he had been fired because a colleague complained he should not earn more than a Frenchman, and how other people had beaten him. (I was very unhappy at this point.) But he said that he was going to stay in France and he was going to become a politician.

Then there was a man from Dahomey, beautiful, he said in Africa, as a kid, he had been scolded all the time by the French priests, and made to walk in lines and salute parades. And his grandmother was against him going away to France, but he had gone (maybe his parents said he had to) and he had had a pleasant surprise, been very happy and had many friends. And two boys, barely older than me, dressed in suits and ties, who worked at the Paris Bourse, really! They were special attendants. The interviewer (hidden behind the camera) sounded like he was going to laugh soon, but very seriously asked them what they wanted to do, later. They said to succeed in their professions, and to have cars. He said would they also have girlfriends and they blushed but kept talking, you always keep talking in France. They spoke just like grownups. Then three sisters, all beautiful and elegant young women, nails, hair, jewels, cigarettes, leafing through magazines at the hairdresser, and had nothing to say but kept talking too, except the dark-haired one. Architects, talking about the best use of a vacant plot, imagining windows, trees, people talking, children running. But you knew it was only a dream.

The most adorable of all was a woman called Lidia. She
worked for the theatre, making costumes and dresses. As she
spoke, she kept adding stitches into little bundles and once in a
while, holding them out – minuscule hats for her cat. There was
one like a small velvet lampshade, with crystal drops coming down
the sides, held with a little bow, and one made of feathers all
curving, like a banana cask, framing the cat's face, a perfect dolly
she was, a grey angora, perfectly calm and happy to be so
important. And the woman said, since the question was happiness,
the only thing I can do to be happy, is create, 'create moments', she
said, do something perfectly, even if it's just thinking of what you
will wear to go to the restaurant. It was like the drinking of a
soothing, unknown drink. She doesn't know me, but I will always
love her, even in a hundred years.

16. How pens must be held – Eugenia's thumb –
    Masolino makes a splotch –
    True colours of Mère Maria Amor

Geneviève says Mozart wrote his music at a dazzling speed. You
can hear it in Alla Turca when it goes like running down
grandmother's stairs, and you cannot stop because you are
intoxicated. Ideas came to him and he had not enough time to note
them, and broke pen nibs and scratched out all the paper, and was
temperamental and certainly it would end up spilling an ink bottle?
I think he had an echo chamber in his head. He heard in his head,
kept it aside, then heard the next bars, all the while writing down
what he had put aside. Double hearing, double thinking, like doing
homework and talking to a friend at the same time.
    I read fast, yes, at dazzling speed, I gobble up and afterwards
feel bad, as if I had cheated, I am a bird skimming the surface of
the lake, catching a sip, a sip, through the whole lake, then resting.
Then I know if I want to start again, reread, and reread, and go
deeper and deeper, and the book becomes part of my thoughts. In
the classroom, I can make it look as if I had read and understood
like lightning, but it's just skimming, it will all evaporate and if the

teacher makes a compliment I'll blush and forget even more.

I also write fast when it's dictation, or copying, from the blackboard, but I must be careful of my *écriture*, and the accents, because my hand tends to make them all vertical, so the substitute nun, a postulant really, and you call them Sister not Mother, thought I had made thirty-two mistakes, and I made an expression like Julius Cesar and said it did not matter because I am always first or second in dictation. But I felt the cold wind of the world outside my little circle, where others will judge you and it doesn't matter that your teachers have tolerated your *écriture* for years.

First it was pens with nibs, and the fearful business of managing the ink, pouring it from the large communal ink bottle into the inkwell. Dipping the pen and writing without making ink stains, and keeping your fingers clean, and not dragging the side of your hand over the wet words. My writing was neither good nor bad. But the way I held my pen could not be condoned. Many a teacher has tried to make me hold my pen differently, but I can't and I don't. I hold the pen like someone who never saw one, with my right thumb sticking up. The nuns say it should be meekly joining the other two fingers and contribute to the movement of the pen. But the pen rests cradled at the base of my thumb and index, and my four fingers stuck together, like a paw really, give the impulsion. I lack rotundity, softness, but I write just as well as most, I know all the capital letters and display them as required by the solemnity of the moment. Sometimes I even do Mummy's special capitals, there is a difference, in the G and the F, and the Z, they curl up then trespass below, whereas at school we do them all above the line, airier, more open.

My *écriture* is the result of me, there is a thin stream of fluid, of thought that goes into the pen and comes out as words. When I write the word 'music', it is *me* writing 'music', not someone else. I have watched myself writing 'music' since I started, all my life, and I have modified the shape of the letters time after time, just as music meant more and different things, and now it is my *écriture*. I await the day it will crystallize, like my parents'. I don't want to be like the others', or like the *cahier d'exercices*. To write diligently is for all the girls who write *Dieu* with an extra-soigné beribboned *D*. The studious and boring girls, with their perfect pen-holding, and where are they? Are they more beautiful in their words, are they more luminous? No, they just write in a way that ingratiates them with the teacher more. They cannot be superimposed on me any more than the sampler matches my handwriting.

I hold my knife the same way at the table. My thumb sticks out. There may be a reason. The reason. It's hard to speak of a very loved friend, which you have to keep secret, because everyone ridicules it. *Méconnu*, unrecognized. I still suck my thumb. At almost twelve. I never could stop, I always was teased for it, and now the teasing has become almost desperate. People are really worried for me. I am too. When I was smaller, there was some tolerance for it, and I did not hide. With a swift gesture, nannies, maids and even Mummy have yanked my hand from my mouth, abruptly, waking me up from my reverie, my absence, my time with myself. My thumb is my centre. It has a taste, of myself. When my hair is long enough, I can twist a strand around my median – it's difficult if you never tried, and I find on my thumb the kneaded taste of skin, bread and myself (the right one, the left tastes of nothing) and a smooth silky brushing on my palm. It cannot be described, like the Holy Ghost. But it's universally despised. It excites rage. 'That thumb again!' Marisa, one of the maids, told me of a girl who was getting married, and disappeared from the altar, and she went and hid in the parking lot, and what was she doing? – smoking a cigarette, I thought. No! She was sucking her thumb. On her wedding day. To avoid the outrage of the hissing wedding party who would discover me curled up in a warm Cinquecento outside the church, I decided I would never marry.

In the smaller classes, up to fourth grade, we had boys as well as girls. Piero my brother never came to my school, and I was glad – how could it have been my school if it was also his, but Ginestra had a brother, Masolino, who was in second grade with us. He was very nice. He wore the same sort of bootlets as Ginestra. His step was noisy as a troop of mules.

We were all officially still learning to write. But some had already reached a level of mastery, having started early, and showed an angel-like angeloid cleanliness and precision, and *belle écriture* it was, right from the beginning. Masolino could not write well yet, and in particular did spots with his pen. He was left-handed, too, and our elbows – my right and his left, would collide sometimes. Already there had been conflicts, the nun had spoken to him and actually held his right hand hard to show him he was capable. He had stubbornly switched back to the left, the second the nun turned her back on him, and she must have felt us smile. To make it extra difficult, if you think about it, when a leftie writes with an ink pen, he travels from right to left, so he drags his fingers over the moist words. But the idea of learning with a ballpoint pen was abhorrent to our teachers and to us.

So once, during a copying assignment, Masolino did a colossal splotch on his copybook. We were both paralyzed by the enormity of it. Mère Maria Amor in a Mosaic act of wrath came down from her platform, tore the sheet from the copybook, to our scandal and fear, and taking a pin from her pockets, pinned the sheet to Masolino's back. Masolino curved, and slouched helplessly on our desk, hiding his face. The page was horrible, and the safety pin. I was even sadder, wanting to protect him and not knowing what to do. Ginestra looked dark but philosophical. A swelling pushed the walls of my heart, slowly depositing a sediment.

Amor did this to show everybody in recess how bad he was. But that time, she showed us how bad she was. Having always been ugly, with a small, round, apple-shaped face, she started wrinkling, she began to cave in, drying up, shrinking. At recess, the girls from all classes, so quick to chirping and making a fuss, although plainly expected to deride him, let him be. Masolino smiled self-consciously for a while, then he forgot that thing on his back, a sort of April's fool. But I could see it, and stayed close by, my hands in a fist in my apron.

Amor kept shrinking, and a few days later disappeared, and nobody asked where she went.

17. Contents of the safe – Christmas in Rome –
     The eel that came for dinner

In the safe, there are four drawers. My cousin Sergio mocked me when I showed it to him. He said, it's just a filing cabinet, so I said it was an armoured cabinet. It's just Daddy's way of speaking, 'Shall we open the safe?' and we all come and watch. He dangles the brass key-ring, three quarters of a ring, with olive-shaped tips, you unscrew one olive (with a red core) to slip the keys in or out.

We look up to the top, inaccessible drawer, as Daddy removes cylindrical boxes covered in white, pale blue taffetas. Those are our christening certificates, more important than any other thing, there is our absolutely precise definitive name. We may have nicknames, people may misspell our names, teachers may turn them into French ones. Here, we exist, perfectly calligraphied: *Eugenia Ada Domitille*, a touch of the magic wand, you will be – who knows. *Pietro Charles-Antoine*, you will travel the world and be a proper Pico della Mirandola. Vanna: *Giovanna Valentina*, fashion has changed and we ran out of grandmothers, so two names only for you, you will be charming and fun. And the names of godparents, those who will take care of us if our parents die: mine are Uncle Elio and Aunt Simone, Piero has Michelangelo and Esmeralda (who was his fiancée, but she broke the engagement, and Piero is a little abandoned), and for Vanna, she had a substitute godmother, but officially, it's Valentina (who was in Portugal, shooting *Under the Sun of St. Tropez*).

Then there are passports, even the old ones, with their corners cut, and stamps in all colours; blue for Mummy and green for Daddy. That they don't have the same type of passport is something Daddy arranged. It seems to me a complication, a cause for worry, I know Mummy really should not keep her Canadian passport, it's against the Italian law to have two nationalities, but Daddy has his own views. Complications do not bother Daddy and he solves everything. But I still worry.

Then the second drawer, the best, containing our chains and medals. My chain has finely worked links, each beaten as with a fairy's hammer, my medal with a mother-of-pearl centre set in blue enamel. The effigy is a St Anthony, fortunately rather blurred. Piero has a chain with sailor's links, he believes it's for captains and commanders. We have our spoon, fork and knife, each in its box covered with a sort of crocodile paper. They are 'kept aside'. Except for Vanna's spoon, which has ended up in the everyday sugar pot, even if it doesn't match, and it looks like it will stay there forever.

I also have brooches, which I never wear (how? when? on my coat?): a spider with green eyes from Mme Volpetti, a small golden palm leaf, given by a very nice maid we had two years ago, a silver filigree butterfly that's not really mine but Mummy lets me have it. Also a filigree rosary in a round box I received for my First Communion, and I never use it, and a watch with a black strap, and my pearl necklace, transported back and forth to Canada by whoever goes there, so that Tante Simone will be able to augment the number of pearls, a given number every year, based on important events – the pearls are small and light, it's almost a hand-length now, and there's a little gold chain on both sides, so I can wear it when I go to parties (if it's here).

Vanna looks at the large silver medal engraved with a portrait of Mary and Child and the inscription 'Sainte Vierge, Protégez Mon Enfant', that used to be hung over her crib, she thinks she is the child in the portrait. Piero tries his fantastic chronometer, given to him by Michelangelo. There is a camera, with marvellous gears and buttons that use up a whole second to happen, *tataclac-tch*, Daddy bought it in Germany. There is a silver letter-knife, with a carved jade handle, Daddy says I can have it some day, when I am 'a young lady with a large correspondence'. I don't get many letters yet, I practise with a knife on Christmas cards. And in the summer, sometimes a visitor will ask me to cut for her the pages of a French book, large, elegant tomes of off-white paper, without illustrations, that must be readied by the first reader. It feels important to carve a book. Some day I will cut my own, like *Mémoires d'une jeune fille rangée*, it sounds splendid.

At Christmas, cards and letters arrive from everywhere. We send some too, but I don't think we keep up, not my daddy, he is too busy, and I *think* he has understood that Mummy simply hardly ever writes letters, or if she does, she does not mail them. If I had all the friends they have, I would be writing all the time. Mummy is different, although she has money for everything, she does not find the envelopes, or has no stamps. I think she *forgets* to finish. Her sisters, away in Canada, know this and just keep writing.

So my parents seem to take for granted this one-way flow of mail. I am not sure how it works, I thought it was very important, to reply. My friends will be stern if I don't reply fast enough. 'You did not reply!' will be the first thing in the next letter.

The same, for invitations, 'We must absolutely have the Brancioris over for dinner,' my father will say, and I know it's because they *owe them* an invitation, and that is a serious thing. It has been explained to me that even if you don't like someone, if you have accepted their invitation, you must *reciprocate* and invite them. If you have been invited and did not go, then you don't have to invite back. If you invite back, and that invitation is not accepted, you are even. That must be a fantastic piece of luck. '*Cumparimmu e risparmiammu*', it's Neapolitan, we appeared to be grand and we saved ourselves the trouble, my grandmother would say that.

Since I am enthusiastic about letters, stamps, cards, messages, I wormed myself into having permission to open the Christmas cards, when I'm home and the mail arrives, brought upstairs by Ovildo. I open them, look at the image, and put them back inside. I can read them only later, when they are up on the piano. Letters are sacred.

The piano is a black Bechstein *piano à queue*. 'What a pretty baby grand,' said Sonny Bonocore when he saw it, and I laughed because I had never heard a piano called a baby, I said, it's a foal, rather. Then the grown-ups laughed because I had not understood, and I said I did not speak American yet. And they laughed again, but Sonny pinched my cheek and said, 'It's OK, it's OK.'

I am the guardian of the cards. I groom them and display them and love them. Once, we had our own Christmas card, drawn by Mummy and reproduced in 100 copies, Daddy kept waiting for Mummy to finish the original and said at one point that the typographer 'did not guarantee the delivery'. It was lovely, black and gold reeds by a snow-covered bank, and I put it at the front.

Some days, it's the modern ones that attract me, the colder ones, drawn in ink with just a little colour – some sent by painter friends, abstract, South American, or the northern silent landscapes, scenes of Canada, of Sweden. After a few days, it will be the warmer ones, the children's Christmas with holly boughs, mistletoe and decorated trees, and fireplaces. Then the serious ones with the Madonna and Child, and the Magi, and the shepherds, naive and astonished. I asked Piero what *was* mistletoe, he says it's a parasitic plant bearing little berries, also that it creates a substance that is a 'powerful glue' to capture birds. Then he started on the rites of the Druids, and I left him talking alone. Bird traps, and kisses traps, as in *Eight Cousins*.

Anyway we don't have Christmases like that. Christmas is not heartfelt in our house. Even my grandmother, who knows the translation of all joys into food, will not, in deference to my grandfather's old age, invite us for the Vigil, but rather go for lunch the next day, here or at one of our aunts'. Becoming a supernumerary instead of a protagonist. Our house does not become red and green. My heart is full of longing when I see images of homes where they know how to have Christmas, where inside is really warm and outside is really cold, like when we are at the farm in our warmest clothes. Puddles have a thin crust of ice, and the grass is pale green. After playing outside, we walk back into the farmer's main room, happy we were cold and now we are warm. I would like a country house, and dogs, and horses. There would be hills, and a bit of forest, just like our farm. And there would be a family of people who are happy together and laugh and chat at the table.

So it's December and nobody knows what to do. The domestics wait for my mother to start something. My mother talks vaguely of Christmas masses back in Ottawa. Grandmother speaks of her times, when children never got more than a small doll and an orange, 'if they were lucky'. Rosalina doesn't know much, but has been ironing her brown dress: on St. Stephen's Day, she will take a *corriera* and go visit her brother back at the village, in Cantalupo. I think that maybe in Cantalupo they like Christmas, they know what to do. The women have been baking thick cakes, and the men look forward to more frequent little glasses of amber wine. They haven't TVs and dreams of far-away decorations. If they dream, it's of more, and a better quality of the things *they know*, a bigger *prosciutto*, many *prosciutti*. More eggs for the cake, more than one cake.

More rum for the trifle. Perhaps more money to purchase yet another square of land. More wool to knit, and that, Rosalina will provide, bringing her sister-in-law dozens of skeins of a fantastically sturdy bottle-green wool, we got it together at the haberdashery next to my grandmother's market.

Rome is no help at all. The city runs in many different directions, customs piled upon each other. Christmas is muddled up with the Epiphany, which is Twelfth Night. That's when the semi-benevolent witch-like old woman, La Befana, flying, goes about distributing gifts and sweets and sometimes the much dreaded lump of charcoal. In some churches, there are exhibitions of ancient cribs, but they are hard to see for the crowds. In Piazza Navona, there is a large fair, have you ever been there? It's a very beautiful square, encased among palazzi and churches, and in the centre, at large intervals, it has three fountains where mythical creatures splash and swim. Before Christmas, the piazza is covered in stalls, unrecognizable, there are lights and competing music and kids blowing in their plastic trumpets. Grown-ups always tell us how nice it is, how traditional, but we don't really take to it, the spun sugar is not as cloud-like as it looks. It even feels a bit sad, all this fun that we don't like, walking with our hands in our pockets.

Piazza Navona, they say, is the preferred store of La Befana, for smaller gifts and nougat that can be slipped into socks. Babbo Natale, Father Christmas, gives larger gifts that come in boxes, bought at Il Sogno or La Galleria San Carlo al Corso. He comes through the chimney and carries gifts in a scrip – and no negative gifts, no coal or blackened lump of sugar. But even Father Christmas has to share with Baby Jesus, whose birthday, after all, it is. And La Befana must share with the three Magi. And the Befana-Christmas must share with New Year's Eve, when people go out and children go to bed feeling they've missed something wonderful. Some children are allowed to stay up and afterwards tell excited stories of playing board games and eating lentils with *cotechino*, a dish I detest. The French girls will speak of their *étrennes*, which are gifts of new clothes, shoes or even money you get on New Year's Day. In our house, children cannot stay up, certainly not till midnight, and never receive money. It is our firm opinion that such children are badly brought up, they are pale and can't climb trees.

Well, we *do* do a few things. At school, we have a choral concert, where we sing old Noels. This washes away the taste of the perhaps not very good marks in our *carnet de notes*. At home, the potted pine gets brought in from the terrace and we decorate it. The crib, made of a wonderful gnarled corkwood, is displayed on a green moss-like cloth, and the palm trees and characters go to their positions. The shooting star. The goose. I listen on and on to our Christmas records. The doorbell will ring with a delivery, as some clients send Daddy cases of wine, or some grand, full baskets, to thank him for favours he did them. The wine cases he opens with raised eyebrows, joking about the fine names and vintages – he does not like wine and says that connoisseurs just pretend to know. The baskets are fine big things, with a showy centrepiece, a china vase with handles and lid, a cut crystal bowl, something luxurious, and some equally rich and plentiful content, fine chocolate, nougats, marrons glacés or marzipan decorated as fruit, miniature lemons, bananas, chestnuts, so perfectly imitated that you gape, from Sicilian pastry shops. Everything gets put in its proper place by the maids.

Two days before last Christmas, there was one delivery, after lunch. Daddy had removed his tie, and was about to have a siesta. As Rosalina was resting, he opened the door. A client was sending him, with great practical difficulties, a *capitone*, a colossal, live eel – in Naples, traditional fare for Christmas Eve.

So Daddy was handed a dampish basket with the eel squirming about. He gave a tip to the delivery man. He closed the door, 'alone with the monster', he says laughing.

And now? Daddy took the most enormous pot he could find in the kitchen, filled it with some water, threw the eel in, put it on a counter, put the lid on, and to keep it in place, put the heaviest thing he could think of – the iron, on top. And went to have his siesta.

At exactly a quarter to three, a colossal boom-ba-da-boom rocked the apartment. Shrill cries were coming from the kitchen. Daddy jumped out of bed, thinking the coffee machine had exploded. The cook and the maid, standing on a chair and the table, were crying *'Aiuto, c'é un serpente!'* as the eel was swishing around on the floor, among debris of pans, gluey, repulsive, looking for escape.

So Daddy woke up the janitor, who woke up Alfredo in the car and told him to get rid of the thing in the Tiber. But Daddy thinks that perhaps the *capitone* did 'die its regular death' – it got cooked on Christmas Eve.

18. When you go to Canada – In the plane with Daddy –
One Christmas – Habitat – Napoleon in Ottawa –
A lake

ONE CHRISTMAS

Canada is the real country of Christmas. It has the trees, the snow outside, and warm homes.

On the first trip, I was only a baby in a cot, helpless and swimming in dreams; on the second, it was summer and there were strawberry fields, and my soft, pretty aunts.

This time it was the Christmas when I was seven. We all went, also taking Anny, our Swiss *signorina*, in a TWA airplane. I was a little woman, with my little handbag.

I had lost consciousness, gorged with artificial foods, confused, tired, asleep. I half woke up. The plane was in semi-darkness, the passengers put to sleep like children during siesta, supervised by a suave hostess, faint night lights on the ceiling.

From the porthole, thousands of tiny lights glimmered, pinned on what seemed an immense blanket of snow. The lights were like buttons on a quilt, softly sinking in it. Was I dreaming? I asked my Daddy, smoking one seat away from me. He said, 'Those are Eskimo houses, Eugenia, with their fires.' I looked outside again, almost pushing my eyes out to augment their range.

That the Eskimo lived in igloos I knew – that igloos felt rather warm inside, I accepted, that is, I said yes, without understanding. That the Eskimo built fires into their houses, to make them very warm, without melting and bringing down the roof, was at the same time true and impossible. You held their picture in your hand, you tilted it. One moment they were real, facing the strong winds, hunting seals, without hot running water; the next, they were in fairyland. In fairyland, the lights would be visible outside, from the interstices of the ice bricks, glowing as from the bedside-table shrine of Mme Volpetti's.

In this silent, majestic moment, while everyone slept, I and Daddy were awake, crossing the night, flying above a place lit like New York, but for Eskimos – such were the riches of Canada, they had Eskimos, their pretty costumes, sleds and igloos, by the thousands.

Acknowledging the polar nature of Canada, we were dressed like Arctic explorers. Vanna and I had thick red coats, with belts, which I thought very glamorous. Vanna had a hood on hers. Piero sported an anorak. We all wore sealskin *après-ski* boots. Someone kept pushing hard on my head a stupid blue hat with flapping ears. This manoeuvre was abrupt, as when someone in a bad mood brushes your hair saying, what a field of asparagus, it's all knit together. I kept removing the hat, hiding the flaps inside.

We went and met every aunt, uncle and cousin in the pictures, they all existed, in individual homes with wall-to-wall carpets and white fresh snow lavishly displayed. The Chéniers, who come to Italy in the summertime, with my cousin Guillaume; Tante Béatrice and Oncle Walter, and my cousin Emmanuel and his dog Tidbit; many more, each with a distinct trait. Dad always quizzes us, when we are driving to the farm, who is the cousin who likes trains? Who wants to be a pianist? Who are the two blond girls? Who is the Irish aunt? Who has a Labrador?

There were labyrinths of snow, much taller than me. For Christmas, I received so many Barbie dresses that I could not carry the boxes. It felt sumptuous. My uncles unwrapped their tapir suède ties, from Roland's, in various subtle tints, wondering if they were suitable for the office. My aunts unwrapped their silk scarves from Schubert's, each carefully chosen. Around Tante Béatrice's table, there were all the variations of Mummy's eyes, cat's eyes, in grey-green, green-blue, grey-blue, grey, with lovely soft velvety complexions. Variations in blondness, platinum to ash-blond. I behaved well all the time. Sitting in despair on the side of a skating rink with skates on. My father buys three pairs of cuff links, one in gold with a bowling ball hitting pins, a 'Lucky Strike', like his cigarettes, a square pair with blue marble and an oval one with a light burgundy marble. He laughs, shaking his head because they are so inexpensive. Playing in a lot of basement playrooms. Good breakfasts. Compliments. Tante Simone lets me hold her arm and look quietly at every charm on her bracelet, and the one with my name, in the middle of a daisy.

AUGUST

This time, it's almost August in Rome, the blinds are kept down in the apartment against the heat, we are piling up clothes, sandals, books. I organize and reorganize my blue beauty case with eau de cologne towellettes, my hairbrush (shared with Vanna), chewing-gum, and an Instamatic camera someone forgot at our house last summer. We are going to visit the World Exhibition in Montreal. Our family is anxious to show us Canada in all its splendour. 'I will see you again in the summer, you'll see, Expo 67 is wonderful,' said Tante Simone when they came for Easter. I would go anywhere, and anywhere she is. She brings cheerfulness and purpose. She has ideas. She is beautiful. Her hands are beautiful, whether she writes a letter, or ties up her sandal. She and Mummy go out a lot together, looking for the best shops. They enjoy doing things together. Mummy has no other special friends, just 'friends', she is very independent.

Everything is hot. On the day of the departure, we drive (in two cars, one driven by Daddy) to the airport, at six in the morning, and have breakfast at a bar known to Tonino – we eat astonishing *maritozzi* with whipped cream. At Fiumicino, Daddy goes from one counter to the other, paying airport taxes, negotiating better seats, accompanying us beyond the gates, with his air of being very kind and at the same time very clever. He is not coming with us, he has to work, he will join us later. As soon as we are inside the jet, I forget him.

We have been transported in a big black car with automatic windows to our apartment, in an ultra-modern building made of little boxes piled up *n'importe comment*.

We look outside from vertiginous heights into the Expo, and Piero immediately spots the Italian pavilion. All countries have brought something they can show the world. What I feel, like a silence, is the newness. The old is silent. Piero cries there is a machine distributing Coca-Cola in the stairways, at the fifth floor. We are given coins. We get the Coke bottles and sit on the concrete steps, a little disoriented after all. The Coke tastes metallic.

There are two parts in the Expo – the Luna Park and the exhibitions. Everybody says we must go to the Czech pavilion. We go to the Indian pavilion. Tante Simone buys me a bright pink bracelet glittering with inlaid mirrors. I drop it and it breaks in five. I tell myself I'll find a way to repair it. We go on a mini-train that runs through the whole area. Adults are ecstatic.

We are given great freedom to come and go within the Expo. Piero, Guillaume and I are told to go to any film we want inside a cinema with many screens and images, meet again at three at the wicket. We watch, standing at a balcony, as images appear ahead, above, below. The boys run to another level. I keep missing the story. The images shock me – a heart, naked, beating – the head of a newborn appearing between two legs. I feel revulsion. It's violent. I am angry.

I go to the *Swan Lake* ballet with a friend of my mother. I fight sleep throughout act two. Maybe I am not ready for adult life.

Another big black car takes us to Ottawa, two hours away.

It's eleven on a very hot day and the housekeeper gives me money to go buy two cans of tuna, ten minutes away. She suggests sweetly that I wear a hat against the sun and I don't dare say no. At the top of the hill, looking down, the asphalt is burning. I feel discouraged, my collar is rubbing against my neck and my summer shoes now hurt in a different spot. The hat is too small, from the fifties, not for a girl, for Florida. Cars trembling with heat drive by. The supermarket appears abandoned. Inside, food of all seasons.

I buy the tuna and a red collar for Tippi. I pay, in English. Walk up the street, the hill. The city is anaesthetized.

I have been invited to lunch. The girl and her mother came by

yesterday, the girl wearing a hat. My striped dress has been ironed.
It is debated whether I can avoid wearing socks.

Voilà, I am a big girl, going for lunch, but I am not happy.
Very.

Monsieur Leonoff and his sister Madame Ménard greet me
with effusion. They used to be neighbours of my Canadian
grandparents', and those were happy times. I feel very shy and
keep mixing up the names and family ties. Eleonora takes me to
her room, very tidy, with a beige-rose quilted sateen bedcover and
curtains. She picks up a perfume sprayer and sprays a few puffs all
round. 'Cabochard,' she says. Eleonora tells me she hopes to go to
New York this fall, for her wardrobe.

She is taller and stronger than me, with large eyes and mouth.
Her fingernails are painted pale pink. She is thirteen. She speaks
French, English and some Hungarian. She is being very nice, very
grand. Boredom, humiliation and discomfort envelop me.
Cabochard pushes hard against my brain.

In the living room, there are carpets on carpets, paintings on
wallpaper, chandeliers, china cabinets, objects everywhere.
Eleonora says her uncle is a great admirer of Napoleon. And now I
see – it's all Napoleon. Mère Marie Léon would be happy, except
that objects here are not historical, rather about history. There is a
copy of the *Sacre* painting. There is Joséphine, pretty, with pink
cheeks. There is Napoleon's head, in an oval frame. There is a
sketch of the house at St. Helen's. The furniture has the imperial
ornaments, the eagle, the Roman insigna, sphinxes, obelisks. On
the mantelpiece, there are two big black vases with handles. 'Those
are called Etruscan,' says M. Leonoff, 'a special black terra cotta' –
I feel a surge of protestation. I know Etruscans, we find pieces of
pottery scratching the ground when we sit at the top of the big hill,
at the farm – it's light and plain, the vases here look like big thick
black crows, *what does he mean?* My face feels very red. There are
painted scenes on plates, hung on the walls, things that always
bored me, 'Enea chasing Helen', 'The donkey and the fox',
antiquity shown in paintings, centuries later, and one is always
expected to know what it's about!

There is a special Joséphine corner, with a harp, lovely, a
display cabinet with little morocco cases, a smelling salts bottle, an

embroidered slipper, and a chair in an exquisite, worn-out silk in roses motifs. 'This should be reupholstered,' says M. Leonoff. Eleonora brings to my notice a group of porcelain dolls and tells me their names.

Our lunch has been put on the table, we girls are eating on our own. The dining table, round, is set on a small raised alcove, hung with dark red drapes – no windows are visible from where we sit. There are eggs mimosa, tasting a little sugary. We drink from red-tinted stem glasses. Then Madame Ménard brings sliced turkey with a red jelly and potato salad. The plates are dark green with a gold band. I dig around the jelly to avoid it. I am breathing little, conserving my oxygen, a sheep being carried by truck, packed, only hoping it will finish soon. Plate too coloured, too full, playing dolls with me as a doll, me as an important visitor and I am not.

After lunch, Monsieur L. drives us around in his golden car to show me the city. The car is refrigerated, and this morning I refused to take my old white cardigan. Eleonora is perfectly at ease.

'*Oh, it's like a museum! They have a harp, and a slipper of Joséphine! And Monsieur Leonoff says that Napoleon was poisoned, there was a conspiracy, because the English were afraid of him. And he made me sit on a chair that comes from La Malmaison, where the Empress had all her flowers and exotic animals – she introduced the dahlia to the Continent, yes!*'

Imagine a world without dahlias. People would be sadder. Without *frites*, without roses. Without yellow roses. Some moods would be missing. Without chocolate, without tea. There would be no lovely rainy afternoons.

* * *

We are on a train to Gaspesia. Gaspésie, Gaspé, Percé. It's a sort of expedition, we brought only half our luggage. We are going to see the Atlantic Ocean, the Rocher Percé, and visit the Audiberts. The train is air-conditioned, that means cool air with a very bad smell of rotten beer. Piero and Guillaume laugh dementedly whenever I say 'rotten beer'. The grownups pretend it's nothing. At every stop, Piero and I get out on the platform to breathe some fresh (train station) air.

The Atlantic is more green that the Tyrrhenian sea. It's beautiful but we don't try the water, we are wearing sweaters, and trousers. Piero and our cousin get extremely excited about flying around the Rocher Percé and my uncle and Daddy say yes. I go searching for coloured pebbles with Vanna.

We sleep in a motel, a roomful of children, watching TV with Coca-Cola and chips. We are noisy, use the internal phone to make phoney requests. The receptionist complains and I am made to apologize, firmly held by the arm by my aunt. I am very unhappy, then I feel wonderful.

The weather has become warm and overcast. We drive through fields and forests, looking for the Audiberts' camp. We go through a mournful burnt-down forest. My uncle explains that it should come back within a few years. There is a lake with stumps emerging from the water. Daddy is pretending to be driving a jeep in the middle of a desert and the boys yell about everything being a mirage.

The camp is on Lac Duvivier. Elsa. We observe each other to verify that we are still the same. We immediately get in the rowboat and go. Seen from the cabin, the lake is oval, with a point on the right side, five minutes away. Behind that, another large, round part of the lake is revealed. I calculate, as always, how far it is to the bank, can I swim it … With Elsa, things are easy. Maybe a panicked joke, if we capsized … Then we'd swim.

The lake is melancholy, reflecting the closed grey skies. There is no wind, no waves. Is it because we have read stories about the poets and nature? We pay attention. Colours go from green to grey-blue to grey-green. Poets by the lake are always sad. But it seems to be a pleasant kind of sadness, since they can write about it. They are born in sad castles, they are sad orphans; they have unhappy loves. And throughout, they walk to the riverbanks with a roll of paper and a pencil and write poems. I tried it, I wore my pink corduroys and a velvet jacket, and went to the big oak tree on the way to the spring at the farm, and sat there interminably, thinking what could I write, sad I had no poem. It was cold. I felt important. I told Geneviève and Mademoiselle Danois overheard me. '*Poète, allez*', she called out.

* * *

Elsa last year gave me a bracelet with grey-green agates glued to it, 'from Gaspé', she said. Now I am here.

So many things to tell, not now. We float. We evaporate to the clouds. The clouds reflect us in the still water.

19. July 3, 1970

I did not do much back in Rome. Instead of calling Phil, for instance, perhaps find out, without asking, what Tommy was doing, or when there would be a party, I just read, and thought and did nothing. Did my reverie. I was still a little in disgrace, which I will explain, and tried to look serious and purposeful. Told Daddy I would prepare for next year, and reread my schoolbooks. Soon it was time again to prepare my luggage.

We are now in Ste Max, in a sort of arbour area where cars are not allowed. We have a mini-apartment on two levels, an alveolus at the top of a sort of whitewashed amphitheatre. Inside, it's a toy house. Feeling of having ended up in a campground by mistake. The Chéniers are just next door. Vanna sent the broom and pail down the garbage chute, never seen one before, big crisis. The plates and cups are very original, a locally made pottery called *grès*, a golden brown, very uneven. They break easily. A daily maid comes in to do the beds. I am always out. I am in a two-week sailing class, Piero and Guillaume are with younger kids, mildly humiliated because there could be no discussion: they go THERE, I go THERE. What peace.

Heavy presence of the French, in France, surprise. *Chauvinisme* (not the same as in English, not Calvinism, nor male pig chauvinism) diminished by comparison with the French abroad. French *regional* chauvinism. Instructor always cursing the Mediterranean for not being windy enough. Invoking the storms of Brittany. Half of the training consists of capsizing and returning to normal. By furious repetition, I have grown rather capable. Two things to master are avoiding suffocation under wet sail, and swinging back on board without scorching thighs. With elegance, no. For the rest, I am not sure where the wind ever comes from, and I am obtuse about it. No drawing can make it evident. Does it have a round surface, a triangle? Does it hit in the middle? How can I feel it on a particular side of a wet finger rather than the other – finger being round, how do you make it to coincide with cardinal points? Am I anatactile?

I like the hum of the sails.

Afternoons, I sleep. I read. This is a sort of holidays village, brand new. On the harbour – with just a few boats yet, there is a night-club, a bookstore, a cinema, three cafés and two restaurants. Everything new and clean. Daddy bought at my request a huge book bound in red canvas about the arts in Paris over fifty years, as told by a man about town. You are *there*. He paid a ton of francs, I felt bad. He was pleased, my daughter reads this stuff. I was glad he was glad. With money Tante Marianne gave me, I bought a fashionable novel, based on the cover, because the author looks like Tommy. One afternoon I went to see *Love Story*, finally.

Every day before dinner, we sit at a café on the harbour, for cocktails, not for me, I order *café liégeois*, then I have no more appetite. Or I have a *croque-monsieur* directly. Later, I usually go to the nightclub. (It's not a dark place for Marseillais thugs, it's pathetically new and clean and modern.) Sometimes I find Daddy there, sometimes with the Chéniers, or other people, and he does the nightclub-goer, never short of inspiration, smoking, chatting, drinking scotch, and I stay mostly in my corner and watch and sometimes dance. Or I sit at the bar, which is so much fun when you are an habitué, you become friends with the barman who looks like Jacques Dutronc and everything is easy, even doing nothing.

I've had a bad fever and felt very weak. It's strange.

My aunt came to see me lying in bed. I felt weak and helpless. A friend of theirs came, too, and she spoke of her wonderful *kinési*, and her *chiro*, and all sorts of things. My aunt insisted on a doctor.

* * *

Mummy drove me to the doctor's, high up in the mountains, in the interior – *l'arrière-pays*. Grimaud, perfect like a postcard, flowers cascading from window sills, old stones. Could we not be there, away from the glare of the sun on the water, the mini-apartments, in a real place. It was a good doctor, fatherly, dressed in white. He praised my good manners no end, at least here was a nice young girl, not like those hippies with all those chains, who come to the doctor's with dirty feet. I felt bad because of the imposture. I was sweating. My fever.

I was afraid he might find something about Tommy and me.

He said something about strain, stress, vague words, things unknown that have a claim on me. I did not have time to worry, the next day I was better.

At the end of the course, our class had a big night out at the Coqueron.

Look at what I was going to send Elsa! Well – hard to write anything on a postcard, or you can encrypt. Bla, blabla, it's wonderful to be here (claustrophobic), I am learning to sail (don't know how to epilate properly), much to tell you and I will see you soon (I met an English boy, just wonderful, next day we were to meet on the beach, but what had seemed a good spot that night had been *invaded* by masses of people, you know the scenes in carnivals where lovers never find each other, I walked and walked in the hot sand, how I despaired and how I hated those people – I never found him again. Absolutely and completely. I didn't know his family name). (Oh yeah, and what about Daddy finding us rather hidden in a corner. He grimaced – I was smoking and beer on the table!!! But the music was too loud for a scene.)

Before I forget. Story of my disgrace, by Eugenia Ceccomori.

Two months before final exams, we had a lecture on psychology. Everyone speaks about it but I never heard an explanation. 'Describe the feelings of Marianne ... How does the author convey the ... Note the importance attributed to this detail ... Show the tightness of psychological reactions in Racine's ...'

Not to be confused with pedagogy or philosophy. It looks like the life of the soul … the mechanisms of the soul…. Not only based on moral sense. I never had so much fun, it swept me away. If only all classes could be like that. Paula too, sitting next me, had big eyes. We communicated by signs and exclamation marks on the sides of a school circular.

Madame Le Gal made diagrams about how – let's say six persons. Each one has to think of who likes her. If F thinks that A and B like her, she draws an arrow between A and F, and B and F. Now, ask B who does she like best; ask A, ask all the others: most times their arrows will be very different! So I might think – suppose – X likes me very much, actually, she might say she does, or behave as she is, but when it comes to choosing I could be sixth on her list!!!

So interesting, and confusing.

I stayed behind in the classroom, very excited. Mme Le Gal's books were on the desk. Impolite, I know, I picked one up and opened it where marked. There were tests and drawings, it was wonderful, all human experience in hypothesis and questionnaires. Putting order and giving advice in the labyrinth of what people do and think: fantastic. The tests were fascinating. I gobbled it all up.

I did not know, or had not understood, that Mme Le Gal, petite and charming in her braided chignon, her timeless blue dress, her soft shoes, had actually been invited to the school to test us for aptitudes. My mother is right, this is a school with modern methods, and what will we do in two years, after the Bac? All this running after the Bac and then what? I remembered the old test we did in seventh grade, and I had turned out Phlegmatic, how it puzzled me all these years. This time I wanted to turn out much more interesting.

Bon. I ran to the refectory to share my rapture with Geneviève, and refreshed myself with bread and carrot salad.

The next day I was on the list for the testing at 13:45, in the library. I really liked Mme Le Gal but I was nervous. All right, no studying required, etc. 'Exactly as you are, relaxed.' But that's precisely my worst, relaxed. Words sputter. My cues are lost. When relaxed I stop. Relaxed-excited is my best. Besides, there was going

to be a casting up of accounts, a judgment, no? But she was a
sweet lady.

We sat face to face. She gave me construction blocks to build a
trapeze, things like that. I was desperate and completely
concentrated (like when we had the exterior inspection and the
exam was on Artaud, but I only got 11/20.) I assembled the shapes.
I felt I was playing for my life. I was asked for words, contraries,
associations and I answered extremely fast. It felt like cheating. I
felt better, but cautious still. I was going to put my stamp on this
ordeal, the stamp of an interesting person. Then came the
drawings. It was the part I had read from Madame Le Gal's book,
something amazing. High peaks for high intelligence, the strong
firm line, assurance, the size of the sun, mountains, trees, I knew
exactly how to do it to be ultra-intelligent. Huge piece of luck
physics exam when the question was on the only chapter I had
studied, and I got an astronomical 17/20 – and MM Loïc thought I
had cheated). Besides I was reading in reverse Mme Le Gal's book
as she gave her instructions. Trees: I made a forest of the thinnest
highest-peaked trees, worse than a mouthful of shark teeth. For
the sun, I made a moon. Asked why, I said coolly there was no sun.
She was not a professor, so it was not impolite. And so on. I was
enjoying myself.

I told Daddy about the test, omitting details, and he said it was
hoped I would not be found out, *dépistée*, he said – he thinks my
psychology is perhaps better left unexplored.

Before long I had an interview with MMC. I was asked what I liked
to do, oh, I said, horseback riding, the guitar. I said I was going to
England soon. Did I feel tired at times – oh yes, I did. I was given a
letter for my parents. Never a good idea, those letters. All hell
broke loose, I can still hear Daddy's Gosh! The nuns had
recommended a one-year break before entering *première*. A pause,
a light regime of study, possibly learning English, riding horses.
They suggested schools in England or Ireland. Daddy was very
annoyed at the nuns, at me. 'You are perfectly *capable*, why would
you want to waste a year?' He wrestled them for a week, during
which I was too excited to fall asleep, thinking about this school of

dreams by the seaside and the boy I'd meet there. I had to make strange promises about becoming more mature, less *fantaisiste*. Unfortunately, I never found out what my personality was supposed to be.

Reveries (3)

20. The English tutor

'And how did you learn English, so well, I may add?' Another
entortillé, a wound-up gentleman, making impolite
conversation, doesn't speak it himself, a perfect imbecile. 'I go
to a riding school, in England.' And we started in *sixième*. And
I don't really speak English – which is the one thing that
counts, but I can read it. And now I have an English tutor.

Clotilde LaViolette is one of a set of six. Imported. 'Shrimp
Cocktail Forks, in a box.' Now discontinued. I confuse them,
forget the genesis the genealogy the geography. Mummy will
say, I'm going to visit Villa d'Este in Tivoli (or the excavations
in Tarquinia, or Ostia Antica) with Mélanie Bergevin, or
Bernadette, they're all the same. They are school friends, or
cousins of old neighbours, or friends of friends. From Canada.
Mummy wears an air of dutifulness about those women, she
tries hard to leave on time, she knows they will be waiting
punctually for her to pick them up, none of them drives, they
are very rational and mostly take buses, have no noisy dogs,
like tweed for their tailleurs, or jersey, it's a thin knit of wool.
You could say their nature, their consistency, is woollen, all-
season, reliable. In the heart of summertime, they are prepared
too, they have made previous arrangements, and migrate to
convents on hills, cool, cold places where they can take strolls
and be patient till the heat has abated. Buttoned-up blouses
and shoes that never lose their shape. Hand-loomed shawls.
Brooches. Sometimes attempting pink lipstick, a fuchsia thread
among the brown of their jacket.

'She is the one whose sister married Ranieri.' The sister
came first. She kept up a close correspondence in air mail
envelopes striped green and orange. Then came the momentous
one: she was getting married. How much fun Clotilde had with
the news, how rich the yield! Weeks and weeks of sweetly
telling all those she knew, and that she was going to the
ceremony, of course. And Ranieri had a middle-sized
apartment in Trastevere (purchased). A stationery-library shop,
Cartolibreria Clodia (almost all instalments made). She
skipped the bit about the defunct parents' home in the village

of Brollio (in shared ownership with his brothers, but she did not explain it all). Clotilde was going for an extended visit, she would keep her rental apartment in Montreal, which had been such a good find. And sublet, yes.

As for what Clotilde could do in Rome, Armande said she could apply to the Embassy, for some part-time work. She could try the foreign news agencies, the press, the radios, many setting up to cover Vatican II, the council discussing the rejuvenation of Catholicism. They would be needing researchers, helpers. She could find a little apartment.

The more it goes the more Daddy wants to speed things up, he is himself more and more busy, no time should be lost, he expects us to go fast, we succeed, dashingly.

He dropped the idea that Clotilde, if she had a little time, would be a perfect English tutor for me. That way, I would get a good accent and learn without effort. I liked that part. It is now clear that my triumphs in French are not extended to other living languages. There is a group in the class who after years of obscurity now enjoy the praises of the professor and dominate the game, throwing words and rejoinders to each other with the benevolence of the professor, MM Andrew. This rising social class is made of the British, Americans, Canadians, Anglo-etc. While others like me are shy and can't pronounce, and learn incredibly childish sentences. Ken is a boy. Then get thrown into books that defeat us. Professors, professors.

Yes, there we were having tea (my contribution to the customs of our house, I caught it from the Agatha Christies, read in French), all happiness, and Daddy throws his suggestion, and Clotilde, who was enjoying her afternoon, takes the bait, swallows it, and still smiles after she has understood. 'If I can get organized, Eugenia can come punctually Wednesdays at five fifteen,' and there it was, Wednesday the sombre-est day of the week, always was, most of the week still to go, becoming even worse. More fences around my freedom. What could I say, be rude and say oh no like a character in a cartoon? I was going to *have to* study? I have been despising all the Italians my age, who must study enormous quantities, their books twice as thick as ours, and many have tutors, and now, me too? You should see how reverently my grandmother mentions my cousins' tutors, a glory to her, rather embarrassing I say – it means you need help, usually for math, Latin – those areas where you cannot go anywhere without a pilot. On the other hand, to have a tutor means you are a good boy ... If pressed, grandmother will confide the hourly fee, with a sigh.

Then Italian schools can be so awful, I know because I've taken Italian exams three times, that's at the end of the year, on top of the *compositions* of the third trimester, it's an old law nobody cared to undo, you Must Be an Italian, study all the geography, the history, the Italian math, everything, until *terza media, quatrième*, eighth grade. *Schifosissimo, no?* One last ordeal before holidays can begin, while the rest of our schoolmates have already left.

In the yard of one of those unfamiliar schools we pass every day on our way to Sainte-Marguerite, appear the other Italians in my class, the exam-fellows. We are revealed for what we are. You can say all you want but you are Italian. Therefore. Ginestra, Santabarbara, etc. etc., some full of bravado, anyway, everywhere. Others are sinking, sinking. Our parents too are pallid and exasperated. My daddy talking with the principal, whom he has picked out unfailingly, putting in a good word, finding common ground, from the family name, or the accent, or someone Daddy knows, someone he spoke on the phone with, he has a perfect arsenal of those, I tell you, even on a desert island.

We are in normal clothes, we hardly recognize each other, the white dress both sleeveless and uncomfortable, it's hot. Here, the fear of not knowing has a particular taste.

Clotilde reached for her handbag and wrote in her pocket agenda, and looked as if she expected me to note the appointment. Daddy!!! He was amused, and I could strangle him. I went to get my *cahier de textes*, and it looked so ridiculous, large as a copybook and days in separate pastel colours. So I put her under next Wednesday. 'Via Girolamo Le Palme, economista', she said, which is how kids say it, that's how it's written on street signs, *Via Girolamo Le Palme, economista*. Or *Via Saverio Mercadante, musicista*, but of course not *Viale Beethoven, musicista*, it's the kiss of death, really. It means you are not famous enough to be recognized. Clotilde does not understand that kind of thing, she wouldn't even if you explained it to her. '*On the other hand,*' uncle Elio would say, 'the people …' Uncle Elio likes to extol education. He says illiteracy is rampant in the agrarian society, and the South (he says *il Mezzogiorno*) is suffering from atavistic neglect. There used to be an evening show, just before dinner, *Non è mai troppo tardi* (Never Too Late) where a professor explained grammar, he had the nice, good, well-meaning, plain way of looking of a cocker spaniel – large moist brown eyes. (I mean, *lo sguardo*, the way your eyes send their message. Le regard. No English for it.) He wrote extra carefully on the blackboard. My grandfather would watch him with pleasure, maybe he liked to think back to his school days. Uncle Elio said once that grandfather is an autodidact, he learned everything on his own, wouldn't it be wonderful, but then you'd miss your friends.

Rome has absorbed Clotilde as a permanent foreigner. 'Lady of indeterminate age and some financial means.' Brisk in dealing with water-pressure problems, or bills sent to the previous tenant, and cleverly using a battery of electric heaters to combat the chilly weeks of November and March that are not part of the central heating arrangements (though she valiantly fights at condominium meetings.) She never gets angry, she is just persistent. By her telephone table, she keeps her address book, which she updates with a pencil, all useful names. She knows, for instance, the man who does repairs to porcelain and other objects, on Via di Ripetta. A reasonable typographer, for business cards. Knows where to find foreign delicacies like brown sugar and peanut butter. She is on good terms with embassy and consular secretaries, and some diplomats. She receives invitations to cocktail parties and cultural events, which she RSVPs and attends. Drinks two gin-and-tonics and avoids the smoked salmon canapés. She makes adroit conversation, she is not shy not ebullient. She meets more useful people.

She is useful herself. Untiring in her efforts to distribute documentaries, television series, children's films. With her chignon, slanted glasses, wattle firmly set, she gives business appointments at Canova's on Piazza del Popolo (except on their closing day, then it's Rosati's) where she actually expects to talk business while drinking *pomodoro condito* in a narrow glass, with three olives. She causes despair and anguish by calling seven days later, to follow up on the notes she took.

She calls the National Film Board in the evening when the rates are lower in Rome and the director of marketing is just back from lunch Chez Vito, Montreal's little Italian restaurant on Côte des Neiges.

'Bonjour, Georges!'

'Clotilde, *comment va dans la Ville Éternelle?*' struggling against the Valpolicella to remember where her dossier is filed.

'Have you discussed the rights of *L'Aube des voyageurs?* Il Dottor Mattei says ...' (something about a series).

Georges Gagnon has many such free-lance agents in Europe, Japan, etc. but Clotilde is the most tenacious. The Iron Violet. He sends her more little cheques in Canadian dollars and cents than to the others. Her voice calls him back from the haze of the antipasto, lasagna, tiramisu and espresso. He gets thrown into activity, walking the corridors of the office with purpose, asking tough questions, cranking up the pressure on the people he calls. At about five, he feels he has done an honest day's work.

Clotilde will not be waysided. Swaysided? I cannot distract her from her tutoring. I walk in as for a social call, and start chatting about the city gardeners unloading the azalea pots in Piazza di Spagna (irresistible). About the traditional beignets of San Giuseppe in the pastry windows. About the posters for a new exhibition. But I cannot make her forget the task. She loves to work. She makes me read the *Herald Tribune* aloud. She talks to me about the parks of Montreal, the Canadian structure of government. She expects me to take notes. She gives me translations into English. She gives me the program of the conferences at the British Council. She says it's time I read English and American authors in the original.

We did *Emma* last year and it defeated me and depressed me. I could not read it. I hate to feel stupid. For books, or for people, you never know if it's you. I told Clotilde because she is the kind you must explain things to, articulating. She got up, rummaged and found an old edition of *Peril at the End House*, possibly original, the dust jacket done in mustard yellow and aqua blue with a suitable sketch of a man signalling with a lamp. Treasure. With fabulous period type and all. 'Why don't you try this, Eugenia. Let me know what you think.' I bounced down the stairs on tiptoes, vanishing like a thief.

21. Back to school – Librairie Française – Martyrs –
    A sense of history

School never seems so attractive as in the days of September when we prepare for *la rentrée*. We have grown, during the summer, we have matured like apricots, and we need new, larger uniforms. We need new copybooks, erasers, pens. For our minds, new, more advanced books. The old faces of schoolmates, scrubbed, hair pulled into ponytails, will return, with a new layer of experience. There will be shifts among friendships, old friends will remain old friends, some will become more prominent, others will recede. Some will become friends of the new girls. A new classroom teacher. A new beginning. We'll go off at the starting line at the first words of the *dictée*, covering the distance of the white pages in our half-confirmed handwriting, mixing the ornate capitals we learned in *onzième ('écriture anglaise')* with the type-like hand of the American girls, or the chunky style, soft and regular, that Santabarbara is showing off. I am still working on my signature, with a Greek E, and the C like a long horse shoe containing the rest, 'eccomori'.

Our parents eagerly participate in this hopeful return to school. They are secretly tired of finding things for us to do, and prefer the well-ordered schedule of school-time. They too, are carried by the September breeze, don't think of the so-so report cards every Friday, constant notes on our behaviour, being on time, wearing the uniform and all the rest. Taking the fortifying medicine after Ovaltine. Being carsick. Dodging the dreaded 'Eugeniá ... to the blackboard' (in math), or smiling at the ironic comments about being *dans la lune*, up in the moon, day-dreaming. Will I escape forgetting to bring, almost every single time, my sewing kit, my gym shoes, my gym uniform, the veil, the prayer book, the white gloves? Will I understand the commands, when we will assemble in lines, outside the Middle Entrance?

Uniform, shoes, books, pens – who could object to those austere purchases? I'll be well-dressed, my socks neatly pulled. My shoes this year are patent black with two straps, the rounded tip is a little exaggerated, is it because they are a size larger. Mummy told the salesman that my feet were enormous. I'll be bright as a new pin. And my books will be neatly covered – well wrapped as a birthday gift, with the blue-bordered labels well placed, middle-centre for the title, lower right for my name. And my writing things will be encased in my *trousse*, my pencil case, the nice burgundy one from last year, with a complete new set of Caran d'Ache pastels, and a new fountain pen, green and black.

School is coming, we need our new things, we go shopping downtown, in the Old Rome. Tourists marvel at the stray cats who live in the ruins of Ancient Rome, among the splendours of the Eternal City. We, too, live like those Roman cats. I know I'm lucky. The dentist has a view on the Spanish Steps. The car is parked behind the Pantheon. By that drinking fountain, there is an Assyrian bas-relief. Around us, freely provided, the perfume, the sweetness of the air of Rome.

We go in and out of shops, with Tonino nimbly leaving his seat to open the boot of the car and accumulate parcels and packets. If the next place is not far, we walk, he follows, not always directly because of the one-ways, so at times he disappears, and even loses us for a while, and my mother remonstrates.

The shoes are done. Even Vanna got a new pair this year instead of my hand-me-downs, 'absolutely destroyed', given away to St. Vincent. We went to Leri for the girls' uniforms. We went around to Campo Marzio to De Magistris, the stationer. At one thirty, we went to a café and had squeezed orange and sandwiches. Then, rather than returning home, while shops are closed, we went visiting the Pantheon, quite tired and unenthusiastic. Then Vanna started crying that her legs were hurting and we ended up sitting by the fountain with the obelisk, in the middle of the square, watching the tourists and the horse carriages turning around us. While Mummy was looking at shop windows, I went with Piero up to a horse munching oats in her nosebag. We called her name, Rondinella, and she pointed her ears forward, so we scratched her a little on the cheek. Time went by, traffic started going fast again around the fountain.

We arrived at the Librairie Française as the shutters were being rolled up. The store is run by Monsieur Jean-Paul and Madame Gabrielle. He is smallish, thin, with steel-rimmed glasses, a shirt and tie and a dark grey cardigan. He is kind, but always starts out teasing me. *'Que veut cette jeune demoiselle?'* 'Would you have – could you look if you have – I would like another book by J-M Trilby.' The one I read is *D'un palais rose à une mansarde*, a darling old book the Larivière girls left behind when they returned to Canada. The drawings are in India ink, very precise, in a kind of Japanese style, and the cover is pale green. It's about a little girl who plays the violin in courtyards. I thought it was excellent. Monsieur Jean-Paul looks doubtful, he's going to say *'Il va falloir faire une commande spéciale,'* with a tone of regret, it's a drag to make a special order. But he darts and ferrets a white, shiny book. *La Princesse Mimosa,* 'with new illustrations …' and it's bigger than the other one. I walk through the alleys, eyeing the *Contes et Légendes.* There are at least thirty. I feel hungry for all those stories. I can perhaps ask for another one, *Contes et Légendes* are quite historical and educational, I heard Mère Marie Léon say. I check one that looks attractive to avoid devil and werewolf stories.

Looking up at the schoolbook counter, I see my mother who has almost made her way through a thick group of clients, and looks around with that air of hers, infallible on Italians, blond, wealthy, distant.

Mme Gabrielle is handing out packets of books (you have to order ahead of time, as early as June), all ready, tied together with an enormous rubber band. When a packet contains all the math, grammar, orthography, science, geography, history, French, English, Latin, Italian, a New Catechism – when nothing is missing, it's quite a thing to be proud of. Still, you must be very prompt to check your own list and see that everything matches. I get nervous when it's my turn to check. The words twist and turn like snakes, I don't understand what I'm reading any more. So, beforehand, I counted the titles: eleven – yes, just like Mme Gabrielle was saying, we have ten, one is missing. I go to the cash, followed by my mother and Vanna with her smaller package. The math book looks cold and sinister with its pale beige cover.

The nuns are very picky about the schoolbooks they choose for us. Mère Marie Léon explained it to us last year. 'To check your history books, *mes enfants*, we go first of all to Jeanne d'Arc and see how she is described. If she is called a witch, we naturally don't choose it.' We were meant to understood that our books must be seriously documented. Now, Léonida is the history professor to all the *moyennes* and *grandes*, seven classes, and sometimes she *must* forget what period she is in, going in and out of classes. Because of course she knows a history book could not say that Jeanne d'Arc was a witch, it could only say that the English, her enemies, said she was a witch.

So maybe as she speaks of Jeanne, she thinks she is down there in Orléans or Rouen or Rheims (north of France), in those horrible years when people would get sent to be roasted. They would, you know, almost like Rosalina's roast beef, tied up, when they got to the stake – no salt and pepper, no bay leaf – oh why, why do I say things like that, it hurts me.

Cruelty of all sorts is inflicted on saints, who are actually gaining from being tortured, because that way they become 'saints and martyrs'. Take St. Lawrence, he was tortured on a rack, I think, because in Italian, we say, easily, 'You look like St. Lawrence on the grill,' if you seem to be on tenterhooks – what are tenterhooks? Saints try to imitate Jesus Christ, who keeps his cross nailed to his name forever, very sad, we are not allowed to forget the pain. They sometimes seek fearlessly to be hurt, to accompany Him in His cruel destiny. Some also seek to hurt themselves, they can for example wear very harsh corsets of spiky canvas, very grating, or beat themselves with whips or ropes. I saw a corset, a cilice, in a film on Saint Vincent de Paul, it scared me because I did not understand, and the scene was half in the dark. And he hurt himself purposefully, tying hard the strings of the torture corset, and crying: aahr! like we do when we cut ourselves and Daddy pours whisky on our cut. And there was a lot of meanness in the film, paupers, people in hospitals, and people in slave ships being whipped, and Vincent rushes to save a galley slave who can't row any more and is being whipped, and embarrasses the captain and other important people he was travelling with.

All this cruelty and embarrassment were terrible to watch, I was squirming in my chair at the special Easter projection in the crypt, all the pupils were carried by the dark flow of passion and meanness, we could not think it was in the past, far away. The nuns think we are very young, our feelings not quite developed, and the saint's story is for our edification. I am not edified, it means constructed, developed, I am crushed, my heart curled up like a piece of paper.

* * *

Léonida the history nun is floating about with her little notebook and her spectacles, not recognized as a modern by the good people of Rouen because she is wearing long robes and a veil, more or less in fashion in the year 1428 or 1438, looking at things with her infinite curiosity, so tiring because she always wants to tell us every little thing, looking with an entomologist's eye at the scrolls on the judge's table, at the guards' armours, the weapons ('... still the old weapons, bows, crossbows, piques, halberds – not yet arquebuses, Guerre des Cent Ans, *excessivement intéressant* ...') How happy she is, bouncing on cobblestones on her way to the cathedral, with her quick step (some also call her Clockwork Rabbit). Popping in and out of houses, 'Just passing!' she says gaily. Noting how kitchens are set up, a man eating at a table set with a tablecloth, a bowl, a tumbler, bread, taking stew from a bowl with a spoon, knife at his side (note the absence of fork), and the wash basin with a cloth hanging next to it. 'This street, you see, is *exceedingly* interesting' – she turns towards us, her little flock, maybe we could be in disguise as well – 'You will note how the wood structure is entangled, completely apparent, and the falling angles of the roofs – obviously a merchant's abode, with very tall gates for the passage of carts…. Oh, oh, the cathedral. Now, *mes enfants*, can you describe the portal?'Looking hopefully at those who are closest, me, and Geneviève, who has been joking with me, but also listening.

Geneviève: 'We have on the right La Tour de St. Romain, on the left, La Tour de Beurre (anecdote on the Tour de B.). The construction lasted from the beginning of the twelfth century to the beginning of the sixteenth. The Western façade is on the whole "flamboyant", a term meaning flame-like, a form of later Gothic style influenced by England, making use of the ogee, that is, double-curve. *Le flamboyant* is characterized by structural simplicity and lavish ornament. The portals of the transept are each flanked by two towers …'

'I prefer Romanesque, myself,' mutters Santabarbara, firmly against the French Gothic current. 'And I am starving.' As for what Santabarbara is wearing, oh she would be the opulent chatelaine, there she is, with one of those cone-like hats and square decolletés, and spotted fur coming out of her sleeves, and a husband with a grand family name.

Of course, Léonida can float from one world to the other. She could be bombarded with questions such as: *Prise de la Bastille?* (OK, easy) *Édit de Nantes? Vase de Soissons? Désastre de Pavie?* – and still know where she is. I know dates more or less. I have tried rehearsing dates before I go to Geneviève's, to impress her dad, he once said, 'Eugenià est une jeune fille cultivée,' because I had recognized a music piece he was listening to. Still, I have written a special Chronology to try and grab the past, make some order.

I get confused immensely with all the Napoleons, the real one, the others, the kings that came after the French Revolution, the real ones, and the half ones, always 'returning to Paris' or running away. There was also a marvellous empress, Eugénie, deliciously pretty and beautiful. Is it the same one Amy sees go by in a barouche, in *Good Wives?* (Such a stupid title, and inaccurate, in Italian it's *The Little Women Grow Up*). You know, when she goes on a grand tour, paid for by her old curmudgeon aunt, with her other aunt and uncle, and cousin Flo?

I won't ask anyone because I know nobody can tell me.

CHRONOLOGY

Adam	Red Riding Hood
The Etruscans	Napoleon
(Valle Giulia and pottery	*Les Malheurs de Sophie*†
in our garden*)	*Le Lac*, de Lamartine†
Nero	*La Petite Fadette*†
Jesus (First Communion*)	Succession War in America
The Crusades	Little Women†
The Good King Louis XI	Wuthering Heights†
The times of the Pashas	Photography
St Francis (his chapel*)	The Carbonari
Bayard	The unity of Italy
Molière (*L'Avare**, I played in it)	*Cuore*†
The Renaissance	Picasso
(La Gioconda*) – Raffaello	My grandparents*
The Baroque:	My parents*
Michelangelo (Piazza Navona*)	World War II
Henry the Eighth of England	– Anna Franck†
Henri Quatre of France	Tintin† all
Bach (*His Life and Music*†)	Heidi† all
Mozart (*His Life and Music*†)	*Fantasia*

(* = things I have seen or done; † = 'read')

22. At Grandmother's – The florists –
The Institut de Beauté

Once in a while, comes the very desired invitation to go and spend
a day or two at my grandmother's. She makes me sleep in the spare
room, on an old bed that is cuddly, warm, soft. Early in the
morning, when she opens the shutters wide, noisily, so that I will
wake up completely, there are plenty of things to do, errands, little
jobs I am a full partner in. Except for things where you use a knife

or big scissors. Endless tales to put the fear of scissors and broken glass into you.

Today, she is not going out till later in the morning. My grandmother asks me to run outside to buy grandfather's newspaper, as well as Madame Volpetti's, and today's bread for both households. She gives me five-lire coins to operate the elevator and the money for the papers and bread, which I keep separate, in my coat pockets. I rehearse carefully what I'll say, on my way to the newsstand, a green pentagonal kiosk, festooned every day with fresh papers and magazines. The news vendor inside is alert, quick, folding the papers together neatly, handing back change. *'Il Tempo e Il Messagero, perfavore,'* and I give him 120 lire. I buy six not over-baked *rosette* for us and a half coccodrillo bread.

Then I take a small detour to the shrine, higher up on Via Cimabue, at the corner with the riverside boulevard. When I was smaller, I thought it was a cat's house. There is a statue of the Madonna, life-size, with a little pale blue cape and a nimbus dotted with electrical bulbs. There are potted plants, and a few little dishes with cat food, some with spaghetti too. And a box for offerings to the Poor of the Parish.

Without looking above, to my right, I know my grandmother is keeping en eye on me from the dining-room window, up there on the third floor. She does it to protect me, and because she always wants to know everything people do. I know, I do, too. I am taking my time, looking at the Madonna. Now I turn with my back leaning on the banister, and facing the other side of the street. There are two shops I adore: the upholsterer's and the florist's. This week, there is a nice small armchair, in blue canvas, with white piping, looking fresh, optimistic. (I can see Mère Marie Albert making an act of this description, *'Optimiste,'* she'd enunciate with three layers of disdain.) Next, the *fioraio* and the pretty sign with a Flora crowned with flowers and leaves. In the tall crystal window, Anita (the daughter of Grandmother's old neighbour) is placing a big vase of perfect red roses on a tall pedestal. She is wearing her caramel dress with three-quarter sleeves and white cuffs. She moves her hands beautifully.

I start walking back home. All morning until one thirty Anita will be working, greeting clients, listening to their requests, making suggestions, deftly plucking flowers from the vases on display, sometimes bringing extra ones from the back room. In her shop, because it's so elegant, you get a special wrapping of crackling cellophane and silver paper at the stem. If it's a plant, there is a choice of pastel colours, or deep green, for the crepe paper of the pot, first, a narrow band at the base, then a thorough covering of the clay pot, finished with a scalloping of the upper edge. The secateurs sharpen the tips of the stems. The scissors snip, the hand-held stapler bites the tissue with force and precision.

The more ordinary flower-sellers are good too. In Rome, they have little green huts (green is the colour of city things, park benches, drinking fountains, taxis, buses). Being outdoors people, they are dressed in layers, more heavily, with a coat or a big black smock covering all. 'What will it be for you, miss?' rubbing their hands if it's a cold day. They have that beautiful way of swinging the bouquet as they fasten it, then put the strands of raffia between the stems to hide them. And they use a kind of waxed white tissue paper, sometimes with a gaudy printed publicity on it, which I detest.

There are so many occasions to buy flowers. For teachers, for the altar of the chapel, for the mothers of friends, for grandmother, for the house. It's funny, my mother never says no when I ask. I'll say, 'Oh, tomorrow is the end of the trimester, may I bring flowers to the Italian teacher?' and she'll say yes. So on the way to school, the driver will stop at a shop, whatever we find open, they all have a day of the week when they close – on top of the Sunday, and I'll hop out, to buy a bouquet.

Really, I know what I like. The difficulty is to get it. So to gain time, and see what the florist is like, I'll start by asking for prices of the bundles, the anemones, something else in pink, then the smallest white roses. I hope with all my heart that it will look pretty, not too big, that the ribbon will be well harmonized, that it won't be spoiled with too many greens. The chauffeur, when it's Tonino, will get out of the car, to stretch his legs, also to show that the young lady is not all alone, in case they are thinking of exaggerating the price. He'll make a compliment, '*Questi sono proprio belli, Eugenia,*' when I rush out of the shop, and put them carefully under the back window.

The teacher – whoever it is, is always overjoyed. I feel very
self-conscious, when I return to my desk, more clumsy than
Zouzou Montrachet, and really happy as well.

It's all about my legs. My mother said, 'Your legs are strong as a
goat's,' and I saw that ugly devil in my cousin Sergio's book
dancing on his hind legs (like a goat's) with a little shepherdess. I
don't know why Mummy was so mean. Maybe because she
suspected I'd just been parading with all her jewels. And the other
day she was very annoyed when I asked whether I would have
them when she died. But I thought that's what always happens,
that girls get their mother's jewels. So I thought about my legs on
and on. My legs are ugly, woody, knotty. How do I hide them?

I'll never be able to change them, I heard Aunt Valentina and
her friends chatting, 'Say what you want, if you don't have good
legs, you're going to have a ha-ard time,' and I know they were
talking about Morena, she is the one with thick ankles, and all the
rest. It's terrible. Trousers are for the seaside, or on weekend
outings, and riding of course, except in American magazines. Poor
Morena, she is quite frank with her girlfriends, trusting in their
good hearts, like a princess with her confidants. Morena is chubby,
cicciottella, with a fine face – but her legs ... Thick, not shapely,
like posts. They are not agile, swinging, girlish. You need face, hair,
hands, bust, and legs!!! That's it. But legs, they have a lot of
power, they say a lot.

Mummy has been going to Elizabeth Arden's for her hair. It
has a bright red door, Christmas-gift-glowing in the middle of a
normal Roman façade, on Piazza di Spagna. I like to go with her to
look at things, but I don't relax in case my mother would tell
someone to do my hair and I would be trapped (I could never make
a public row) and I would come out a curly poodle, as it happened
once. It's an Institut de Beauté, but only if you are beautiful.

Lights and mirrors everywhere, shining counters, staff in white
smocks, castles of creams and perfumes. I trot here and there. In
one alcove, a woman is lying on a day bed, face down. An
beautician plunges a large spatula in a bubbling pot of dark mud,
like the lava of the Vesuvius, takes it out smoking, waits a moment,
then spreads it on the woman's leg in a broad, sizzling, sticky layer.

It looks horrible, like a potion, it could be the contrary! Instead of beautifying, it could make you ugly, sticky, spiky, muddy like a frog! Then the solidified mud gets pulled away with a tremendous tearing noise. The client says absolutely nothing, she must be reciting at super-speed, *'Chi vuol comparire, pur qualcosa ha da soffrire,'* 'to be beautiful, some suffering is in order,' '... suffer-suffer-doesn't hurt ...' or maybe thinking of the divine young man who'll pick her up tonight, and: what shall I wear? From under the lava, her legs emerge, pink, beautiful as if they had been born from the foam of the waves, like the Venus on the laundry room's calendar. Of course it was worth it.

I continue looking for interesting things. In an alcove, a large lady, bandaged like a mummy, is lying down, her face painted blue. Next to her, a friend is having her hands manicured, chatting volubly, looking like she's talking to a friend who just died and she hadn't noticed. The boy from the coffee bar next door arrives with a round tray of drinks for the clients, who pay without asking for change. The bandaged lady looks like she'd love a drink. A blond woman starts making a fuss because she had asked for a Cinzano, she says, and there is only a Crodino left on the tray. My heart boils over with defence of the downtrodden and unmasking the wicked. But the annoyed lady lets go, she has to decide on the nuance of her next tinting, the boy continues, flustered, I follow him, thinking I will help him if the ladies are not kind.

Here we are in the salon where Jacques does his famous cuts. There are also some other coiffeurs, assistants, shampoo girls and manicurists. He is nice. He calls me Miss Mille Frutti because he likes a shirt I once had, with little rows of berries, apples and oranges – now it's too small and Vanna will wear it. He wears his hair with a bang, and over his ears, a little bouffant, like the singer Antoine, do you know him? It's terribly difficult to explain things when you are at the hairdresser's, words lose their meaning, you say cut a little here and they cut a little everywhere, then a little again and again. Or, I'd like that cut, and you show a picture on a magazine, and they start putting rolls, hurting terribly and bake you under a hair dryer and you still hope until the result humiliates you and you are too broken and red in the face but you must pretend and smile at the mirror.

Jacques is styling a woman who must be a princess, never unbeautiful, not with wet hair, not with rolls, not unbrushed, and now, blond and more beautiful every minute. Her perfume is Mitsouko, inexpressible, divine on her. Jacques chats, smiling, clips a little, pins a lock, imagines layers, volumes, brushes elastic curls and locks it all in place under a whirlwind of hair spray. The client puts down the transparent shield she was holding and breathes. I breathe the hair spray and Mitsouko. Her eyelids go down once, twice, judging herself all over again, all or nothing. Then smiles delightfully to Jacques who's been immobile, with folded arms, ready to agree. His mouth curls up a little as she puts money in his pocket. He lights a cigarette, takes two puffs and pushes it into an ashtray. He goes to his next client, ruffling my hair as he goes by.

23. Naples – First meeting of my grandparents –
    Street scenes – The port of Naples, the port of Capri

My grandmother always speaks dreamily of Naples. It must have been beautiful to a newly married girl from a sad little village in Campany. It's called Andrinopoli and you should see my aunts' dubious expression when it's mentioned. Respectful but ready to giggle. She was seventeen years old, composed in her demeanour, but still a girl, capable of vivaciousness.

My grandfather, in what was far-away Sardinia, had been using his head to leave his native mountains, getting into the armed forces, being posted on the Continent, in the North, in the South, at random at first, then gradually to larger cities, helped by friends whose names I found in old postcards. Friendships cemented by solidarity. As Sardinia receded, as well as the memory of the people who had brought him up, adopted, treated as a son then would be, as hard as a servant – the fact he was Sardinian, a man of measured words, prudent, reliable, hard-working, became more evident, proverbial.

Grandmother will also say, 'I used to be a beautiful woman, elegant, slim,' and show me a picture of a plump lady in a Charleston dress and cap, against a draped backdrop, with a potted palm. A younger grandmother, yes, but not very different, like a Pekingese will be a Pekingese, young or old. She says, 'I had lovely red hair,' but of course it's a black-and-white photograph. I feel miserably unable to compliment her. I know, chubby women were appreciated, it was a sign of good health. It's like for Naples, I know she loves Naples – it's hard to understand, like I know Africans love manioca, a terrible gluey soup, and I feel I am being stupid and stubborn, but won't budge.

So if she was slim and pretty, Naples was beautiful. It is the past.

Pietro had been posted to Naples in 1920. He was beginning to feel comfort in his position. The war. His class had not been recalled, of the six hundred thousand Italians dead most were no more than twenty-two. The consequences of the war were becoming less acute, the invalids, the jobless – still jobless, had a few more lire than yesterday. He had spent the war posted in Livorno, and Calabria. For years he had heard stories of the war. In the cafés, the songs had been about soldiers, return, separation.

He was thirty-three, getting heavy-set, sitting at a café of Corso San Carlo on a fine afternoon. Naples. The luminosity, the caressing breeze surrounded him. He was on his way up.... He allowed himself to dream, even to feel nostalgia. The mountains of the Nuorese were turning into a sweet memory, the face of a particularly kind aunt, an object of longing.

He saw Ada walk by with her mother and her sister Rosalia. She was flushed with amazement at this, her first visit to the city. They were buying things necessary to Rosalia's trousseau. He got up and followed them. He saw Ada drinking water from a water vendor, and dabbing her cheeks with her handkerchief, her dark red hair, her pale eyes.

When mother and daughters came out of a mercer's shop in Via Cisterna dell'Olio, exhausted, laden with packages, he darted forward offering to find a cab. He helped the ladies climb up. He wordlessly reminded the driver of their agreement. There were thanks, and goodbyes. He looked at Ada long enough that she would understand. There was no time for anything but standing there, filled with hope.

* * *

A few months later, accompanied by a retired colonel who had befriended him, he was making the journey to Andrinopoli to make his proposal to Ada's parents. Was accepted, of course. Coffee, cookies and barley water partaken of with enthusiasm. Back to his room, he felt the full brunt of his joy and his chest almost bursting, having no mother, no brother to speak to.

My great-grandfather is very *flou*. I think he had no particular occupation. He showed alertness only in vetting the household accounts. A small, bony man with pale red hair, he had a flotilla of daughters with rounded chests. He also had (another thing you don't pay for) a fine harmonious name that commanded obsequiousness in the small town but not much else, a house on the piazza with a dignified façade of yellowish stucco, and a field of hemp, ugly at all times, and smelling badly after a rainfall.

He did the necessary breathing and moving expected of the living. His mildness was interpreted as kindness by his wife, who spared no pains to show her gratitude, milling around in constant activity, managing to preserve the meagre family substance. 'Cleanliness and order don't cost anything,' and no house was more clean. The girls, in various degrees of cooperation, were drawn into grand cleanings, dustings, washings, buffings, polishings. (This woman, Clemenza, my great-grandmother, I was taken to visit, in an apartment of Trastevere; me, microscopic, barely a toddler, beside my grandmother, who held my hand; she, shrunken and very old. Clemenza, Ada, Enrico, me. She belongs to a place so distant that I have to invent it. So far, in a house that does not exist, a world that is gone. A sense of greater distance, of void, because of the kinship. Clemenza, I only know your name.)

So the chiaroscuro of the sitting room, with the dark furniture and the white flat cloth against the window, had an air of dignity. Saint Anthony in a painting on glass looked towards heaven, interceding for lost causes, with the eyes of a madman. Three short calla lilies phosphoresced in a vase.

The fiancé-to-be had appeared in his white state uniform, broad-chested, strapped up tight, mustachioed. Light reflected in his black-brown eyes with white flashes. He listened as the colonel spoke of destiny, faith, nuptials, everlasting affection. Then gave his service record and legitimate expectations. He said, 'I put my heart and my capacities at Miss Ada's feet.' The father, half-swallowed by a wooden wing-chair, turned his head right and left and gave the expected agreement in the same breath as he exhorted the guests to have a cup of coffee. "O caffé, eccellenze, 'o caffé!' Ada presented Pietro a dish of aniseed *taralli* on a napkin. 'I did those,' and Pietro felt this must be the food of angels.

Naples is suffused in pale blue and gold in those watercolour prints of early Ottocento, idyllic, the waves are gentle, breeze is sweet and fruit aplenty. Little Cupids flutter about, holding the curtains of this lovely theatre. 'Splendours, Delights and Wonders of the Most Noble City of Naples.'

In the first year, before your grandfather was posted in Cagliari, we rented two rooms in the apartment of an officer, the windows opened on Via Caracciolo, a fine street....

Vedi Napoli e poi muori, if you are Italian, by the time you are ten you'll have heard this dozens of times, it means, if you see Naples, your heart has nothing left to wish for, you can die happy. (Does this mean Naples is so beautiful? It could be more about how passionate Neapolitans can be, or how strong a spell the city casts – perhaps not strictly a matter of beauty.) The immense perfectly arched gulf, the Vesuvius, blue-grey, noble, immanent, in the background. In the fine old paintings, there are 'Fishermen under the moonlight,' where the surface of the sea seems oily, 'Boats by Marechiaro,' with the moon appearing behind a dark cloud; night-time emissions of the volcano, with a little orange lava to create more light. In a book of songs of Old Naples we have, it's all about the joys and sorrows of love, the eyes and mouth of the girl, trying to get her to love in return, and so on. I don't really understand Neapolitan, I have to read it aloud, and start over, like a car trying to go over a hill, taking a run up to understand it more – I throw in anything I know, Latin, French, Roman dialect, English. To listen to the songs, the singer is never complaining about anything going wrong but his love affairs. He lives for the love he is singing to. He sings, well-dressed, from a sunlit platform, or under a balcony, in the lukewarm breeze of a night.

His words, his emotion are all that counts.

*La Signora Ceramelli, the landlady, had a beautiful chest of
drawers, painted all over with flowers and gold fillets, in the hall,
and she kept telling me about it, saying it belonged to her
daughter, now gone with her family to Turkey, and that she had
said she could sell it for her. Oh how I wanted it, it was so
beautiful. But your grandfather said no, he said it was gaudy and
how would it look among our proper furniture, once we would
move into our own house, when the day came.*

I have remained resentful at my grandfather, for being so serious. I
saw him in a new light. My grandmother's regret was still there,
after all these years. My own sadness at the lost *cassettone* pricked
me. I felt helpless. This object I loved, I saw, delightful, painted
dark green, with flowers at the corners, in red and blue, pretty,
light, a touch of silvery gold here and there, delicate as good
artisans can do it. It was gone as in a shipwreck, in a earthquake,
in a bombardment. And what could my grandmother do, she who
now had to prove her qualities to her husband, older, wiser. He had
said no. You couldn't do anything.

*The city was lively, gay, the carts, the charabancs went by,
painted in bright red, the boats were painted. Stalls and street
vendors everywhere, much of the life was outdoors, in the street.
People and voices everywhere, Neapolitans love to chat. Foreigners
say they are noisy, excited. No, they are lively, but calm.
Foreigners, Italians, don't understand them. You must learn the
language. The street vendors each have a cry, do you know any,
here in Rome? We had more before the war. Yes, there is the rag
man, the umbrella repair man, the knife-sharpener, some chestnut
or olive vendor. In Naples, they were everywhere. Here: 'A tengo cu
l'annese e o limone, acqua bella gelata 'e stagione!' This was the
water vendor, selling both aniseed and lemon scented water. And
the fishmonger, he'd say, 'I have silver in my basket!' Tomatoes,
they'll call out, 'they are black' to say they are such a deep deep
red. Ah, they have a turn for words, and it comes out like music.*

* * *

The fruit they have in Naples, there is nothing that can compare.
The best come from the hills of Posillipo. Six different types of figs,
delicious peaches of a sort they say come from Asia, at least four
sorts of cherries, and what about plums – asinine, damascene,
armeniache – *and oranges, lemons, citrons, with their leaves. The*
women of the people, do you know how they call the merchant if
they don't know his name? Bell'omo, *fair man. The people of*
Naples are delicate, sensitive. The cart driver, when he has to tell a
person to stay away from his wheels, if it's an older lady, he'll call
out: careful, young lady! If it's a soldier, he'll say, watch out,
corporal! And a priest, zi' cano', *he makes him a canon, more*
important than he is. Anything that sounds like a compliment.
And the pazzarielli —

Lello did a *pazzariello* show for us, he explained that's a kind of fool
who goes around the streets (once upon a time), advertising for a
new shop or a theatre. He wore a red waiter's jacket, with a big
paper rose coming out of a pocket, and three ties flapping about,
and a bow-tie, and a yellow vest, and a Napoleon paper hat with
ribbons streaming everywhere. He held a big stick. Piero, wearing a
straw hat, followed with a little drum. 'That's my band,' he said.
    So he marched to the middle of the living room, swinging his
stick. He called out:
    'Battalion!'
    Boom! (drum-beat)
    'Fanfare!'
    Boom!
    'I raise my baton!'
    'Your attention!'
    Boom! Boom! Boom! .
    'Wait a moment I have something to tell you!'
    And he began, telling everyone, men and women, spinsters and
wives, large and small, noble and un-noble, rich and rather poor, that
in Vicolo Scassacocchi there is a new wine tavern, and the owner, Don
Gennaro, who is a good man and has a heart, at the cost of losing of
his own money, has told him, cost what it may, the people must enjoy
themselves. So he offers his new wine at one lira per litre.
    'Hey, folks, enjoy, enjoy you must!'

Boom, boom, bada-baboom, Piero followed him, half-blinded by the hat, inebriated by noise, drumming the loudest he could since this was clearly a once-in-a-lifetime chance.

Afterwards, I took a book from the bookshelves in the alcove, on the second landing, where things are always in half darkness. *Voices of Naples*, about the cries of street vendors, with some very blurry photo-images, about *pazzarielli*, and the manners of the charming girl vendors. Then, as it happens when you read a book that is more or less not for you, a dark cloud. The author explains how the *malavita*, the malefactors, those of the bad life, used to call out to each other in the city, like birds in the jungle, communicating aloud, in disguised language.

'It's the song of prisoners, of outlaws, a song of passion, of hatred and revenge, with intonations that make your blood curdle. They'll say, 'Listen, you bird in the cage, this song is for you,' then tell him how there is news the judge will be ill-disposed, or how it seems the prisoner may be sent to another jail.... It starts like a lament, or a lullaby, then gets closer, becomes a chant at the top of his voice, and when it seems to be about to disappear, another voice, hoarse, lugubrious, picks up again from nowhere.'

This was very unnerving. But worse, they called this kind of song *'canzone a figliola,'* the song of the young girl – why the young girl? It's an enigma that in itself turns the world upside-down. I don't know the language enough. A song that carries despair. It anguished me.

I had a nightmare. A pazzariello, loud and crazy, not playful, waving a bottle, scaring me.

* * *

We go to Naples every summer, on our way to Capri. Depending on our numbers, whether we are going with a nanny, or also an au pair, and whether the Chéniers or Aunt Valentina will join us later, we take the train, or drive. We now take triumphantly the new Autostrada del Sole, smooth like silk, and Tonino thinks nothing of going a hundred an hour.

From year to year, with Piero and Vanna, we comment on the novelties, a new Esso gas station, the fields by the highway, artichokes, fava beans, hemp, grey and damp-looking, quite smelly, and stunning sunflowers.

We were driving in two cars last year, and the new Alfa had a breakdown. My father was not amused. Oncle Bernard, showing strong leadership, decided that by going on the other side of the highway, he would double our chances of flagging down a tow truck. We watched in horror as, with a few steps, as he is very tall, he crossed the middle line, past the oleander bushes, and got on the other side, just as a police *milledue* drove by. So my father, disgusted at having to break the road regulations in full view of the police, but quick to the rescue, crossed to the other side too. The police, who had started explaining to this crazy foreigner that this was the Autostrada del Sole and didn't he see how dangerous it was to cross it, now had my father too to scold and fine. But Daddy had come to extricate Uncle Bernard, to clear up a complication, as only he knew how. '*Per l'amor del cielo*, for heaven's sake, what are you doing, this is the Honourable Chénier, a Canadian, a senator –,' end of the remonstrations, the lunatic is actually a honoured visitor and the police give us a ride. I feel the pride of Canada being like America, but better.

By the time we have reached the port of Naples and its smells and fumes, I am carsick. The water of the port is black, oily, surely poisonous, even pestilential. A couple of boys swim gamely from one of the colossal clove hitches to a fishing boat at anchor. It's scary to think that this ink, only one hour and a half away, mixes with *our* transparent sea of Capri.

I hold my breath, my heart, my thoughts, until I set foot on the pier of Marina Grande, legs wobbly. The representatives from all the hotels are out in force, in their caps and uniforms. 'Hotel Quisisana!' 'Hotel Augustus!' I finally can breathe, dispel the fumes, look high above, towards the Castiglione, to see, far away, our house, white with green shutters, look, it's her.

24. Cristina and Eugenia plan an exchange – Consequences

Cristina and I have an idea. I want to be a boarder, and she would prefer to be home. Except that she can't, she knows, her parents will say no, she must learn foreign languages, and to do that she must study at our school, away from home. So we have thought, at least she could be at my home, better than being a boarder, and I could take her place as a boarder. We haven't asked yet, we are just preparing.

So I tell her everything.

'When I go to bed I leave the door open just one palm, it's better, that way I don't hear noise and I see just a little light, from inside my father's closet.'

She says, 'On Tuesday evenings, they serve eggs, but if you are a *régime*, a special diet girl, they give you a wonderful pudding instead. You only need to say *'régime'*, the nun will serve you without asking.

'At breakfast, if it's a lucky day, fresh bread will arrive just in time so you can have fresh bread and butter instead of rusks.

'The dormitory nun gets replaced sometimes by Mademoiselle Danois, she stays in her room, listening to radio and never goes on rounds, so on those nights, you can read in bed.

'If it's Tonino driving, in the morning, he never minds stopping at the baker's, to buy a snack, you must have the money ready and be really quick and get your square of pizza *bianca*. Get some for Vanna, too.

'There's a nice nun in the laundry room, Soeur Marie Estelle, she doesn't have the white habit yet, she wears a kind of pale blue apron, and a small veil. You should see how much work they give her! I go talk to her sometimes, instead of going straight to piano practice.

'My bedroom really is my father's den (he never uses it). I have started putting my books in front of his, on the lower shelves, instead of the children's room. And there is a strong box, just behind my bed! but don't worry, there have been thieves only on the ground floor, and we are on the fifth.

'At the afternoon *goûter*, if you come back for seconds, sometimes the nun will give you an apple, or a second chocolate bar.

'If you say you have piano practice, you can leave the study room, for a half hour.

'Beware of Mère Marie Christophe. She walks completely silently. She is the worst.'

Our plan occupied us. It was a secret, but I told my grandmother, who knew Cristina. She always listens when I explain something. She was very impressed. She asked feebly what would happen on weekends, would I go home, and where would Cristina go? Details were a bit complicated.

Then came the Easter holidays. One afternoon, when my father was driving me to my cousin Lea's birthday, I told him I wanted to be a boarder because I wanted to study more. He said, 'We have been thinking about that.' This stunned me. I explained our scheme of exchanging residences, Cristina being in our house, and I taking her place in the dormitory. He seemed puzzled. He said he thought that anyway Cristina's parents were moving to Rome to open a coffee bar near Via Nazionale, and leaving the Capri business to an uncle, for a while. So Cristina would go home every afternoon, after all, to her parents' apartment, next year. But that had no bearing on my situation – which was that the nuns thought it would be good for me to have more time for homework, to have less distractions, to be more *concentrée*, less *dans la lune*.

All this seemed sufficiently close to our original plan to be fine. When Cristina returned, we had half forgotten our idea. We understood confusedly that adults were going to steer our destiny and anyway summer was not far.

I saw Cristina in Capri, twice, that summer. Large-scale events overtook our normal holidays. There was to be a trip to Canada, to visit the family.

Cristina had by then grown used to being a boarder and would not have minded continuing. Myself, I was not used to decisions.

When we returned to Rome, at the end of July, to prepare for Canada, a massive letter had arrived from La Mère Économe. Roneoed in blue on paper that smelled of alcohol, and felt almost damp, long and minute lists detailed objects, linen, clothing and rules for boarders, *demi-pensionnaires* and *pensionnaires*. It seemed we would each have a small-scale household in our little private rooms. The bulk of the properties was called a trousseau, as for a newlywed. I had visions of the trunk Uncle Alec brings back to Rosie in *Eight Cousins*. A frenzy overtook me. I would wake up at night wondering at all those things soon to be mine, labelled under my embroidered student number, III.

My mother took me to the official purveyor of the school. Everything was to be bought there, an expensive children's shop on

Via del Corso, to simplify. My grandmother said there would have been better quality near Piazza Argentina, at moderate prices. There were to be upper, lower sheets, pillow cases, heavy and light blankets, bedside carpet, towels of various sizes, in bee-combed cotton, and linen, which turned out to be very disappointing, as they became wet and did not dry you, leaving you cold. *Débarbouillettes* (things to give your face a quick wash), not *débrouillettes* (things to help you fend for yourself), which is a French invention, instead of sponges.

For clothes, there were to be two pale blue aprons (I kept my old one, in cotton, and Mummy bought another in the new, modern-looking, jumper-style); six shirts, white; two pleated navy blue skirts (a luxury, since I'd always done well with one); regulation cardigans, one with a round collar, awfully unbecoming, and a normal V, buttoned one; dozens of long socks, blue and white (we skipped the awful beige); underwear. When it came to petticoats, my mother pronounced no girls were wearing them any more and that was it. I tried for a while to squeeze into my prettiest one, soft, quilted and smocked on the upper part, trimmed with taffetas. Then my sister started using it when she and her little friends played fairies and princesses, and it became a thing of the past.

25. Wolfgang – Love – 'Ballet de cigales' –
     The cicadas according to La Fontaine – Other fables

Do you like to run? I like to run like dogs do, scampering and flinging their limbs about, no, that's horses when they go from obedient and harnessed to allowed to be wild. I enjoy the springs in my knees. Also dogs in their spring dance, running in circles mad with happiness. If a dog does it, I join in. I like to run downhill and bounce. And the other way, always surprised at what quick work I do of the hill.

The staircase of Palazzo Doria-Pamphili, where our ballet was, had many flights of large white slices of marble, it was no effort at all, it led to Paradise. On those steps one morning I became aware

of being alive. Happiness and movement. I was light, and lightly I
leaped from step to step, with my small self, my waist tightened by
the belt of my loden coat (red, before it was dyed blue). Under the
coat, daringly I thought, I wore the black leotard, and flat little shoes.

It was a large room with wooden floors, and enormous
windows looking to roofs, churches and palazzos. We put our
things behind a wooden screen. We *piccole* would arrive when the
medie were finishing. The mothers would lower their coats on their
shoulders and sit on plain chairs. There was a piano
accompaniment, and sometimes a xylophone. I love the bim-bim-
boom, the round-tipped hammers that tap on distinct points of
your rib cage. Wolfgang explained steps and postures and we
imitated, as much as we could. It was a mild-mannered course,
nothing military. We would exercise on the floor, not so much *à la
barre*, ours was a combined method, said my mother, much
superior. (Of course today Santabarbara, has a way of taking a
third, then a fourth ballet position, absent-mindedly, in the middle
of a conversation, she went to a proper classic course with a lot of
barre work.)

We had Wolfgang. He was gentle, strong legs in his grey
maillot, pale, dark-haired. He was Polish. His was the face of
someone who receives bad news with every morning mail. He
spoke with one of those accents, that sink, and make you laugh,
but of course you don't. (But you wouldn't be laughing *at* him, you
just would be laughing because accents *give you* laughter and fun.)

Small as I was, there was an even smaller girl, graceful as a
doe. We were arranged by size, and she'd go ahead first. I liked
that part, when I'd follow her. At the end of the lesson, we would
do a little dance, which was immensely satisfying. We were proud
of our ballet shoes, leotards, body tights, and to be taught by such
a fine teacher, who gave us the impression of being important,
Wolfgang so kind and assured, the palazzo of marble and columns,
and just so very happy, dancing and moving.

LOVE

In the same period I was sent to a succession of kindergartens. I
was always a little mystified at first, and tried to keep my coat on,

ready to leave, but the continuing presence of my mother reassured me, and I would relent and play. There would be games such as I always liked ever after, Montessori cubes and sand paper letters you could run your fingers over.

This was the last *scuolina* before I was sent to Sainte-Marguerite. We specialized in letter-writing and had a little internal post office running.

One afternoon, with lights on as it must have been winter, in our makeshift classroom, lightly sweaty from excitement or the overheated radiators, we sat on the wooden floor, waiting for the mail. I was waiting, hoping in the vaguest way possible. Hope of nothing, of something marvellous. A beige puppy half-asleep in his basket who dreams perhaps someone will come and tickle him.

The postman, a boy with short blond curls, was delivering letters to the children sitting in a circle. What was his name? He stopped in front of me smiling and drew a letter from the mailbag. His smile helped me understand. He had chosen me to be his correspondent. It was from him to me. Was it a drawing? Maybe it was a proper letter – with much help from an assistant teacher, in that case – but I don't remember, whatever it was, it would have been blurred, what with this flaring of feeling, this plunge into the universe, and me barely reading, and him barely writing. Was my love for him instantaneous, or was it the conclusion of many small kindergarten kindnesses? Had he perhaps shared with me his Cioccorì?

We were small, and we did not have the vocabulary. But it was love, dwarfing my size three frame, size five shoes, my three and a half years of age. It sparkled and burned, raised my fever, beaded my brow. It turned on a fiery pink-orange-purple sunset over Rome. It launched a declension, 'of Eugenia, by Eugenia, from Eugenia', went to Martial, Terence, lost its way, erupted in poems, prayer songs, and schoolyard riddles.

'... *Voici donc les beaux jours, lumière, amour, délire ...*'
'... *Il pleut, il pleut, bergère, rentre tes blancs moutons ...*'
'... *Toi, Jésus, le seul Seigneur ...*' and some rather yelled words from a song you would still hear in coffee bars, that year, joined in the fun and din, '... *Le mille bolle blù, blù-blù-blù ...*'

* * *

Love flooded the playroom, the present and the infinite.
It paraded, and swirled, as he sat next to me on the wood floor,
shoulder to shoulder. We were all smiles. We were in Paradise.
But our minutes were counted. Unable to face the riot it had
launched, having worn out its battery, emptied its well, lost its
voice – in the desperate gurgle of a tape being rewound on a
recording machine, this love, panting and exhausted, made for a
chink in the windows and slipped away, to refresh itself in the cool
winter late afternoon.

The Cicada and the Ant
BALLET IN TWO ACTS

I was registered at Sainte-Marguerite, at the top of the register,
along with Ginestra. Mummy drove me in every morning, and
every day, I would leave at lunchtime. This was civilized. I had my
first copy-book and worked in a class-room with a blackboard and
little desks, and left when things would threaten to become too
serious. I went to dance lessons twice a week, at four o'clock.

In the enthusiasm of the first Christmas of the school, a *spectacle*
was planned. I was the youngest in the smallest class, and I was
chosen to be *le nain* Rikiki, a part of immense prestige. There was
music, and there was dance, and I gave all my heart to it. There
were many rehearsals and I thought that, a little dance here, a little
dance there, school was going to be very pleasant.

Le nain Rikiki was a mischievous little thing, dressed in red,
who came in at all intervals between tableaux of a ballet called *La
cigale et la fourmi*. The costume was Standard Elf. A pointed
bonnet, a cape and black tights. My ballet shoes. The music was
played on a portable record player covered in a kind of pale-blue
and grey cloth. One nervous nun would lift the needle from the
record between every music movement, to allow the narrator
(Selenia Redding) to explain. The story was as usual about the
hard-working ant and the frivolous cicada, but there were other
insects, and it was set in the streets of Paris. The cicada was a
singer with a guitar, the ant, a fruit merchant. I did little steps
criss-crossing the stage, and bowed and smiled. I was not supposed
to sing with the rest of the choir something that rhymed with

'… *par ici*' and ended with '… *le nain* Rikiki!' At the end the cicada dies (no food in the pantry) and is carried away by a dragonfly angel.

I was not really used to nuns yet. They pretended to be quite normal, but they were quite a shock, with their headdresses and costumes. Their faces framed in a triangle of white and black cloth seemed to have no equivalent in the real world. Some were kind-looking, most were reserved or severe. All had a task, a lesson to give, rules to follow and to apply. They were guardians. If they took you by the hand, it was with the intention of taking you somewhere, rather fast. They were busy and hard-working. Ants.

On the day of the show, they sat in one long row, in strict hierarchy, Mère Prieure, Mère Supérieure, Directrice du Petit Pensionnat and twenty others. We were nose to nose with them, dancers and singers on the same polished grey marble as the audience, in the Great Room. The school was still so small that all girls were employed in the opera-ballet. (Although there must have been, even in those Arcadian times, an outsider, at least one, tone-deaf or barely arrived from Finland, or the last-minute culprit of something, barred from having fun.) They did look a bit like the insects in the play, a whole congregation of ants with a veil that took no beauty away since they were ants, on one of their rare moments of repose. Large, small, pale, pink, red or dark, some with a white veil, most in black with a white jugular, immobile. Tremendously enjoying themselves.

Their eyes were shining. The Mère Générale had large brown eyes. You call nuns 'My Mother', every nun is 'My Mother'. As I got closer and closer in my little elf fluttering, and smiled all the time, perhaps the nuns thought I was a sort of 'My Daughter'. When the last '… *nain* Rikiki!' rang out, I made my last reverence not very far from Mère Générale. Applause.

She was the Queen Nun, the Top Nun. Her majesty was heightened by the rarity of her appearances. She said, '*Embrassez-moi, mon enfant,*' and I kissed her, naturally. I moved aside because I knew Stella Buongiovanni was arriving with a bouquet, and Mère Générale said to her: 'Kiss me, dear child.' Stella didn't want to. She said, very distinctly, 'No, because your beard will prickle me.'

It's true, you can ask anyone.

School started again, after the holidays. On the first day, when the one o'clock bell rang, I walked to my peg to take my coat. I lined up behind the others before the very steep staircase, which took you to the refectory and the parking lot, where Mummy would be coming. I almost made it to the top when a refectory nun saw me and said, 'Where are you going, Eugenià?' and told me to remove my coat and put my apron back on. Worried, I started crying a little. I was told to go to the refectory. There, I cried and cried as loud as I thought was allowed, simply wailing throughout lunch, giving it all, in front of the Arcoroc glass plate and the sad food. It was all over, I knew it. They let me cry.

FABLE

Cicadas are the secret spinners of a pale gold braid, they start only at the right point of warmth. They begin when perfect conditions have been confirmed. They won't begin just on any given blue day. You may think it's time, but they are the only true repository of summer. More reliable than a Swiss banker. If you can catch that first song, you're lucky. Afterwards, they will be singing all summer long, according to their own schedule. They will confirm your happiness: Ah, the cicadas are singing.

Maybe you don't know the story of the cicada and the ant. It's a fable by Jean de la Fontaine we all know. The Italians say it's Aesop's. There is a hard-working ant and all summer long she mills around collecting seeds and victuals for her pantry, you know how they trot and climb obstacles, and drag big weights without tiring. Meanwhile, the cicada, dizzy with sunshine, sings along, apparently thinking only of the moment and not caring about eating – maybe a little something here and there, but not putting aside any food for winter. So when winter does come, the cicada, who did not save food or money, knocks at the ant's door to ask for shelter and food, and the ant sends her away very impolitely with these words: 'You sang all summer, now you can dance!' But it's not the cicada's fault.

'You know how the cicada was singing all summer, just having fun and singing, and the ant, the hard-working one, toiled and carried food back to her lair, never stopping, never having fun. Then fall comes, and winter, and it's cold, and the ant is closeted in her lair, with a little shawl on her shoulders, and a stove going, and she munches on roasted seeds, sitting on her armchair.

There's a knock at the door, and who's there? It's the cicada, wrapped in a fabulous mink fur coat. *"Formichina!* Dear, dear ant, how are you?" she cries. "Hr, well, I'm well ..." says the ant. "We were just going through the region, Georges and I, back from Monte Carlo, and on our way to Paris, on the Hispano," says the cicada,' – and Lello makes a wonderful face, puckering his lips. He explains that she is smoking from a cigarette holder, and looking wonderful in a Schiaparelli evening dress.

'The ant says, "Going to Paris, are you?"

' "Ye–es," and the cicada shakes the ash from her cigarette.'

Lello stretches out his arm, you really see the long long glove, and the hand of a very sophisticated lady.

' "That's where Jean de la Fontaine lives, isn't it?" "Why, ye–as, I believe so," says the cicada.

' "Do me a favour, will you?"' Lello calmly leans on a broom – ' "If you see him, tell him – on behalf of the ant in the Fable – tell him to go to hell!"'

But I don't do it as well as Lello.

26. Father Ratinoux on a beach outing

'O quante belle figlie Madama Doré, o quante belle figlie ...'
('So many pretty daughters, Madam Gold-on-everything,
    that golden dust covering everything, so many pretty daughters....')

There are three girls exactly. Pretty in some photographs, some more pretty, more often, at other times caught just after a whining about their socks that keep falling, or their ponytails that are too tight.

Eugenia is showing the photo album to Père Ratinoux, who
has just arrived, early, for lunch. He is immensely interested.
'There you are, Eugenià, and here is Vannà, oh la la, she does not
look too happy, and Anna-Chiarà, charming, *elle a un petit air
malicieux!*' he says. Who would have known Père Ratinoux could
make a mischievous lilt? Like everybody, he adores the little sister,
always dressed in white or pink, a little doll, so dark haired.

'Those were taken in Capri, Mon Père, have you ever been there?'
Father Ratinoux has only been to Sorrento, but is ecstatic
about it. Sorrento is another one of the resorts near Naples.
Eugenia and her siblings, with cousin Guillaume, had become
strongly insular about it. Capri, the best, the only one. The other
ones were imitations: Sorrento, Ischia, Procida (this one sometimes
mentioned by their grandmother as a grand beach frequented by
relatives.) And Capri is not to be confused with Anacapri, the more
mountainous area. 'Obscure rivalries subsist from the time
Ubaldino stole Ubaldone's prickly pears,' says Ingegner Ceccomori,
raising his eyebrows. The children actually like Anacapri, where
there are always discoveries to be made, but their ground is Capri.

Père Ratinoux had been visiting his brothers' seminary in
Castellammare for two days. He had brought administrative
documents for the Father Bursar to discuss, and was preparing to
return to the House of the Pères Blancs, in Rome, Via Giovanni
Piccolomini, the quiet gardens, and monotony, set among the
scalding sidewalks. Seeing a providential sign for Sorrento, listing
rates and hours of departure, gave way to a recurring half-hatched
dream of his, to spend a day at the seaside, like everyone else.

On the hydrofoil the breeze was heady. The coast approached
like a majestic fruit basket. At the harbour, things looked greasy,
smelly, but with an awakened sense of adventure, he went looking
for a path, a sign, a pergola, and he found a little beach, a
restaurant, a pergola. And sat down, and ordered, yes sir, *spaghetti
alle vongole, fritto misto* and white wine … While his espresso was
being made, he went walking awkwardly on the rocks. Then, with
a resolve of 'now or never', he had to arm-wrestle with himself to
decide for a swim, embarrassed and pale, in his polyester blue
swimming trunks. The surf was inebriating. Healing. He sat,

thought for a minute about the ancestor Claude Ratinoux dit
Laforêt who had gone and settled in the snow of Trois-Rivières,
Québec, as a compromise, you could say, for the Promised Land.
No, some people were Nordic. (Some tough people were Nordic.)
He was. That is why this sea was enchanting. He beatifically swam
and admired everything until he started feeling tired, and gave
thanks, floating on his back as Jean-Germain had taught him.

27. Looking from a fogged-up window in the traffic

It is not all fun to have a driver, because you have to go and pick
up others as well. The worst time is after school, when you have
been waiting because the car was tied up in traffic on the way
there, and you are faint with hunger and have hallucinations of
bread, butter and jam. On rainy afternoons, we barely seem to gain
ground. Tonino's head is sunk into his shoulders. Although tired,
he has at least the distraction of worming his way into small spots,
advancing, shifting, braking, while we have nothing to do, floored
by school, hunger, the smell of our damp coats. Reading makes me
carsick. And we have to pick up Piero at a schoolmate's near
Piazza Barberini. We don't protest.

I look inside any window I can. Sometimes striking gold,
seeing someone, something interesting. A secretary taking
dictation. A large old painting in a gold frame. A nun of an
unknown order. The flash of a red dress. The blond head of a small
child who can barely reach over the windowsill, looking outside at
the cars in the damp afternoon.

28. Rome, July 20, 1970

Sputters and *borborygmes*, dictionary says rumbles (in one's
stomach), pathetic pallid translation. I am a little lost. I thought
we'd go to the apartment, instead we are at the new house. Home

with half my seaside things in the suitcase since I have insisted I'll do it myself. I brought back a blue shirt with Indonesian flowers in white and red, dotted, a jungle of flowers that interconnect.

I should be doing all sorts of intermediary things during this interlude. Call grandmother, all right. Call Ginestra, what's the point, we always meet again in September – social relations heavily insisted upon by Daddy, apparently a normal person makes at least two phone calls a day. Drop my black sandals at the shoemaker's. Buy *Bridge over Troubled Water* for Elsa, and guitar strings. And, I don't have enough functioning *mutande*, 'those that must be changed', knickers that is, exactly: I want to wear a superior style of knickers. How can I avoid getting the ribbed cotton ones with a thick elastic band (and avoid the guilt because I could perfectly just replace the elastic in my old ones? Unfortunately, I know how to). My ideal would be the kind of pretty pastel ones the French au pair forgot last year.

Found the cool shade of the house and its light scent of wax. The house, a living organism. Found letters and postcards. Delia wrote a thick one, in pink, the gall! She thinks I am interested, she so overemphasizes, embellishes her life. No, it's not optimism. It's a disease. She is the soupiest, the soppiest, immured to irony. When smaller we thought her stupid. Not stupid, but with a peculiar deafness, tone-deafness. Such a long time with us that some have taken to her as an inevitable sister. Geneviève would reply. Unbearable Delia!

Letter from Elsa. She says I am crazy, unique and wonderful. This embarrasses me. I can do anything I want, as long as I'm happy. She asks, in my old letter, what was the matter with my marks? She went to Bretagne with her parents, it was OK. There was a family they know. There was a certain Éric. She loved *West Side Story*. She adores Arsène Lupin. She is reading *Le Grand Meaulnes*. She says the sea is freezing there. Her father is going to be posted in West Africa, next. I wish we had a system of pneumatic tubes for sending letters back and forth, at the speed of thought.

The swimming pool. It's almost Olympic, not quite – in order, I thought, not to be too sports-like. Then I noticed that those proportions left enough space for the grass, for the benches, for everything. It's pure and simple, with a travertine frame, and cabins and showers in a toy house. It connects to the garden surrounding the house by an in-between garden, more wild, with a few rocks, bushes of this and that. It's quite away from the house, which I particularly appreciate.

Others do, too. Lello goes to have a quiet sun-tanning, if he can escape us. He takes a floating mattress and very carefully, trying to stay as dry as possible, pushes himself away from the sides. He looks so happy. We will wait for him to become nice and hot, then ambush him with tremendous splashes of cold water and shrill cries. It's a miracle he doesn't hate us. He looks so *désolé*. But we cannot resist.

My mother has the most exacting standards for the water. Eliseo must make the difficult calculations about the proportion of *the chemical*, as he calls it, that is the chlorine, which he carts in his wheel-barrel. It used to be in some sort of barrels, but since he has found out that chorine is more or less common, down-to-earth *eau de javel*, bleach, he has found a wholesale place where they sell it in very undignified demijohns. It looks like the gardener is bringing in about fifty litres of white wine to sustain him during his travails. Not elegant. My mother expects the water to be like mineral water, not a leaf, not a blade of grass, not an ant. Not a dog! (which, regretfully, happens.) The other day, when she came to check things prior to her swim, Piero just had to take a running jump and do a *bomba*, splashing her, because he had spotted a live lizard which he wanted to rescue before she saw it. A merciful veil on the aftermath. But a grateful lizard thinks of Piero every night before falling asleep.

I come to this place alone, to be alone. Decided a hundred laps will be my customary length. In case I'm asked. But – tiring, and so boring. Poems come useful again, on top of being portable language lessons, they help pass the time from one lap to the other. I do 'To be or not to be', 'La pioggia nel Pineto' – the one about the divine myrtle and the salty and burnt tamarisks, and *Je suis belle, ô mortels*, which we've started doing with killer winks like chesty divas of the Belle Époque. Anyway, not expression, memory, you keep a tempo, let's say the breast stroke, 1-2-3, *Je-suis-bell/o-mor-tell* — Also do not get carried away because you will drink, chlorinated, transparent water.

Swimming and wearing out your skin in vitriolic water seem like a bad idea between lap 23 and 47, and from 51 all the way to 92, I noticed. I don't know enough poems, even if you include 'Le Corbeau et le Renard', learned in third grade and ingrained in all of us. What a rich scene the time Baby-lana stood up and recited it – only she would dare, in her ungainly, somnolent, outrageous, disquieted rodent way. Mustn't laugh. Who is this woolly Baby-lana, you'll say.

29. Little bands – Santabarbara – Baby-lana –
The hill – Delphine

When recess bell rings, imagine a bag of marbles spilling on the ground – all going a different direction. I may be walking with Geneviève, following the *grandes* on the Hill, coming across a group from our class, or being netted by the Italians. I like all of them, but not together. G and I are interested in what the other thinks and says. Our talks are at a certain wavelength. Then, as we walk and talk together, a marble might hit us and stay, sometimes it will whiz by. We annex another girl, or keep walking. Sometimes, the marble shatters our unit – usually, when the Italians arrive, and G leaves, automatically.

When I say Italians, I always mean a group that lasted about two years, when we were twelve-thirteen. There was Santabarbara; another girl who struck poses all the time, another who was nuts; *her* best friend, very pretty and very spoilt, both living in a nearby residential development, where boys, parties and mopeds were rife. A girl who was smooth, bored and insipid, but somehow necessary. Two sisters from a Veneto village, whom the group took on out of charity.

S, the exuberant dark-haired Italian in comparison to whom we all seemed pallid and tranquil. Queen to those who wanted a sovereign, she was handled with caution by all others. Her nickname means gunpowder room, and made me and Ginestra very merry when we came up with it. It was soon spreading, anonymously. One of my first successes, but it came with a little shiver. Another thing I know and S doesn't, is that she looks rather like Louis XIV, in subtle yet overwhelming ways. This is the extent of what I've ever been able to hide from her. Two years have gone by and she is still fantastic at knowing things.

She had access to extremely flammable life material. Which she shared. Supreme as she was, uncomfortable as she made me, she shared. It was a system: she liked to have a little court, the little court told her all. In return she told her little court all she knew, beyond the group, beyond the school. At the same time, she was prudent. She kept up appearances. The nuns suspected but she was brighter than them. In the classroom, she was organized and knew what to study, no more than necessary. At home, she had phenomenal privileges, it seemed to me, having a stipend, buying her own clothes, driving with her sister's friends. Whatever she did beyond her privileges, she was never caught. She would be shopping with irreproachable Bettina. She would calmly explain her schedule.

Although she did have a Bourbon nose, she was irresistible in a dark and soigné, Oriental way. She had a fair amount of young girl jewellery, the first of us to move away from the childish into the young adult. She seemed to receive gifts she really liked, another indication of her formidable organizing skills. She was a trendsetter. One of the first to have an elephant-hair bracelet, soon followed by the gold version. Rivulets of dark hair framed the pendant on her chain, an ebony and gold cross, to which the nuns could object nothing. And it was the fashion. Roman jewellers must remember those two-three years as a bumper crop, selling truckloads of little things, enamelled charms, ladybugs, scarabs, medals, rings worn as charms. They bought apartments, paid for sensational wedding parties and stately cars with our articulated enamel fish, coral hearts and filigree sandals. If there was a symbol, though, I'd say the Rolex wristwatches – dozens sold by the Via del Corso and Piazza San Silvestre franchises on the occasion of – any occasion, but anyway before fourteen, in steel, gold, or two-metals.

I never had one of those – which is perhaps the reason why I was not totally affiliated. Of course, this was intentional on my father's part. My father being a tremendous conformist, and original, a snob to end all snobs – and a hater of snobs. So no Rolex, elegant status symbol and *also* nouveau riche, expensive and cheap. (The only way to be sure of any of my father's responses is if it falls within frequently repeated principles. For the rest, there will be so many elements fighting each other that his reactions are impossible to anticipate.) To be a snob, you must have or do a combination of things you like and things you can impress other snobs with. Or embellish a lot. OK. You like to read. You must not say what you really like. You must be able to use your inclination in ways that impress. Anecdotes, aristocratic characters, flamboyant, outrageous, the hidden side of things, original but not erudite. If you are talking to French intellectuals (too specialized, boring), you squish them with little-known writers from the Caribbean. If you are wealthy, you drive a mini-car. If you have no money, you have a very dilapidated, muddy, Jeep. It will be uncomfortable though. It's a game actually. Snobs do not show their true feelings, not more than poker players. You can be a snob of the Catholic school, of the bohemian school, of the international consultant school. Of the Oxford school. Of the postal office school. They all have their rules and their little conventions.

The Italians followed a particular path, using the interior staircase through the immense, empty garage. It was an original, but authorized route. The schoolyard has many places: the middle passage, in case of rain; upstairs, the front of the garage, the sports fields, the alley to the parking lot. For the smaller classes, the *petites* yard, the playground, and *la pinetà*, with the nuns' accent, the pine grove. And the Hill.

Baby-lana I described in short as the crazy one, you could call her Woolite, that's what it means in English. Her grandparents were 'of the Bianchi wools'. She was too of the wools, but what would they do with her? She sat twisted and slouching, she was always blinking, she bit her nails and her fingers. Her hand was sweaty and twitchy. Her writing was small and knotted, Arabic. She was very strange, and she shocked me and embarrassed me. But we had, I don't know why, a half-friendship. Besides, we were, we are still both Eugenias – there is no reason why she would not be alive, although, doing what?

We would tremble contemporarily when our name fell: 'Eugénià ... Bianqui' and it was her turn and my salvation. She was a complete disaster, you could see that even if she had studied – and not roamed about on her moped, nor gone riding, nor hung out with the swarm of boys and girls who lived in her enclave – she would have looked as twisted and about to collapse, her hands in her apron, her pointed feet pointing at each other, her elbows flapping, and not really understanding what she was supposed to be doing.

She did not understand when we were asked to learn a poem of our choice – 'of our choice'! We were not used to such frivolity. We all learned a brand new poem. And what did Eugenia B. do? She did 'Le Corbeau et le Renard', a piece for children really, which we all learned five hundred years ago! She knew it well, too. The professor was rather taken aback. That was pure Woolite.

As a benchmate she was tremendously unnerving, because she whispered rather loud, and could not be stopped. She was neurotic, that's what she was. She would tell you the adventures of her little clan, repeating the same words like an sheep auctioneer.

'I went to the jumping show with Massimo Alberelli – *conosci?* And Marco del Ponte, *conosci?* Barbara Ratti won first prize, *conosci?*

She meant, 'Know him? Know her?' – all the time!!! And she said 'all and sundry', all the time.

'We went to see this new moped, and it needed new brakes, and all and sundry, then Marina Santi came, *conosci?* And she invited me to her party Saturday, and she invited Marco, and we thought we would go, and all and sundry.'

They were always together, and always looking for things to do and buy, and it seemed you could never have one moment to be in peace.

One thing she did normally, it was hating to have to go and visit Gorizia, the northern town, cold, damp, where the family factory was – and having to behave like a good little girl. I would have died. I would laugh with her at the latest advertisement on the walls of the city, urging people to buy Bianchi blankets – as if people need encouragement to buy blankets. (But this kind of humour displeased Daddy, when I told him I would hate to have the same family name as a salami (I meant to be humorous) – he said I was very pretentious indeed, and why would one be ashamed to be in an industrialist's family. And what kind of bizarre ideas was it, was it not pleasant to have money to do the things you like? I kept for myself my explanation that I would not have minded to be a Peaches in Syrup, or even a Banana.)

Baby-lana spoke all the time. She told me both the constant moped-ing from one place to the other and the salient episodes of their lives. For instance. An expedition to the pharmacy of Ponte Milvio, a large one that stays open late at night. They descended upon the pharmacy, and Baby-lana herself gave the pharmacist a folded little paper with – she made the drawing as she spoke, during math class – what she called *un cazzetto*, which she represented a sort of softened pistol, as she panted in her mad way, so descriptively that I could not but understand although I did not quite understand. But I was flattered that she thought I would *know*. She – of the wools, a girl in my class, of my then age of twelve, who rode horses like me, and all and sundry, had actually requested a condom in public. I was shaken. Condoms were for military men and for the absolutely brutish. We were, imminently – and some were, *tout court*, of the Pill. I never could understand whether this exploit was a lark or a game of forfeits or just a particularly pleasant thing to do – in her opinion.

With such aptness for risk, Baby-lana lasted one year by miracle and did not finish the second. One afternoon, during a test, she was found reading – her mouth somnolently gaping – a gossip magazine with 'The prohibited images of *Romeo and Juliet*, the film where, as everybody knows, the actors are naked. As the nun walked up to her, she did not even notice. Three enormous suspension points hovered above the class, boom boom boooom – then the nun performed the practised snatching of the offending object. To see them in rather streaky black and white as M M Andrew took the magazine away, with what seemed to be black elastoplasts everywhere, Romeo and Juliet looked pained and ashamed, rather like Adam and Eve chased from Eden.

I really worried about what school would take her.

* * *

In Rome, there is the French embassy, and the Academy at the Villa Médicis, the French Cultural Centre, the Alliance Française – the Palazzo Farnese, continually referred to for its beauty. Italy is not France, but many French have a weakness for it. A toy Napoleon tried to have – and they are still trying to, in a friendly nonchalant way.

But there is no tableau of French girls. It never incarnated, or I never noticed. I see them scattered everywhere, not in groups. They speak French, but no better than some of the others. They generally have the ugliest shoes. Some of them don't mind the dirty-beige stockings in the school uniform. They are not surprised by jam for dessert. They don't quite know how to peel oranges. I heard one say: *Ça, c'est un vrai ciel d'Italie!* which surprised me, I thought the sky was the same in France. Apart from that, they are like everyone else. Slightly defensive about the school, in a mild patriotic way.

But when they are bad! In second grade, perhaps, I met a sliver of a girl, small and nervous. Sophie de la Motte. The absolute first girl I ever heard swear, almost openly! So small! When we were waiting in a line – not such hardship, and bang, 'I'm fed up!' and not in a low voice either. She said slang words, I assumed. I did not know, since I had *never* heard them. 'I'm fed up! Those *bonniches!*' She meant the *bonnes soeurs*, the nuns. I was petrified and scandalized. Being fed up!!! *J'en ai marre!* What a little demon! But I also heard the verbal caress in the word, and what pleasure in her vehemence! It was self-explanatory: she meant she was bored. Not only was she saying it in slang, she was saying it out loud! How could a girl like that exist?

Three or four years later, when we graduated to the Grand Pensionnat, we started using slang – later becoming virtuosos and Nobel Prizes of all the slangs of all known languages. I recognized that the little mischief-maker had been a sort of prophet, and fashion avant-garde. Sophie de la Motte, and she was fed up!

The Italians, and yes, I was one of them, along with Santabarbara, the sisters, the crazy one and the idiot, had their own circuits. Walked holding each other by the waist, four by four. Would go to the *grandes*, not in the open, but on the Hill.

The Hill stood and still stands as one of the many protuberances on the school grounds. It was left to itself, without buildings or structures, our only modest wilderness. A path leads straight up initially, then mid-ways conveniently turns to one side and disappears from view, among the grass and the weeds.

Mysteriously, the Hill was not forbidden. If I was Daddy, I would suppose some legality, a right of way that can be preserved only if people use it. The mild climb can perhaps be construed as good exercise. Or the nun making the rounds likes the promenade herself and insists with her superiors that it is not misused. The reputation of vipers nesting actually kept most girls off. The thistles. And *grandes* smoking.

There were sentinels, but we would be greeted without hostility. Only a few actually slipped cigarettes from their shirt sleeves or their knee-high stockings. Their calm, self-possessed expression, more than innocent. Faces of marble. What other actions will they conceal? Rules, interdictions. It is forbidden to smoke. To smoke on the Hill. To go to the Hill and talk. Talk freely. To think of going to the Hill.

They sat on some low carpenter's timber, gathered by their worker bees, legs stretched or folded. Santabarbara would easily strike up a conversation, connect with someone about an invitation, a social event, a dinner. Some common friend. Compliments on shoes or stockings or a bracelet.

The feeling of danger. Apart from smoking. I used to come here to supply some girls with books that had not been authorized. I did this not to be philanthropic, but rather to be appreciated. I would pick up whatever I could recommend, or titles that seemed appropriate for sophisticated *grandes*. So it was *Tom Jones*, and *Roxana*, something called *The Game of Hearts*, and old mysteries with titles like *The View from Pompey's Head*. Any Françoise Sagan, Maurice Druon, which I had by the truckloads. Whatever I could find in whatever language. A certain Edmund Crispin was much in demand for a while. And *The Vicar of Wakefield*. It was not hard to slip past the few scattered nuns with a book in the front of my apron. I was good at pretending a great joie de vivre, and a need to run, running away from scrutiny. But I grew tired of the obligation, and my father complained the bookshelves, which I pretended to be tidying, were always in a mess. When I switched to an apronless uniform in eighth grade, I stopped my life of contraband, with infinite relief.

There was a harem idleness on the hill. Some would be brushing their hair and tying ponytails, or making braids. There might be one carefully plucking her legs. Of course you need longer than one recess for that. Someone would be explaining the sugar and lemon paste used by a Lebanese friend for hair removal. A Turkish grandmother's Izmir childhood would be evoked, and the fifty ways to prepare eggplant one had to master in order to be marriageable. Since those were the first years of the war of the miniskirt, the nuns' latest diktat would be discussed. The moment an order was given, the resistance would form. How so-and-so had got caught. We heard of the horrors of an American school, the Mary Mount, where girls were made to kneel and measure four centimetres above the ground, the tolerated hem of their skirts. There would be a line of absolved and a line of punished marching away. (At Ste-Marge, they chased us individually. Much more fun.) Chewing gum, mints were distributed. Some would be reading a carefully shared Italian newspaper. There might be a guitar. The girls names would be Sveva, Lorenza, Marina. Valentina, Ortensia, Olivia, Ottavia. Esmeralda. Veronica, Ann, Denise, Beverley. Morena, Rona, Soledad. Marie, Catherine. Lorraine. Caroline, Sybille, Marie-Ange, Arielle, Delphine.

Delphine was luminous. '*Belle comme les amours*', beautiful as cupids, as putto-loves. Light brown curls falling from a halo into ruffles, delicate nose and mouth, she had the brightness of a hyacinth. She wore her shirt's collar up, and her cardigan had a softer curve, a rounded neck-line, almost a décolleté. So beautiful, you could never quite get used to her. She was French, but her true country would be a chateau in a valley – small, compact, delicate, like Azay-le-Rideau, of which I have a postcard, set on water in the white winter light. Painted by Fragonard or Chardin.

A famous actor, whose tanned face, grinning under a leather hat, was plastered all over Rome, came to pick up his small son from kindergarten, and there was a well-behaved tumult. In the classes with a view of the main entrance, the girls who had lingered after the four-thirty bell massed by the windows. It was Thomas

Morgan himself, dressed like any young man, polo shirt, loafers etc. He did not wave or anything, behaving seriously like any other father. He did not dare, scared of the nuns, I think.

After all the fuss died down, Delphine stayed looking at the main gate from the chemistry lab, dreamily. She was in her white smock, holding a test tube, vaguely looking at the tube, at the gate. Utterly thrown away from her natural place. The Chemist and the Gentleman. The Young Girl with the Hyacinth and the Western Actor.

Isn't she beautiful? The nuns must be careful lest someone steal her.

30. The new house – Rollei and the magnolia

The new house in the countryside has been finished since February. We can spend weekends and holidays there now. It's very beautiful. 'Take the Flaminia, past the suburbs, about half an hour from the city, just past a red house on the left, there is a road …', Daddy has a standard explanation and truly they often get lost but they all get here, each one of them, we have so many visitors.

It begins with an alley planted with pines on both sides, it tells you: you are going somewhere. You will arrive by car, surely. You'll reach the top of a large, lazy hill, from where the rest of the countryside begins. *There*, said the king, is where I want my tent.

You will see a sea of pink-red roofs. You will see wooden structures of massive chestnut, and heavy-set grey stone walls. Trees and bushes. My father calls it mostly rustic, Spanish, New Mexico ranch. You will stop your car under a carport, made as beautifully as an indoor room, with a huge wrought iron lampion hanging from the transverse beam, and a terracotta floor that tickles the eye, to show you are welcome. There is a passage covered by the same type of roof, with smaller beams, two smaller lampions, flanked by little walls. The wind, the breeze or the still summer air will accompany you to the French door. Welcome, welcome.

The *cameriere* will be waiting on the other side because your car was heard. You walk in an anteroom and the stone, the wood and the terra-cotta are continuing. Inside, the terracotta has been buffed and waxed, and it gleams in a pattern of squares framed by diamonds. Things are large-scale: paintings, orange-red carpets. What you see ahead, beyond the living room, is an interior garden, and beyond the garden, more roofs.

You are now in a room that you could never forget. The ceiling has shot upwards, it's double what you expected, and the beams are now chasing each other, golden brown, rich, essential to the roofs like masts and booms to sails. The roof mirrors the various chambers of the room, it moves and sets above two sitting areas, a corner with a Pleyel and books, a dining area and a plaza – dancing place, cocktail party space, a village square – in front of the fireplace, with the largest of the carpets, thin, red and green, Anatolian says M. Audibert. Above it the bronze patina of the three-tier enormous chandelier with vague roses.

On cue, Daddy will appear, going a fair speed, from one of the corridors.

'*Carissimo*, how are you?' (You are supposed to answer, 'How are you?' – nobody is to know how the other is.) And things will flow from there: a visit perhaps, the introduction of more guests, the arrival of Mummy, the scotch whisky.

But where is he, where are they?

I am in the middle of the living room, in faded trousers, and Rollei Polsen, regal in a white djellaba and some clink-clank on his neck, has just arrived. He is a famous photographer, and his subject right now is Italy. A monumental book will be published. He is friends with the whole *beau monde*, he drops names all the time, phenomenal memory he has, and he has seen many fine houses and gardens, the permission to visit obtained after much chatting at cocktail parties, and phone calls, and appointments with ancient gardeners or princesses, difficult to handle, live grenades. But he is a perfect prize for any party,

Also called 'Old Roly-Poly'. (He does not care for me.) He was hoping my parents would be home. (He is quite hot and the djellaba is uncomfortable.) How nice it is to be in this oasis. (It should be easy enough to have a little countryside repast in this big barn.) No, he has not eaten yet, actually, yes, it *is* one in the afternoon and Rome *does* seem a long way to drive, doesn't it.

Never show you are bored when you are bored, or happy when you are happy. I am completely unhappy. Aniceto in the kitchen is grumbling. There are never unexpected guests for lunch, and never never when the Ingeniere and Madame are not at home. (*Il ristorante è chiuso*, he mutters, the dining room is closed!) But the show must go on. Very well, I'll do things my way, a sort of dolls' lunch.

Anna-Chiara, the mosquito, has appeared, sensing some excitement. I say, Rollei, would you like to stroll in the garden with Anna-Chiara while I have some luncheon prepared. I want him to look away while I prepare, he would expect to clap his hands and have it all done. I can't ask Aniceto because he is busy setting the table for the children in the *office*, that's English Italian for den.

There is a spot where nobody ever goes, except for breakfast sometimes. A magnolia tree grows there, marvellously prosperous. Leaves dark green and gleaming, flowers white, regal. It's in the shade now, the light falling brightly around us. I bring my jug of iced tea. Mummy says 'Too sweet!' and 'Tea makes you nervous!' not true, *she* makes me nervous. I go find two little cantaloupes in the garden, one is not enough, and a bottle of port in the bar. I get Aniceto to take down a prosciutto hanging from the rafters ('A sight to behold,' says Daddy, sounding like a pig-breeder of long lineage), some bread too, I ask for it with a tough face, he just *has* to obey (but sometimes my orders don't pull the trick, they are not even *heard*). I make a tomato salad with vinaigrette, Tante Simone told me, two parts oil, one part vinegar, one small spoon mustard, salt and pepper. I get from the pantry a dusty box of Turkish delights.

On the table, two stem glasses etched with birds and garlands all over, survivors of a hopeful time; two green dishes shaped like a strawberry leaf that are kept as a decoration and nobody ever uses. The linen set with embroidered lemons, but I can't find the napkins, what would Grandmother say. Salt, pepper, water, white wine, bread. Towels. Some white and pink flowers from the oleanders. Pillows from Mummy's boudoir for the iron chairs.

Mr Polsen has meandered back and is now sitting in the shade.

Some magnolia flowers are open and cascading, fleshy, vulnerable, some are closed, vertical. The obverse of the shiny leaves is of beige velvet. The tree, full, shapely. The dogs have come to say hello and hope for some prosciutto, or bread if no prosciutto, they don't ask for much even from a rich guest with gold rings and a black coupe. I tell Rollei about the dogs, the history curriculum, and Latin. I drop all the names I can think of at my school. He knows everybody! I tell him what we found under the house when excavations were made for the foundations, and how Daddy had all the vases and the marbles stuck back into the dust of the millenaries, too afraid that the Fine-Arts would stop the construction. But he could not help keeping two superb small black vases.

Anna-Chiara has finished her lunch and is rehearsing her Argentine tango on the piano, going softly on the pom-pom-*po-om* as I told her. Roly-Poly thanks her for the music, 'so refreshing,' and goes to his car.

He returns with his big Hasselblad. For a while he walks around the magnolia tree, pacing, walking up to it as if to talk, as if to climb. Then focusing, releasing the shutter, focusing, rewinding, stepping back, looking, seeing, not ridiculous any more.

31. Cleaning boots and saddles – Corset-maker to the stars

In the room, on a chair, my mixed-country outfit – underwear, undershirt, jodhpurs, a green check shirt, a thin grey sweater and boots. Boots and leather care are very important in the army, and for horse people.

I'm a maniac, my first pair lasted me four years, and this one (still short, still black, but with an elastic at the ankle and no strap) is so beautiful I wear them all the time, sometimes even with trousers at parties. I clean them and shine them to death, they get warm from all the polishing and brushing. At my riding school, in Guildford (Surrey), where I go riding and learning English, they teach you how to clean the tack. At first you snort because it looks like a trick to save on grooms. Then you understand this do-it-yourself thing is very very 'in', the mucking of stables, pushing super-colossal wheelbarrows up the muck heap, cleaning tack, grooming horses, you are being taught how to be self-sufficient, don't worry, *you still are a spoiled girl who will find a groom back home*, whom you will drive to distraction with the new methods learned in England.

Take your saddle and bridle, which are personal to the horse that has been assigned to you. Poor, *poor* Billy Boy, *povero*, it's enough that you change riders every week, your tack is just yours, yes, and your stall. You assemble clean rags, a sponge, two buckets of warm water, and soap. First you clean. You wring the rag until it's merely damp, remove all visible mud. Now wash the rag in one bucket, rinse it in the other, wring it; rub it, with and against the grain, to make the leather sweat and render its particles of dirt; rinse the rag. Now you nourish the leather. You rub a barely damp rag on the glycerine soap bar (a misnomer, it just *looks* like soap) and apply a thin film on the leather. It smells good, clean, a little like dried ferns. You let the saddle dry, then you shine it. April or Mr Parks will inspect it, by scratching here and there with a nail (same test as for a clean neck), so you must do it properly. But you never know: sometimes, you have worked hard, and they still catch a greasy film, so you look like a slob, sometimes you get away with a slapdash job. Same thing for grooming, sometimes your horse is a dust factory, the more you brush the more the skin breaks and releases particles, makes clouds, it's endless, and you're hungry for breakfast. I have tried new methods, like using a damp cloth to keep it down, it works until April goes by with a brush and does a quick lifting of the hair near the neck. Once I stayed brushing until I started coughing and sneezing and they came to get me because breakfast was being cleared. The horse was barely clean and I was covered with dust.

Horses are such fine things. They let you be associated with their beauty. You can walk proudly.

You can walk proudly until your breasts start growing and showing. The undershirt does not hide them much, so you start rolling in your shoulders, and you lean towards your desk in the classroom. Other girls seem to have easily rounded that corner, and you admire their neatness, the way they hold themselves, the way they wear their breasts, the way their bras fit them, become one with them.

I don't know. I am unsure. Since our first times in the countryside Dad has shown us how to play rough with the dogs, to look war-ready. He made us practise '*I am a rough and tough*' in a gangster accent. But I also like dresses and jewels, things. I like to dress for the place, I suppose, in the countryside I wear boots. In the swimming pool, I wear a two-piece swimming suit, I could not believe my eyes when Valentina gave it to me. At school, of course, it's the uniform, more than ten years of it. Like an old housecoat and slippers. My mother gives no advice about navigating all this because she is always angry at me and me at her.

I was small, maybe seven, at the mountainside, and I had tried on huge skis that morning, and failed. The sky was woollen, grey, and low. I was alone in a large room with a bay window, there was an immense pool table. I had been sent inside. I was immobile, doing nothing, chewing on my inability. There was a little boy, curiously looking at the table, the holes, the cues. He went all around the table, then came up to me. Finally he said, kindly, are you a boy or a girl? It was a scientific question, I was in ski *fuseaux* and with my short hair, hailed enthusiastically by Dad as Geppetto's style (Pinocchio's dad, first of all *I hate* Pinocchio, then why does a little girl have to look like an old shoemaker?) But the little boy mortally offended me. Was I *a boy?!* So I was a girl.

To my mother, I kept saying nothing, not a word, I was not even thinking of speaking about it, I only smouldered in resentment. I started wearing the top of my bikini, under sweaters only, it was bright orange and green, impossible under shirts, but my mother's friends must have told her, and I bet she did postpone it, forgot, and I feigned indifference, in fact I was very nervous about it, I wished it would appear one day magically, by my bed, but there we were, one day we went to Brighenti's, the corset-maker to the stars. I have been there often, but *not for myself*, in the wake of my mother or Valentina or Tante Simone. It's lovely to look at the ruffles, the slippers decorated with a little white powder puff, the crepe dressing gowns from the outside. It takes courage to walk in. Those who go in are women who have strong motives. Women who know the importance of the bedtime, the sun-tanning one, the lounging by the swimming pool, half dressed, half undressed, and if undressed, by wearing the *déshabillé*, the négligé, confirming: why, yes, I am half undressed. You can't be shy when you make that affirmation. The body as a bouquet, held properly.

It's busy, inside Brighenti, with clients, and little drawers, and dozens of framed photos smiling down to the clients, Lollobrigida, Loren, Virna Lisi, Sandra Milo, the Kessler twins, they smile and say 'To Brighenti, affectionately'; 'To Brighenti, with love'. They all chose self-explanatory pictures, 'How could I look so lovely if not for *this* (turn a little) and *those* (lean a bit), and how could *those* be seen, presented, appreciated, savoured, if not for my splendid corset, my superb bra, my lovely bathing suit, my embroidered kimono?'

They have this freshness, a freshness that tempts, calls for being grabbed, picked, crushed, consumed. Crisp croissants, a freshly folded newspaper, a starched shirt, a full dahlia with all her alveoli. They give newness, strength, enthusiasm. Yes, men, women, *anyone* would like to be close to them. Champagne and felicity are never far.

Oh the pale green petticoat with the foaming white appliqué.

The clients do not look like the beauties on the walls, but that is not stopping them. They are determined to participate in the combat against other women, against indifference, against a job that takes too much of a man's time, with a spirit of sacrifice, sacrifice of money, for everything here is costly, and perhaps, having overcome the limits of their purse, they'll have to explain to their husbands, and have an argument over it, but mustn't allow it to ruin everything; sacrifice of physical comfort, too, since they are ready to shorten their breath and compress their movements. The saleswoman will find their size for the girdle they saw in the shop-window. It may not suit them, but they will then think of another colour, and of judicious alterations. The saleswomen are another notch below in glamour, with their simple dresses, but they know just how much the glamour of that bodice can be stretched to include the client.

'I have seen you a little thinner in the springtime, you are going to reduce again, you say? (...) But yes, we do have it in *mordoré*, it would suit your complexion, I am not sure though' – she rifles through a pile of boxes behind her – 'that we have the same model, ah, this one comes down lower on the thighs ...' and she displays it on the glass counter, it is appealing, this sculptured silhouette of embroidered game of light and shadows, *this* will be *you*, an idealized body.

My mother is parleying with a matron who looks tired but is not giving an inch.

'But, Signora, this is the model most young ladies are wearing, what more would you want, look, good Sangallo, simple, pretty, white, we are selling them by the dozen.'

She walks over to me and pulls my shirt from behind to evaluate me.

'With a bust like *that* you cannot go with an elastic model, it's not appropriate, it flattens the bust.' (We keep it for women who are *flat*.)

It is clear that the saleswoman is on my side and Mother is not. Mother has decided, the beige elastic thing is right for me. Argue with my mother? She would embarrass me so. And really, am I one of the pretty young ladies?

I run to the cabin like a dog with a bone, and try the bra on (made in USA) with a sense of triumph, some day I'll walk in with my own money, and the saleswoman will take me under her wing if I make myself endearing, and explain how you wear this and that, and what is more becoming, and show me all the colours of the season.

32. Eliseo and the season of flowers

I was eating a slice of bread and butter and cherry jam by the French windows. In a corner of the garden, Eliseo stood watching the mimosa tree, in his shirt, unbuttoned where his drum of a belly could not be contained, and his nailed boots, one partly fastened with rope. His round brick-coloured face was contracted in contemplation of bad news. For all his strength and shovel-sized hands, he was just like a pitiable large ogre afraid of the mean-spirited little fairy.

He sighed. 'Euge',' he said, 'now Madam is sure to come and yell because the flowers are a-fading and tonight there is the party. *E mo', chi la sente?*' he added, with feeling. 'Who can endure that?'

I knew. It's not my fault if she is like that, but I feel as if it was. And my father is never around in these crises. He will show up *afterwards*, to pick up the pieces. He too, behaves in a way I hate.

Poor Eliseo. I kept chewing on my *tartine*. A cup of tea would go well with it. Eliseo's problem ... I could run an advice bureau, like Lucy. Almost said: five cents, please!

Mimosa tree – Japan. Japan – kimono! It was only nine thirty but perhaps Zia Valentina would be up, reading the newspaper on her small terrace among the roofs of Piazza Cairoli. She responded admirably. Yes, she knew where to find Japanese lampions, she would come early for the party and help me. I went and found Vanna, and asked her if she would like to be 'like in a play', and wear my kimono costume tonight. She said yes, enraptured. I asked her to go and make a pot of tea for me, for practice. My mother. I found her playing solitary. Odd. I fell upon her with an air of irresistible eagerness and helpfulness. I said we could do a little Japanese corner in the garden with lampions all over the mimosa tree, it would make it look 'fuller', and Vanna would have a little table under it, in a Japanese costume, serving tea in little bowls, with a pretty fan, fanning herself – I'd sit down with her, and make one copied from my *Japanese Tales*.

Oh, wonderful, for once the impossible big sister would do bricolage with Vanna, and Vanna was all happy to play the little geisha. When Eliseo was summoned – he had disappeared to visit his rabbits – it was to go buy cut flowers for the house, and the mimosa's insufficient yellowness had been forgotten.

During the day, there was much fussing and almost falling from a crooked ladder, and gathering the most oriental accessories for tea, and doing a special maquillage for Vanna. When the evening came, the mimosa looked just enchanting, quietly glittering. The guests were mostly international people from the FAO and the Embassy, in silk suits cut in Hong Kong and tweeds, and the old standbys who always come. Zia Valentina held forth on Japanese cinema and hand-made rice paper. There was a rice salad, which I adore. After an initial success, Vanna became tired from the excitement, and cold, and went to bed in my kimono. Gérard, 'the French tenor', kept bringing up that we could go to Venice next week-end with Aunt Valentina, 'the three of us', plaintively, which made him look pathetic, his tie knot and his teeth particularly. So after a little, I sneaked out to the library with a plate of olives and petit-fours, and sat on a large leather chair which makes me think of Christopher Columbus. I stayed a long time listening to the wood-worms in the beams, a nice sound – except I dislike the dust, and pulling out the most curious titles, like *English Eccentrics* and *Portrait of the Artist as a Young Man*. Thinking of this and that. Then I remembered a satchel of silver coins Daddy gave me when they went out of circulation, a long time ago, which he told me to take great care of. I thought I had put them behind a black collection of German philosophers, and took down the whole row, and a whole *History of Italian Literature*, but only found dust. Felt bad about my absent-mindedness and unreliability. Then went back to my room without meeting anybody.

33. Approved reading for maids – Bluebeard – Photo stories

I don't know if you know Delly. Not to be confused with Magali. Delly (man or woman?) is awfully proper, no burning kisses. It's almost always the same story, only the settings and the adjectives change. It would be 'proud Provence' or proud Ardennes. It's attractive and nauseating as hard candy, which is never good for long. There is always a secret, and a sacred trust or a betrayal, and a woman in a situation of inferiority, depending, very depending on others. The woman behaves fearlessly, according to her moral principles. She can be rescued only by a very powerful man, an officer, count, knight, well-born, who initially treats her with contempt. She insists on being reckless. At some magical point, he starts showing some surprised admiration for her. He always is ahead of her, he knows something she doesn't. He knows. He has a

superior knowledge of women. He knows how to distinguish them.
He has experience. Odd, because you hardly can imagine him
being as ordinary as being in the same bed as someone else. Going
to the bathroom. Nakedness that would reveal him. He would not
be naked. He would be naked-but-in-his-uniform.

M. de Tarlay is talking to Mitsi (his son's governess, an
orphan): '*He seemed to listen with unfeigned interest to Mitsi. But
an observer would have become convinced that this interest was
almost only for her appearance, that fine face with its velvety
complexion, under which ran a lively blood, those brown eyes with
gold specks, under the shade of long dark lashes.*' He is not far
from the slave buyer. Her appearance becomes *detached* from her,
and captured. It is taken and manipulated.

He calls her 'little girl'. He bestows forgiveness for behaviour
that displeases him. She is inferior socially. From the beginning she
has trusted he would eventually come to know her admirable
moral traits and not destroy her. She confided in God and sought
guidance throughout. She has trusted him – in spite of all the signs
of sadism and anger. If he had been a Roman emperor, she would
have been a Christian martyr. But the Roman emperor turns into a
soul redeemed by love. Her trust is rewarded when the nobleman
elegantly (it's an innate trait) requests her hand.

Ode to Bluebeard (you know Bluebeard): Bluebeard is a dear,
dear man. I write this because I am being 'very difficult'. My
mother is stupid. It's one of my *contraries*. I say contraries to
distract fate. Bluebee, my dear Bluey. Another contrary: if you are
in a perfectly safe situation, you imagine the organ crashing down
on the altar. No danger, it could never happen. It's just when
moments *hold* too long, when there is no swing, the air gets filled
with thoughts of destruction. It's a distraction. 'The pause that
refreshes.' You risk nothing by just thinking contrary thoughts; to
say them is more dangerous; to write them more dangerous still.
But this Bluebeard thing, there is absolutely no danger. What could
he do, actually arrive here? And what? He would mistake me for
one of his wives? No, he would be pleased that someone has kind
thoughts for him.

Nonsense, wonderful nonsense.

The books of Magali are just a little more daring, in French it's risqué, risky, risk of blushing, risk of showing something you don't trust. Risk of straying. Something I have but don't recognize. I don't speak about. First of all, with my friends we keep it hushed up, we exchange the books etc. but we know they are what my father calls utterly not presentable, not unlike photo stories, which the maids buy with glee and snatch from you if by any chance you find them. And *fotoromanzi* you find, torn, scattered pages, in places trampled by prostitutes.

How do I know, it's very simple. First, I notice any kind of readable things, anywhere. Second, '*quelle*', 'those' (pious veil on the noun) are here and there, judiciously scattered, and it's inevitable that the car will stop, sometimes, in one of those places. For instance, some of their territories lie at the curbside of the road from school to our countryside. Odd, isn't it? We pass by them in our blue car, driven by Tonino who looks straight ahead as he goes by, we in our blue uniforms, thinking of our lessons. We do not pay the slightest notice, we don't make comments, it would be unthinkable. We don't have the words. Outside our vocabulary. They are so bizarre, so outrageous in their white patent *cuissardes*, their thigh boots, their trench coats, their heels, so crazily vulgar. Caricatures. If we do need to stop, it could be because we have a flat tire, or someone is carsick (it's a very winding road), or there is a beautiful pair of pheasants in the field (it's all fields, along the Via Giustiniana), we would stop at crossroads, not, if possible, on a dangerous curve. We stop where others would stop, too. There would be grass, kept short by patient road-menders (who live in houses painted Pompei red), gravel, a bit of mud. So I know. I can tell you they are very careless with their magazines, there are pages scattered, crumpled, damp, and they don't read *Playboy* or *Playgirl* or what is the other one. That would be boring, since they are into the same line of work. (Would that be a busman's holiday? I must ask Clotilde.) They read *fotoromanzi*, photo stories, like the maids. Maybe not exactly the same, there are different classes. But that's what they like. There they find their models, and their ideals of fashions. Like the maids, and ladies at the hairdresser, they also like Farah Diba, the student who becomes Empress. I know exactly. Although. We are not. In the same world. (Unless they remove their costumes and go to the bakery, buy bread and ham like everyone else.) I know exactly where they wait for cars, even if they have left their spot for a while. Even if they are not *there*, they are not really absent, they are not far. Sometimes a small brazier fire, waiting for them.

Now when we are not in the car, not at close range, there is occasional, good-humoured mention of *quelle* at home, by one of our cousins who has found a way to mispronounce a Roman slang word. Saying it and not saying it. *'Migh-notte'*: the sound is funny, disguised, and mentionable. He will say, 'You should see on Tor di Quinto tonight, what huge brazier fires, and a brisk trade, you would not believe what the *migh-notte* are wearing!' It must be said that on Tor di Quinto the prostitutes are hard to miss, they parade as on a private stage, they own the street. As you drive, you must be careful not to bump into the car ahead, which is prone to go very slow, then brake abruptly. I heard Daddy say to Tonino, 'Beware when you drive there, men go crazy, they go crazy!' I think rather they have fits of laughter.

Delly, Magali – I would not bring them up with anyone. It's a sort of contraband, vice. The books are obtained wordlessly, between readers, all of them Italian girls, by the way, there are none at the Librairie française. You buy them at the more plebeian *cartolibreria*, the stationer who also sells books. You put them on the counter and Mummy does not question. 'A household name', 'romanzi all'acqua di rose', novels with a bland rose-water flavour, and that is *perfect!* Daughters must be blandished and un-agitated. But there is an invisible ink under the rose-water perfume. You don't tell anyone, also because you can't describe it, you are not sure what makes you want to read more, it's impalpable, a little tickle, more variations about the young *comme il faut* daughter of an uncertain mother, who has a name that used to be but is not quite – She is proper but there is something about her gorgeous skin, and the silken shoulders ... it's a girl, it's her and it's you ... you start thinking of her skin and it enraptures you ... If you spoke about it, it would become a problem, which you know is not solvable. It's a jungle that no explanation can clear now, there is a necessity of not speaking, of just continuing going on reading bad books, in a sort of paroxysm.

Delly and Magali, pretty names on a beribboned swing, who share amiably the market of girls' afternoons. There is no substitute for the bland chatter they spin, the company they keep, and the constancy of their credo, you will love, you will love. But since the story is trite (how otherwise could it be Books for Everyone, in the sense of 'No Danger'?) and no apologies on their part, the quantity at least must be unimpeachable, the flow constant. In short they must work hard, otherwise how does one churn out *L'Infidèle, Mitsy, L'Intrigante, La Princesse à l'oeillet*? And us, panting, reading without reading, struck here and there by the 'slight pressure of his palm', or 'her slightly matte skin'.

Where is that pink beehive? Mesdemoiselles Delly and Magali, they can only live in Nice, or Sanremo; under a mild climate, with palm trees and gentility everywhere. A timeless place, a zone of neutrality. To the point you cannot tell Delly is a man or a woman, I think, rather a woman, although there is a man who writes like both, Guy des Cars ... or is it Cesbron ... oh la la. And Magali, with a woman's name, could it be a man? The only certainty is – with those cover jackets, and those titles, no boy ever will read those.

Delly lives on a hill in a delightful villa with her poodle, and Magali lives in a little *hôtel particulier* with her Persian cats. They are in their fifties, plump, unmarried, intelligent, diligent, extraordinarily fond of comfort and custom-made shoes. They have cooks but like to do their marketing on their own. They wear dark pinks and maroons, lots of crêpe, hats, gloves, parasols, beribboned purses. Nougat the poodle goes on the market promenade, a dark brown mid-sized dog. The authoresses call each other on the telephone, always for tea and bridge and things like that, never anything in full measure, like a proper dinner. They prefer to spend their day writing or plotting, with walks and some light gardening, and eat their meals in peace. They are very fond of each other, as simple as that, *tout bonnement.* A few old friends, some neighbours, come to their little gatherings, and there are nephews who come for Easter and bring *marrons glacés*, one is a jolly Jesuit and the other, an agricultural engineer.

The day I started thinking of the authoresses behind the books, the flavour of their books became too faint, and nothing would restore it. The list of titles that used to read like a musical scale gave a hollow sound. I disliked that row and a half of books as much as I hate Delia when Elsa is here. And what if someone I wanted to impress was to see this river of mawkishness.

My younger books have migrated to Vanna's room, though I still keep an eye on them. I wanted these disappeared. It would take twenty-three days, one book a day, hidden in the waste-paper bag, though the maids, who are informed of every scrap of garbage, would not allow it. They would return the book to your bedside table, scowling that so much gets lost in this house, they are not surprised to see *a book* fallen in the garbage by mistake. You cannot throw a book away, no more than bread. Not make a gift of an already read book (Daddy very sarcastic when I as much as glance at a book, or record, bought as a gift). But somebody who wouldn't mind, the farmer's daughter, or Eliseo? I'll pretend I am a good soul and offer the whole collection to the Bazaar.

I was sucked in, and made to half-wrap the 'lots' to show the contents and make them more attractive. Stick huge ribbons on the leprous pots of the unwanted plants, lugubrious sentinels of apartment landings, sanseveria, ficus, monsteria. Rejuvenate picnic baskets that came with Easter delicacies, and now contain less glorious chocolate boxes and ceramics made by the *dames patronesses*. Hand-knitted booties and baby coverlets, a little scraggy. My pink and pale blue collection of twenty-three had enough ruffles and rosettes for a Flamenco dress and was among the first to go.

34. *Peter and the Wolf*

Look, admire how calm I am, listening to the 'Step of the Wolf' in *Peter and the Wolf,* delightful ballet designed to make children die of fear.

I am lying on the mottled black Techno reclining chair, parallel to the mottled white chair, on the curly brown carpet, sprawled like a very large Téo, the Hungarian shepherd. The black record is turning, disquieting, with sinister gleams, on the retractable record player, record turner, which you learned to handle very carefully, turning the ornate green key, lowering the vertical panel, pulling out the tray, the buttons, the arm with its *diamond* needle. The forest of albums also enclosed to be summoned one by one, with a light finger.

We have *Edith Piaf à l'Olympia*, Paul Anka and some Hawaian singers, we have Rosa Morena, Quando Calienta El Sol, Sapore di Sale, samba records with feet patterns and martini glasses on the back cover, *Misa Criolla*, we have the Passion According to Matthew but without the part I like. 'These Boots Are Made for Walking', brought by Sonny (and Mummy frowned), I listen to it all I can. We have Léo Ferré singing Rimbaud and Verlaine, with barely any music, which gives me the goosebumps because he sings from an empty, bare room. I learned some of those, the easiest way, with music.

Il patinait merveilleusement,/ s'élançant capiteusement …

Je fais souvent un rêve,/ étrange et pénétrant,/ d'une femme inconnue/ et que j'aime et qui m'aime,/ et qui n'est chaque fois/ ni tout à fait la même/ ni tout à fait une autre/ et m'aime et me comprend./ Car elle me comprend,/ et pour elle seulement,/ mon coeur transparent/ cesse d'être un problème …

We have Glenn Gould and Wilhelm Kempf because Mummy plays the piano. Mummy plays Fauré, Liszt, and Schumann. Schumann more often. I used to sit under the piano and wait for the right chords, and a good occasion to cry, and think of my dead grandmother, the Canadian one, whose photograph is on top of the piano. We also have Noel songs and the life of Schubert, Mozart and Bach for children, on three-quarter size records. Schubert has the nicest illustrations and music. I cannot understand how with so much music inside him he died young. Why he had to die, since he already suffered from loneliness. We have *On a marché sur la Lune* (the Tintin story – 'Allô, allô, ici la terre, fusée lunaire, répondez …!' and the silence all the way from the Earth to the Moon, terrifying and thrilling). And Radu Lupu, which I don't listen to because I used to think it was another wolf story.

A howling in some kind of clarinet can be heard from afar, the trail of Peter's wolf is tortuous, he half-crawls like the farm dog when he wants to catch a lizard. It does not matter that the woodcutters afterwards will catch him, and kill him, and take him around hanging from the legs. Even after he is dead you know he was alive before and very dangerous, as in *Red Riding Hood*. And since it's a story, he is never *completely* dead. If the record starts again, the wolf will begin living again. If the book starts again, the merry-go-round will re-begin – Red Riding Hood, like a candy on the record, will turn faster and faster like a skater, a fuse, a flame, a shadow, sink in the record, disappear inside the story with her picnic, her basket, the grandmother with her bonnet ... All characters dancing in a ring, holding hands in a merry-go-round. In the end, all go down, eaten, swallowed, finished. Only then, rescued up to their feet, and the story can re-begin. Called back to live, disappear, return.

35. Theatrical success – A case of acute envy

It feels great when I can rehearse. When the moment is known. It feels safe. I know how to feel. I don't know *le trac* – the panic. Poetry, theatre. At school we do a play only every two years, every year would be too exhausting for Léonida, the absolute *metteur en scène*, reigning on the stage as by divine right.

We accept her as inalterable, from year to year. The way she directs windows to be opened or closed, as she walks in a quick step, pulls at her thick compact beige-y shawl. The way she manipulates markers in the books she brings to class, perforated strips of sheets of stamps, and rectangles salvaged from waste paper. Her nail and finger plunge in the thick of the book and push hard to open it, lifting the marker and holding to it for dear life, then sticking very deliberately the marker between the next pair of pages. The way she says *excessivement* instead of *infiniment*. 'Exceedingly.' She says it often. An older sister of Geneviève's has told us it's after Proust (the sublime writer that is being kept for our last year), but we would never dream of imitating her. Her oddities, her passions. It's a treat to hear the passion for history, her subject, in her voice, too bad that the program is so broad, it's impossible to keep the pace. She also, of her own initiative we suspect, makes side lessons of history of art – another set of manias about the projector, and the way to handle slides, and this and that. I learn not much but I adore her lessons.

So thoroughly – so exceedingly does she immerse herself in a theatre production, that MML needs a rest cure of plain old history teaching, interrogations, exam marking and prayer. I think she puts Molière's soul in some of her prayers though. The theatre is extra-curricular for us, and for her too, after all, straying from her everyday duty and her spiritual path.

Then, as time goes by, owing to her infinite readings, living in that world of hers where not a name can be pronounced without bringing in a cascade of others, and the map of history is a giant pin-ball game, she starts toying with the idea of a tragedy, or a Claudel, 'next time'. The compliments from the last play are rehashed by the nuns, all fierce theatre lovers, and bang, it's too late, her fever is contagious, authorizations are secured and the title of the next production is announced.

In a way, it's part of the curriculum, we study about five plays a year, almost all of Molière, Racine and Corneille. (Almost all our professors will at some point confess they prefer Racine, but shyly, as if unpatriotic.) We have interrogation on poems and excerpts, that is standard. On alternate years, those who want to can play scenes for the rest of the class. So in *troisième* we did a little 'spectacle', starting with Herminie saying *Le lac*, and three scenes from *L'Avare*, with Frosine, and with Cléante, and the monologue of the stolen silver. L'Avare is Harpagon, a horrible old miser who makes life miserable for children and servants. We were to tour our half of the school. We had no costumes, no props, Aunt Valentina said it was 'terribly modern'.

Léonida, our handler, led us from class to class. All the *grandes* and *moyennes*, all seven of them, during French lessons. We were presented as a sort of special treat. Benches were pushed, and chairs were put in a semicircle at the bottom of the room. None of the normal artifices, no lights, no curtain, not even something of a stage.

I pretended to play the other scenes, but I cared for nothing but my monologue, standing in the semi-circle, alone.

There it was. I mentally beat the measures of a pause. I waded in the silence and found it not terrifying. That empty space, I appropriated, I knew it was done by great actors, and now I was doing it because I knew how. The audience was now an audience, not girls in the same uniform as mine. They were not thinking of homework or interrogations, or of the shortest skirt they could get away with. They were at the theatre.

I took a few steps, stooped and grim. They giggled. I raised my head and looked at the audience without seeing them, entering Harpagon's hallucination. I felt radioactive. Fluorescent. I was feeding on them, and distilling my precious lines, a nectar, a royal jelly.

They saw l'Avare saying the lines I'd learned maniacally – and loved, and they followed, from laughter to pity to chiming delight, they listened to the illusion and laughed. L'Avare was a crazy old man, with a morbid love of his silver coins. His madness was repulsive but Molière had written it knowing it could be droll. I was being a good interpreter and it worked. Wafting to me, the girls' attention, their favour. There was alchemy, of which I was a prey and a master. The play had transformed me and the girls into a fluid, an essence of flesh, the rarest bit, nose-membrane or ear tips, or even tendrils of sea urchin. Of this we drank a sapid succulent brimming spoonful.

They applauded and cheered. I rolled blissfully in their corollas, I was proud, I knew I had done 'something'.

In the corridor, all sorts of unknown girls would say hello. For weeks thereafter Léonida greeted me, misquoting I thought, with 'Mon *cher* trésor!' She would have liked me to study more for history, but some things are impossible.

Arpeggios still waft in.

* * *

The Barber of Seville this year. The full-scale production with costumes and props and the theatre in the Crypte. They had meant *Polyeucte* but there were objections. No part for me. They took Madeleine Reynas, a *première*, for Figaro, it's meant to be a play for the last two classes. I thought I could be Bartolo, but nobody asked me. Madeleine! She didn't even think much of it. But I just wasn't going to say a word. It wouldn't change anything and I would expose my true heart and risk more wounds. I would seem envious. I would not speak calmly. I would end up crying.

A yearning for the death of Madeleine materialized. Something that would *impede* her. I was badly envious, and knew it was despicable. I wanted what she had and was prevented by various rules and inhibitions from grabbing it from her, or, better, if possible, taking it by stealth. In the swimming-pool, I beat everybody in breast-stroke, so inflamed was my rage. I was inside an invisible prison, my own temperament. Nobody could see it, nobody would save me. I suffered as much from the events as from my own rules of laissez-faire, elegance and politeness. Instead of helping me, my system compounded my problems. I felt it inevitable that I would burst.

One afternoon during Cathechism, I was struggling to recover the last rhyme of 'Eleanor Rigby', to put my mind off my torment. To no avail: I half-sang 'all the lonely people', still I was hurting, my breast crushed by an ingenious killing machine, two massive slabs of marble closing in inexorably.

I was scared by the intensity of the pain, I wondered what would become of me. I tried an ultimate effort to free myself, and forced myself to consider the facts, one last time. Between severe pangs, I saw with stupefaction that, with a free hand, I was steadily turning the handle of the torture machine.

36. Piero's friend – Coins and cameos – The Tiberius Agate –
    Antiquities on Via dei Serpenti

First you hear his laughter ('yak-yak-yak') or his imprecations, very loud and never in earnest, he just seems to be practising his Roman slang. '*Te possin' acciaccà, Toni', ssi te prenno te scanno!*' that is, may they squish you, Tonino, if I catch you I'll bleed you – all because Tonino has made a pretence of running him down, very slowly, then braking two centimetres away. And he walks with big steps, exaggerated, like a wolf in a comedy, or is it those big cumbersome feet, not sure he is really allowed to be here, but it's his apartment! '*Sono Rembrando,*' and he shakes hands, pumping with enthusiasm. You know he says it to make you laugh, because Rembrando, it doesn't exist. But Piero has told me he, Rembrando, thinks it's Italian for Rembrandt, that's his name, and he really thinks he can disguise as an Italian.

Piero met him at the numismatics shop, he just wanted to have a look at some coins, like collectors do, and meditate fruity swaps, also have an answer ready in case he's asked what would he like for his birthday. And Rembrandt, who was sitting looking at catalogues, gave him some tips, so when Daddy came to fetch Piero they spoke, and Piero now goes and visits Rembrandt, they always have some trafficking going on, books, coins, images. Today I went upstairs with him. He lives on the fifth floor of an old building facing the sunset near Via dei Serpenti, in the Monti neighbourhood, not far from the Forum. The floors feel elastic if you run, but it annoys the tenants below very much.

It's a house for things you like and nothing of the rest. Books vertical, horizontal, and tables against the walls, with trays and boxes, and large photographs on thick crinkled paper, copybooks, catalogues. Chairs and just one sofa, with a sheet thrown over, and white walls. There is a plastic basket with empty wine bottles by the door. He has more pencils than the stationery shop, big bunches of them, kept in old tomato cans, scrubbed and cleaned, I looked inside.

He speaks like this, in Italian: 'Want snack, miss? Want banana?' And he laughs, because everything is a game to him, this thing of being in Rome, learning the language, going to the money exchange with his pounds and coming out with lire, working in the Vatican where he can study the most fantastic coins and cameos, his other hobbyhorse. He eats mozzarella and tomatoes all he can, and sits at the wine shop with the old locals, and although he does not have friends yet, he knows everybody's name and he has many teasers, which is a beginning.

'See this cameo' (and already you know this is an amazing cameo, his voice is echoing like thunder in a grotto) 'the stone is *sardonica* and the cutter had to study how the layers would react, be white, light or dark, as the cut went deeper, it's a good piece, the head of an emperor perhaps, Claudius perhaps, and – oh, *guarda!* you see, this is the Great Cameo of the Sainte-Chapelle, the largest of antiquity, generally considered the finest. Also called the Tiberius Agate. It was in the hands of Pope Clement VI, one of the popes of Avignon, then when Clemente needed money, he sold it back to the kings of France, and *mannaggia, porca miseria*, we lost it. Just look at this, *incredib'le, ragazzi, incredib'le.*' Rembrando has a strong esprit de corps, he works in the Vatican on some study, and he has come to consider himself as part of it, 'We lost it,' indeed.

The picture he holds (you translate into colours automatically) is a summary, says Rembrando, of who was the most noble family and who should be a Roman emperor at a certain point in history. A masterful carver was probably given an imperial command – the emperor wished it, or perhaps it was the artist's idea in the first place. You had to take a chance, with those capricious masters. You stuck your neck out. The carver explained how many images could fit in the cameo, he had to insist (carefully) on what was possible, keeping in mind this was an irreplaceable stone (not a wall for a fresco, which you could whitewash if you made any mistakes). 'It could hold about twenty figures, master, as you can see from this sketch … It is not clear what the stone will reveal as we start carving … assuredly, it is splendid, Yousef, the Smyrne merchant, said it is unsurpassed … to recognize the likenesses of the august emperors and the gods, they could not be carved much smaller … Yes, master, it could be attempted to make them smaller …,' and much sweating.

I would have ended up with three small pieces of stone, each with a single figure, and escaping from Rome under a cloak in the darkest of all nights. I cannot plan, although we must. PLAN our redactions, our compositions. Limit your élan, don't rush. Think, and connect and develop. Do as they say. When we were smaller, you could just write about a visit to the countryside, a thing you had seen. Now you must consider, reason, be a thinker. Even if it all gets dizzy.

Piero can imitate Rembrando very well, he is funny, he keeps quiet, then he shows you how clever he is. He calls him *il professore inglese*. Rembrando knows how to use Daddy's camera. He's just as fascinated by things as Piero is.

I thought that cameos were what you see in the shop windows, not very far from coral necklaces and opulent bunches of cornelian beads, displayed to flow from madrepore conchs. Those cameos are pearly white on beige-rose, a stone very close to flesh tone, set in gilt, or gold, and there are animated discussions between ladies about which ones are 'authentic'. I am a little ashamed because after all those glorious masterpieces, I still would like one of the plain pink ones.

'Cameo is the work in relief, intaglio would be cutting into the stone, cameo and intaglio are the two arts of glyptic – *gliptica*, no?' We don't know this word, but if he's suggesting it, it must be wrong. '*Gliptica, gliptica* ...,' he sings. 'From all corners of the Empire, stones would converge to Rome, agates, carnelians, onyx, ashen agates, agate-onyx, bluish sardonyx, and the Romans had Greek and Oriental craftsmen to carve them, and do fine bas-relief on their monuments, to illustrate their history. You know relics, the Byzantine emperors gathered an enormous number of them, the Holy Cross, and the crown of thorns, and many other precious objects. That was the imperial treasure of Constantinople. In the times of the Crusades, it fell into the hands of the Latin emperors, until one of them, needing money, had to sell it to Louis IX (King of France *and* Saint). He brought it to Paris and housed it in the Sainte Chapelle. So the Grand Camée started as part of the treasure of the Caesars, went to Constantinople, to the Byzantines, then to the Latin emperors, then to Paris, to the popes in Avignon, then back to Paris, returning to the collection. And myriads of objects, liturgical or pagan, were gathered. The kings of course rather liked them, but they also felt a responsibility as custodians. Louis XVI, the one who was guillotined during the French Revolution, as late as 1791, although practically a prisoner, expressed the royal wish that the stones of the Sainte Chapelle, instead of being sold would be stored in the Cabinet des Médailles. That was really lucky for us, because revolutions are dangerous times for people and for symbols of wealth, and things change hands, get stolen, dispersed or destroyed.'

I became nervous when Rembrando started talking about revolutions, he might have expected me to know interesting facts about the one of 1789, and I had never heard there had been another one in 1830, I would have seemed ignorant, which I am. And I think there is another one too, after the Prussians besieged Paris, it looks like there had not been what is called 'a good war', that is, a sufficiently exterminating war, and angers kept simmering, since they were not extinguished with sufficient, durable, terror.

'They have something like 300,000 coins' (I stopped 'seeing' and lost count, but Piero, on his own internal Viewmaster, he saw a parade of them, each one splendid, curious or interesting) 'but what are numbers, we are not impressed by numbers, it's rarity, beauty that matters.' We were solidifying as one unit, an unruffled group led by *il professore inglese*, whom we'd follow unhesitatingly, a small, very good, archaeology team, dressed in white or beige, looking for treasures, and finding them fairly often, at frequent intervals, so that we would not get bored. In Assyria or Babylonia, where no homework would reach us and cast its shadow.

Coins are not carved by hand, they are cast, but, if very old, they are almost handmade. And they carry images of history, always a face, and something else. 'Somebody would decide to have a coin cast to Crispina's effigy, see here, Crispina Augusta, wife of Emperor Commodus, *pazzo furioso, eh!* and on the obverse, a goddess, to create an association of virtue – to put her in good company, here, we have Juno Lucina, the goddess of Light and Childbirth; or Venus, and here, Concordia, peace, of course you know that, *te possino*, Latin is easy, eh!' He turned the coins in his fingers, slowly. 'She was sent into exile to Capri, and later assassinated.' It saddened me to think of the evils in the times of the Romans, I only went once to the Villa of Tiberius, left to abandon although it's a beautiful spot. Capri seems to have left it to itself, you know, people say Capri is a happy island, nothing really bad happens, Tiberio and his friends were bad so they've been abandoned, the villa is only ruins, washed clean by sun and rain.

Piero is thinking about the satchel of drachmas he has, rather worn out, but from the fourth or third century B.C., with eagles, the nymph Chalkis (he makes it sound as if she was extremely famous) and other effigies. I am thinking of the Grand Cameo and that it never got lost over the centuries, someone always *had* it, guarded it, hid it, never lost it.

It's not a very fine afternoon but foreigners never notice. Rembrando said we were going on an expedition, *una picc'la spedizione*. He takes us to the courtyard, then through a thick wooden door, to a walled garden, a sort of vegetable garden probably tended by the concierge. It's on a slope, with the usual bits and pieces of ruins scattered. We are wearing our school shoes, the grass is wet.

Rembrando whispers, 'I have reasons to believe this property belonged to Muzio Caravanti, the friend of Corizio ... in the golden days of Rome, during the papacy of Leon X.... Before the sack of Rome.' 'Fifteen twenty-seven,' says Piero, absent-mindedly. 'Rome then was a city of many gardens, and men of letters would give dinners in the open, some women came, too, or they'd meet here and there, on the Palatine, or at the temple of Vesta, anywhere they wanted, and write poems on a given theme, and the food and the poems would go on all night. They'd have tables brought outside, and all sorts of food and wine, and fruit, grapes, they called their gardens *vigne*, vineyards, and have a lovely time. This Caravanti was a merchant of marble and a patron of the arts, he met all those sculptors in his shop, and he became a connoisseur, and when he could not afford to buy a statue or a painting, he'd tell Coricio, who actually was Johannes Goritz, a Luxembourgish prelate, a powerful man in the Vatican. They enjoyed latinizing their names then. Vincenzo lends me his shovel because I say I need to exercise and I'll help with his potato beds, but *attualmente* I do a bit of digging here and there. I have found an inscription, come, help me turn it.' It's a long flat piece of pale grey marble. CARAV. AED. MDXVI. If you walk back every day of those five hundred years, you would find it above an imposing door, the main door to a house, and the people inside.

'What is possible, mind you, just *possible*, it's that there would be something actually buried here, I mean when the Lansquenets came and pillaged every house, the owners hid things by burying them. Some of these treasures have been forgotten for centuries and found quite by chance.' He stumbles on a rock. '*Porca miseria!*'

Piero is digging. Rembrando sings something that goes '... Yonghi Bonghi Bo.' It's much harder to dig than to buy something from a shop, but you can tell a much better story.

37. In the bathroom

What would you like to see, madam, the Estée Lauder, the Helena Rubinstein? Payot – we received their latest just yesterday. Dry skin? This is the Hydror line, day cream, night cream, eye balm, cleanser, tonic.

And nail polish? (I don't have the fan with all the shades of pink, orange and red, unfortunately, but I can still manipulate all the little bottles, glick-glick. And shake them, there are two little balls inside, another delicious sound, tic-a-tic). You could try this, it suits your skin tone, a little warmer, *voilà*, it's the Rose Mozart. Not quite ... the Stravinski Trio then.

Oh, you prefer Elizabeth Arden for nail polish ... no, we don't sell it.

Cotton balls, the pastel-coloured ones, and salts for the bath, and L'Oréal hair spray. Ah, the little girl likes the enamel compacts, would you like to see this one, little girl? Just to have a little look? The bright green and blue pattern? (There are so many in the window under the counter, it's dizzying. If I had to choose one this moment I would suffocate. Not a chance. I may perhaps ask for a small scented soap ...)

'*What are you doing with that face on, Eugenia?*'

If only she would not be so angry. A bottle falls, I jump from the stool to collect the pieces, and I cut my hand. My finger is bleeding, and hurts, and now Mummy starts scowling and reaches for the medicine cabinet, and holds my hand tight, it presses and hurts, and I am crying and yelling. She wants to pour tincture over my hand, above the washbasin, and I scream and she hurts me, she fights to keep me still, to control me.

Anger buzzes in my head. The words come from unknown places: 'She is – a devil. I hate her – like a devil.' And stop, afraid.

38. Dictionaries are not all

Throw me a word, and I will return it crumpled, elongated, denatured, unrecognizable. Long hair, tanned, strange beads and a foreign accent. Or I will hide away where I can *rosicchiare* the word in peace. English professor jumps two feet in the air. What! Italianism! Foreignerism! Barbarism! And calls for reinforcements. Mme Juliano, and MML soon arrive with pitchforks and cries of Gallicism! Anglicism! Frenchism!

Rosicchiare: to nibble, to gnaw (but better because of the sound 'zeekk', sound of dog rasping bone). In French it would be *grignoter* (too human, this nibbling, too dainty, mouse-like).

So I was going to look up *ronger* (in the French-Italian dictionary) to see what was the difference, but I did not go far, I got stopped at *rosat* ('of rose'), besides I had gone to the *wrong* dictionary. Then it became urgent to verify *rosarian* from English to French, then to Italian. Unavoidably got entangled in *Rosicrucian*. Then, almost inevitably, carried by the rhythm, *saracinesca* – into French. In the sense I have in mind ('rolling shutter'), they offer the bland *rideau métallique*, which is an insult to the very possible, flavourful, 'anti-Saracens device'. Then, perversely, found *sbolognare* ('give you a false coin, or get away', implying that in the city of Bologna people had strange habits). But *rosarian* was still in a fold of my brain: *amatore di rose*, in Italian ('rose lover'), not bad. In French: nothing. No French rose lovers. Incredible. They just skipped it. Another case of translators asleep at the helm. Very disappointing.

My life is an infinite translation.

On the map, Italy, France and England are neighbours, with appropriate natural fences. More proximity would be asphyxiating. Oh, you're having a pleasant sunny day today, Madama Rosetta, and poor Mrs Watson, it's pouring rain, the butcher has no nice cutlets, I see. And what will you be having for lunch, Madama Rosetta? Liver sausages? Why are they blue-green all over?

And you would always have to explain everything.

It's not the Tower of Babel, just a modest turret children play in. But there is noise inside my thoughts. A field of *interesting* weeds, not a lovely herb garden. Hardly anyone can understand. I've always been like that. I cannot really explain. People say of a blind man, he doesn't suffer, he doesn't know what he's missing.

I think my professors are crazy.

I have been repeatedly told not to use *translating* dictionaries. Where? What a question, I was always only at Sainte-Marge. They say, *read the definition in the language of the word*. That way, we read more, and suffer through the attainment of the word. Suppose the word *surmise*: instead of finding the Italian translation *(sospettare, congetturare, cercar d'indovinare)*, I'd have to read the English definition ('infer doubtfully, suspect the existence of; make a guess, try to divine something'). After reading the English definition, the translation would simply spontaneously pop up in your first language. The problem is, because I have two main languages, I always use words instinctively, or averaging two definitions. So for years I was always *assuming* translations from English. One day I asked a translator from the Geneva School of Translation, and she was nonplussed. Why did they ever make you do that, she said?

So until I found out that my professors were crazy, every time I needed to exchange a French word for an English word, I've had to go to the Italian first. Open the French-Italian, then the Italian-English. One day, I discovered that *Concise Oxford Dictionary* meant English and all that amazing etymology. By then I had the acrobatic flea habit.

And there is the matter of my *analphabétisme*, a word the English have missed, 'illiteracy' sounding by comparison not *knowing* letters, and I know letters, it's the *alphabet*, the *order* of the alphabet. There are reefs around the PQRSTUV. You don't believe me. See it in lower case? – pq rst uv – p and q are practically the same, and the u is spelled v in Latin inscriptions. Besides the u goes after the p so often in French and Italian. And what about the J and the Y in Italian? That is so stupid. J is '*i lunga*', pronounced like an I (that is pronounced like a long E (ee) in English). And Y ('*i grec*' in French) is not '*i greca*' in Italian, but '*ipsilon*', a foray into Greek just to show off. So for my alphabetism, extenuating circumstances. They extenuate and you say, yes, yes, I beg you, stop explaining.

How is one to say omino? Ometto, omuccio, omaccio, omone, omaccione. Ominide?

Omino would be a small man, but with a implication of pity. A poor little *bonhomme*. Large man, I would say for omone. Large-and-ugly-menacing man, omaccione. It's not the same as adding adjectives, it is not a man who is large, his largeness is kneaded with him.

I'll give you one Sonny told me. In Toronto, Italian kids call the English ones, richer, with money for pastries, 'mangia-kékk'. Cake-eater, but in a two-language word. 'Torta-eater!'

I am not a mangia-kékk. Mangiagelati, maybe. But I really do not want to be having ice cream while others are just looking on.

Generic insults are fine, they mean nothing. Cretino. We children in small coats pretending to be playing in the park under the contemptuous eyes of our nannies are acutely sensitive. The insults will be ambiguous. 'Your Rs are not Italian.' ' ....' 'Say "Roma".' 'Roma.' 'You see?!' I say it fine but this particularly insistent boy is on the offensive of the impalpable echo of other places. Roma. I say it fine.

They have noticed I communicate with my sister with foreign monosyllables, intended to be secret. They hate not to be in. They feel they will never get the accent. And they hate not having a secret language. Hardly anyone speaks more than 'English Spoken Here'. I hope they pay them more. Maybe that is what I will do, be a shop interpreter, called here and there, from place to place, in a nice street downtown. I would get to know all the names of precious and semi-precious stones, and the materials.... Nannies speak German or French. Misses and au pairs speak French or English. Maids, who are Italian, usually also know a dialect. These other kids, we see them five times a year, we barely know their names, there is another Eugenia, a neighbour, in the next building. The park is intended as a place for becoming friends. We get there for lack of better things to do, and our accompanist is not so happy. Eugenia, don't just stay there like a pole! We are expected to blend, play the universal games. *Giro, giro tondo, a cavallo impe ratondo.* Then everybody down, it's supposed to be fun, an idiocy because you fall slam on your tailbone, and, of course, if you are a girl, your knickers will get green with grass or mudded. 'Eugenia has no sense of humour.'

'Giving a party is not all play; the hosts are not there to amuse themselves, they have to work so that the party works.' Decidedly gloomy. My father admonishes all the time. He does not find me a dedicated worker. Frivolous. By now (fifteen and a third), I should be having business ideas, a script in my drawer, or a novel (tac, you open the drawer, tac, throw in manuscript. Manuscript in drawer), be poised and sophisticated like the women he most admires. He hurries me so, he rushes me so. I have found my manifesto, 'I like to watch clouds, the wonderful clouds,' and tried it with him to see if it absolved me, but he snorted and was not amused (maybe a little, though). I barely have time for my own *minimum vital*. I sleep less, I am more tired. It takes oxygen to do things.

What work, anyway? He is chatting, laughing and making laugh. People around him are like batteries on charge, drawing from his vitality. My mother has another cluster around her, people who listen and think ' … *but* her eyes …,' '… what can she be *meaning?*' 'What fabulous turquoises!' Aniceto, with Eliseo, who's been slipped into a white jacket too, circulates with trays. And in my own way, half hiding near the fireplace, vacant-but-present, I am doing my part.

Party. Groups of guests are scattered artistically. Good-looking, or elegant, sitting, standing by little groups. A skinny guy at the piano is adding his musical reveries to the buzz and laughter. The house is alive. Piero is darting back and forth to tell me what grand cars are parked outside. 'A Maserati! A Lamborghini!!! Michele de Mauri and his Bentley!' 'Don Massenzio! In his Land Rover!' Here is the top of the top, undeniably, and one glance is enough to convince you. Don Massenzio, prince Carrà di Quinterio, has just arrived in the middle of the party, limping, and the torches are burning brighter.

He can do and say anything he likes, it started when he married a Scandinavian starlet without his father's consent (nobody paid attention to what *her* father said.). The headlines in the gossip magazines. Italy then still had a foot in the other century. He got the label of half-crazy, and the freedom that goes with it. Sonorous, a couple of large medals on his terracotta chest – recently escorted by a fabulous model, reputedly Chilean, mute. Since he keeps marrying nationalities, and not having a proper occupation, except for hereditary functions at certain Vatican ceremonies … well, he is a playboy.

His family is more ancient that the Caesars. No contest, right? Zio Elio says any family is as ancient as you want. Daddy likes him, he likes Daddy. Daddy admires him for his ultra-relaxed countryside manners, which Don Massenzio can afford being a first-class prince, not very rich in cash for that matter. His castle is rather a blockhouse. He has collections of ancient pottery and coins, and gets burglarized all the time. Just to give you an idea, he greets visitors in his kitchen, a huge place with beams, and a table for twenty-four, where he sits like a countryside innkeeper serving the local white.

'*A' Ceccomo,*' (that would be my dad, who is greeting him fraternally), 'look at this foot! I almost fell inside a tomb! Giggetto er Tombarolo made a mistake and it was all for nothing!' (He goes hunting for Etruscan treasures, on his land, not a legal activity, not quite illegal either).

'Don Massenzio, *ma cosa mi hai combinato?* We must find you a bodyguard! Eliseo, bring us some wine!'

By the fireside, the son of Don Massenzio tells me how it went. It was a night for the hordes (*una notte di tregenda*, it sounds better), full moon, wind, dogs barking – awful job to find this tomb with sounding-rods. Then an aperture is scratched away, and Giggetto is lowered in the tomb, alive, you understand – very hard because of his girth. More light is flashed from the top by his assistants – Don Massenzio, Valerio (the son), and two English friends. And from the entrails of the earth, come the *smadonnamenti*, the Madonna-slandering, '*porca miseria, porco qui, porco lì;*', pork this, pork that. They pull him back up, and the boss emerges furious, he had already 'visited' that tomb, well, sorry, folks, I'm really losing my mind …

Valerio and his English friends couldn't care less, they were running and hiding, playing ghosts.

Undaunted by his strained foot, Don Massenzio is going to make his 'Vodka Spaghetti'! Frisson. Barely suppressed delirium among the guests. In the era of the grapefruit diet, people still eat.

Numerous country inns and rustic restaurants have opened outside the walls of Rome, and grilled things are all the rage, more than ever. It is almost nine. I am hungry, and so is Piero. On the way to the kitchen, the Gourmet Prince catches me by the arm, singing some drinking song, that's how he is. In the kitchen, it is not one of those times when you say, dear me, there is not much in the cupboard! All the deliveries have been made. Flats of San Marzanos, basil by big bunches, and fresh sausages from a special maker. And the vodka. Don Massenzio does everything himself, he brought his own knife and oil; he splits sausages and tomatoes, swiftly, talking all the time.

'Where can you find a sausage-maker like his, I ask, nowadays? He is worth gold!' And is the water beginning to boil? – this to a separate front, the stove where Elvira is in charge.

'*Eugenia bella*, tell your mother' (yes, yes – as if she cared) 'I must bring you some of my vinegar, it's almost a hundred years old, you only need to keep it alive,' an amoeba flaccid and muddy living at the bottom of a bottle, and a taste of dust that will make me sick.

A silver-lidded fine lady in yellow and black stripes has commandeered one side of the stove, sipping from her highball, he's noticed her, but he has the fabulous Chilean, and he wants to know, from Marcello behind him, how will the wine be this year. He keeps the fire very high, stirring the meat with great panache, to seize it, while on the right he gets the tomatoes to sizzle in a hellish noise of oil, all with great swigs of wine and moppings of the brow. And finally the savage flambéing, well-timed with the bellowing of the draining of the pasta, and carefully making portions for maybe forty *piatti fondi*, he insisted on those, although *flat* dishes are now all the rage for pasta. Mysteries of the annals of china. Power of the prince above all snobbisms. In a class by himself. Imitate at your risk and peril.

The glistening, inflamed nests are passed rapidly from hand to hand. Lively cadenza of forks swirling on plain white dishes, with much exclamations of those who know about food, and those who don't.

Marcello comes closer. With his hoarse voice: 'Do not underestimate the importance of these spaghetti, Euge'. Do not underestimate.'

'Porca miseria!' That reckless Santabarbara is tilting her brouillon from another bench so I can read her commentary on the exam subject. Pig misery! Misery is a porker! 'Explain and comment on this thought of Vigny: "I can only read books, now, that make me work. On the rest of them, my thoughts slide like a plough on marble. I like to plough." What enrichment has been brought to you by difficult books, no matter what the subject?' The alternative subject ('Analyze and comment on this page of Sainte-Beuve on Pascal') is even worse.

The sky is medium blue outside the large square window, rather like my ink when you tilt the bottle. The blind, paler, between air mail paper and my slippers, is rolled up almost to the maximum. The sun won't hit my desk until later.

Vigny and his plough! I'd send him down a marble hill on skates. Why doesn't he stick to poetry, or what was his thing, the Bible? Did he *envision* the consequences? Twenty-two girls must write a whole huge dissertation about a little declaration he made in the middle of a salon, admirers fawning around him, which a secretary jotted down respectfully (as useful for some future biography) – and we now have to fill up a minimum of eight pages of exam 'copies', the large format. 'Right margin; space above, use ink only, write intelligibly, do not eat or drink, no books, no dictionaries' (as if we didn't know). 'When finished walk quietly to your classroom and do only homework. And these are not empty menaces. You have exactly four hours.' This was the exam preamble of Madame Sassi, our math professor, the one who is usually so humorous, but changes completely here in the great study room. Well, Mère François Xavier did not say the plan is required, I hate that, plans are a waste of time.

Inspire air. Let's begin inspired. Expire words.

There was a time when the ability to write was a sign of wisdom.

And now?

* * *

There was a time when the ability to write was a sign of wisdom.

People would ask scribes to write letters for them, and respect those who, whether they were priests or lawmakers, knew the gods and the rules. Those were societies – Ancient Egypt, Rome – where equality of all citizens had not even been elaborated in a philosophy. Then came schools, accessible to greater numbers, as potentially useful to society as a whole. Then, after millennia of tablets and parchments, the art of which was held by very small numbers, came the invention of Gutenberg, the printed word, which allowed far greater distribution of ideas and learning. The printed word started as a very serious (the first book was a Bible) and labour-intensive process, born out of a long gestation, then, as it became easier, writing covered the whole spectrum, from futility and vulgarity to immortal pages.

So Alfred de Vigny, – half-point perhaps for knowing his first name – *born in France in a well-off –* or so we assume – *noble –* this is guaranteed – *family in the XIXth century, was given presents of books for the New Year, and his imagination started galloping and conceiving the first verses that gave him immortal fame –* for our greatest luck. *What kind of books would Madame de Vigny give her son? What would a French boy like?*

Now I need to establish telepathy with the pages of our literature book, let's get the century right at least, eighteen hundred = XIXth, and the captions ... illustrations – 'Death of Atala', held by a bearded old man, a Greek athlete holding her knees, there are two crosses in that Indian cave, no no, that is Chateaubriand ... Lamartine – and his whippets, hateful dogs, always the same trousers, for ages, *they all wore the same trousers* ... Musset, that's George Sand's friend, she was rather crazy for her times, even for now, did he have a beard.... What did Vigny look like, any detail, anything different, yes, a red cassock, pudgy cheeks, boyish, in a uniform, very French face ... that's him! And was it *Lamentations d'un cerf,* and something with the Bible ... '*L'homme sera toujours un nageur incertain, / Dans les ondes du temps qui se mesure et passe ...*' – What was it called? *Is it* Vigny? How do I stick it in?

Because the starting point of this thought is set in the past, it is, in my opinion, of interest (??????) to examine what was considered as 'books that make one work' in three rough epochs, and three perspectives: for a child, before Romanticism, Vigny's literary movement; for a cultured man, in the times of Vigny; and today, in the personal readings of the author. That would be me. Do I dare? Oh yes, think of what Santabarbara will say! I will, initially, try to examine how the 'degree' of a book (a book that makes one work, or a difficult book) can be measured.

The degree of difficulty varies from a person to the other, is relative. A glass of Scotch whisky will be almost deadly to a baby, it will produce coughing in a man who doesn't drink, and it will perfectly pleasant for the Scotch-lover. Can we talk about 'alcoholic content' of books? A cup of tea, on the other hand, is mild, non-alcoholic to anybody, although horrible to some and very pleasant to others. Oh, what is this, how will I get out of it?

Let's therefore establish some subjective points of reference, for example, in areas of interest to literate people. Suppose this forms a pyramid. At the base: most adults find comic strips easy, if not pleasant; most read the newspaper; some read easy novels; a smaller number read novels that are more original or complex; fewer read more difficult novels, essays, and poetry; even smaller numbers read many of these latter in the original (two to four languages); a minuscule number, at the tip of the pyramid, can read in Latin, Ancient Greek, Hebrew, etc. Those are, to paraphrase the English, the 'learned few'.

So to a reader in the last category, would only ancient codes in Hebrew be sufficiently alcoholic? Would his mind 'slide on the marble' of a very stupid novel, like those of Delly – treacherous, I know. But it could be conceived that this personage (call him Erasmus Offmanbach Rasmunsson Ceccarelli) might find an important subject of study based on 'The idea of eternity in the novelettes of Delly and Baroness Orczy'. Therefore books don't have an absolute value: it is, rather, the reader that injects them with a value. The reader can make a dull book stimulating.

The statement of Vigny is a statement of taste, not a maxim. We can envision the celebrated poet reclining on a récamier, or sitting at his desk in his study, his portrait in a red officer uniform in the background, surrounded by a group of young people, trying to forge their minds through readings that expand their experience. Was it a time when Paris applauded a succession of

*light, easy, silly, naughty books, was it a particularly hollow
season? Perhaps.* No idea about the historical moment(s). *But to
his students Vigny would not say: read the easier books, or follow
only your inclination. He would say, you must read all sorts of
books, study them, not only enjoy them. And he would say: you
must read. In a recent interview, the American actor Dustin
Hoffman gave this advice to aspiring actors: 'Read till your eyes
drop off.' He did not say: watch movies. He said: read.* Zia
Valentina thinks he is wonderful. *We are not very far from Ancient
Egypt here: the ability to read and the habit of reading seem to
open all doors, and confer knowledge and wisdom. Vigny does say:
'I can only read … now,' he makes concessions having seen his
taste mature through the years: he has become more
discriminating and frivolity seems frivolous.*

Not sure M. François Xavier will succumb to this…. But I
don't have much to show, and I might as well try and impress her.
As Santabarbara, in one of her chilly down-to-earth dictums, said,
'The nuns want three things out of our dissertations: knowledge,
reasoning and style.' I don't have anything to say, I can only write.

*His statement is not a maxim, but it does have the ring of a
master's exhortation.*

This could get me an 'OBSCUR', or, worse, 'REMPLISSAGE'
(empty words).

*And is it not a vivid image, the one of the plough, since after
all his words are concerned with 'culture', the field that needs
cultivating?*

This is more like it. Applause.

'Eugenia, always do first-class things.' This is Marchese Isola,
who often lunches with Daddy. He is funny. I am not sure what it
means but it sounds wonderful. I'd like to see him in my shoes.

*What did little Alfred and his friends have in their bookcase?
As books 'that make one work', or serious books, certainly, a
missal, a Bible with the New Testament. Schoolbooks, too, would
be in that category. On another shelf, the books that are
considered 'for children', like the Contes de Perrault, and some
poetry perhaps. It is probable that old French was then not
transcribed into modern French as it is now, and a man of the
XIXth century could understand it better one of the XXth century.*

It is even possible that they considered the poems of Du Bellay as too easy.

'Déjà la lune en son parc amassait/ un grand troupeau d'étoiles vagabondes ...'. *Did Vigny, even then, prefer the page that resisted being understood, sentences that need rereading, that he had to plough? Vigny studied Latin and Ancient Greek as a matter of course. Considering the man he became – ??? – he must have felt, as a child struggling over his first versions, the pleasure of unravelling a problem.*

Let M F X believe I am attracted to effort, at least that I have a moral notion that effort is good. The nuns like those gleams of a sense of duty. They like you to buy *Missionaires d'aujourd'hui*, and you like to buy it to make them happy. They like you to read all the *Brigitte*, but you read with a black patch on one eye, to avoid the religious exhortations, you read them because they are modern, Parisian, they are well written, and tell you how people *live* in France, and tell you about writers who sound interesting – as you eat *panettone* skipping the green candied fruit.

Nothing to eat here of course.

What did Alfred de Vigny read, and what would have stimulated his thinking? What did he consider stimulating thinking? Like many others, he found models in antiquity, either historically sound or as objects of his creation. He read Ovid, and Homer. His other great preoccupation was Christianity – as in 'Catholicism', ... I think the nuns, subtly, select suitable authors for exams, it gives them good points with the bishop, redeemable for holy images, seats at Vatican ceremonies, discounts on purgatory....

What did Romantics find in antiquity? How was their interest different from all the previous rediscoveries and reinterpretations of antiquity? And the 'Bataille des Anciens et des Modernes'? How often did literature, until then, detach itself from antiquity imitation, inspiration?

Masterly, except that I don't know the rest. What next. At cocktail parties, you just start something and the other one will continue. Or the waiter will come with a tray and interrupt. Or the music will start. Not at a 'sit-down' dinner.

Vigny had naturally a complete culture of French 'Classical' literature. The word here is used not to indicate classicism (the period preceding Romanticism) but the books whose recognition has been a lasting one. I will attempt to list a few.

Return mentally to the covers of our Lit books. Middle Ages, I don't know. Skip that. XVIth, it's the Dame à la Licorne, I remember. XVIIth there is something like Ruth and Booz, who cares, I know the authors, Molière, Corneille, Racine, Pascal, Descartes, Boileau, Bossuet, La Fontaine, Sévigné, Madame de Lafayette, who is NOT there? XVIIIth, I've lost it, I cannot see ONE, not one – except Marivaux, 'inventor of marivaudage.' *'Century Disappears and No One Notices.'* What happened between Classicism and Romanticism????

Rabelais, Ronsard and Montaigne are the main writers of the French Renaissance. Marot writes delightful epistles to make the King laugh and release him from jail ... because his valet stole his money ... because he ate lard ... because he attempted to rescue a prisoner ...

He did not succeed but at least he tried. Do you know the names of their houses? La Devinière, the house of guesses, and Montaigne (the Mountain). I'd like a name with coral in it. Do you know Marot, Rabelais and Du Bellay were rather heretic and played with fire? Agrippa d'Aubigné, he is famous for it, completely Protestant, austere and sombre, a warrior poet during the wars of religion, very serious, invoking God, fighting by the side of Henri IV ... Don't you think life then was a risky game, a match of chess with rules that changed as you played, you had to keep playing while the smile of a marquise could mean a midnight rendezvous, or her taking you into an intrigue, or being knifed as you walked home, danger, love or fame. You said something witty and they would all laugh, or some would and others would touch their dagger by their side. Was life more flavourful, did you just die of happiness as you woke up alive, did wine taste of roses. You always needed to be able to jump on a horse or unsheath your epee – for women I don't know, they had a ton of rules, you had to be very brave, reckless, to undo them, or very clever. 'Play your cards, Chevalier,' I would get all garbled. I would faint a lot. I would have tried to hide somewhere in the countryside, away from the court where you always had to be something, and favour would change from dinner to supper, and a fresh bed of hay be prepared just for you in a nice cold dungeon. Awful times for people with a pessimistic turn of mind. The one thing that could help you would be to die admirably, to make one last good show. Unless they killed you in private, which was really horrible because nobody would *know*.

Indirect quotations were made for the likes of me, who can only ever remember the gist.

Of the seventeenth century, Voltaire said that it was a marvellous time, when you could go from the theatre of Racine to the theatre of Corneille, or Molière, on the same night. You would be there, breathing the same air as the authors, the burning wax of the same candles, standing in the stalls. You would in a sense be part of the creation of Le Bourgeois Gentilhomme *or* Le Cid. *Isn't the first series of shows called 'création'? Aren't the names of the first actors printed on the booklets of the plays? So the audience of the first nights too has a special place. Yes, Voltaire sounds a little wistful ... but why? Did he not think the philosophers like himself make the XVIIIth century illustrious?* (Thank you, philosophers, re-emerging from the fog, you were there all the time but I had lost you because they list you as *writers*, funny, no?) *Voltaire himself, and* Candide, *or* Zadig; *Rousseau and Émile, or* Les Confessions; *Montesquieu, and the* Lettres persanes. *Well, Voltaire was right, in retrospect, the past seemed more gay. Le siècle des lumières is a century of research and study, that ended in revolution and fear. The only writer who had time to spare for frivolity would seem to be Marivaux.*

At least, she won't say I didn't give her *names*.

I see the *petites*, snacks in hand, coming outside for recess, could it already be half-morning!!! Forty-five minutes to copy all this, forty minutes plus five for incidentals, and last-minute genius for the conclusion, no, ten, oh la·la, there is barely an hour left. I see distinctly Santabarbara's broad handwriting, and she is making a separate sheet for the plan ... *Horreur et damnation!* I will make a plan *afterwards*. No time to lose. Calm and concentration. I hope for shredded carrots for lunch. The sky is bluer and ruthless. Blue is a strange colour ... Madame Sassi is looking this way ...

For myself, I have often been wondering how to keep the books you have read orderly in your mind, as in a bookcase.

Diary (4)

41. Rome, July 26th, 1970

My suntan is disintegrating. Swimming pool not as good as the sting of sea water. I should do the things others do. I am in the category of women, but without the resources. Find the creams, the little things, obtain the money, the time, the know-where-to-look. Know *how* and be organized enough to lacquer, oil, smooth legs and various parts, without attracting attention, which is the last thing you want. My mother talks to the little girl, my father to the intelligent girl. Both elide me. Ask my mother when at the profumeria? She would never play along. Her capacity to embarrass atrociously. Beautify therefore underground.

My mother: 'You put on anti-perspirant right after your bath?' (and so does Vanna, secretly). *She* belongs to the smooth, the delicate, the un-perspiring. I am slightly repulsive. Having a fifteen-year-old daughter is. Scandalized cries – *'Oh how can you!'* One can never say anything.

Daddy gave me an envelope with pounds, for Mme Audibert to apportion, and a few bills to Vanna, and I gave her some of my old heavy pennies.

'Don't buy only sweaters this time,' he said. 'Speak English at all times.' 'Make Vanna participate.'

I did not sleep very well. I saw myself at Harrods and at Moss Bros and I would buy everything. Daddy is right, Shetlands and corduroys have been our mania, boys and girls, a very long-lasting one. Shelves of the most divine shades of pink, grey-green, pale blue. The irresistible ones in two tones. Eyes have the same mystery, three types of specks that draw you in more and more. Eyelashes that start brown and end up blond. I have a burgundy cardigan (with purple-blue specks, very rare), and a thicker one, beige. I will look for, and find, the eternal and reassuring Lyle and Scott. A small leather-embossed sign to be found in shop windows, a promise of quality. Wash in cold water, don't allow to soak, dry between towels, 'away from heat sources'.

LONDON, AUGUST 1970

I am at Moss Bros on King Street, inside the place of dreams.

Declensions on everything I like. All the hats, all the sizes and the colours. All the riding sticks. I have a list. It's altered by the faces of those I wanted so much to leave behind. In the distance, glowing, idyllic. They did not get to come with us. My apology, my affection, in packets of chocolate biscuits and riding cravat pins. Each horse whinnying in his box is expecting something from Eugenia. Passing the time in their stalls, waiting to hear friendly footsteps. Titus, Marlboro, Vol-au-vent, the unpresentable Géraldine. The new Arabians, flown in from Scottsdale, Arizona. I can't think what it must have cost Daddy. Suppose someone gives you an emerald tiara – you are pleased but a little uncomfortable. Apparently a cargo plane is the simplest way to bring horses from America. A grey stallion, and two ginger mares. Whatever the price, you get fabulous, rare horses, born at Villa Aladdin in the desert of Arizona – and a story you can dine out on for a while.

A bridle, a bit, a new undersaddle, a halter of the new coloured braided nylon. Curse pounds and shillings. Well, just round it up. I am here principally to buy my first black hunting jacket. 'You ask Moss Bros about the number, shape of buttons. Don't discuss it. Just order what they say.' I do explain to a puzzled tailor the kind of hunt I went on near the Appian Way. The jacket is perfect. This is how men feel in their suits. It will show who I am. More myself.

Piccadilly Circus. Great big iron fountain, and hippies, in black cloaks, ghost-pale. The ones we see in Rome, and imitate, are the American Woodstock model, more joie de vivre, plumper, whether carnivorous or vegetarian. But the British hippie seems more 'advanced'.

Monsieur Audibert takes us to the antiques market in Chelsea, where he seems to know every vendor.

'Papa, you are not to bring home another one of your lamp-posts "on approval". Mama will not approve, I think. You still have not decided about the "Unusual Empire ormoulu watch on marble pedestal",' says Elsa, quoting him.

'Nonsense, it's perfectly decided, my dear.'

I think he comes here for relief from the Ambassador. Daddy says that diplomatic life can be very stressful. We go from stall to stall. How I understand him! But my nerves are not as steady as his. Dozens of objects beckon, and at every step you find other objects of your affection, which you did not know you needed one minute ago: a carved dove with only a little chip, the moulding of a hand; a music stand, walking sticks with silver knobs of dog's heads, a vase just the right size, a teacup with a little firework painted inside – the furnishings of desire.

'An Aries charm in orange enamel, festooned, mh, late Victorian,' said Monsieur Audibert. Words firing as much as the object. Victorian! It can be mine, I have the money, but will Madame Audibert approve? 'Of course, Eugenia, it's a perfectly good buy.' It's not quite a Capricorn, only a horned animal, bouncing about the Zodiac. Close enough. The purchase, solemn, buying gold. Also a silver locket for Vanna, engraved 'V', hoping there won't be a fuss at home because her name is Giovanna really.

Monsieur Audibert wants us to call him Jacques, he can't be serious.

We must send a postcard to Piero, lost, with Guillaume, in the wilderness of a Canadian summer camp.

Dear Piero,

We went to a Ceylonese restaurant and ate curry. We saw the speakers on their soapboxes in Hyde Park.
 Say hello to Guillaume. Attenzione alli alligatori.
BEWARE of Big Foot!

V&E E&V V&E E&V

We visited the Elgin Marbles at the British Museum. We bought stickers and cards and signs about Carnaby Street and the English flag, all sorts of *things*, decorated tins of tea, dish towels called tea towels, we stocked up on cookies from Marks and Spencer; we ate avocado.

We were having too much fun to notice this did not look like summer. We became used to distinguishing fog from muggy weather. It finally *was* England. We re-counted our luggage to now include Elsa's; said goodbye to Mme Audibert, who trusted us to do stupefying things such as switching trains to Shropshire. We had the school's address, tickets, the name of the Canadian and the Italian consuls, change for telephone calls, our boots, our hard hats and sticks, and what else.

No need for the extreme cunning required on the Rome–Naples. Everyone fell in his proper slot. We settled down to play cards sluggishly. Elsa and Vanna slowly drifted into making nonsense jokes, playing 'war', pretending they were chicken. How tiresome. I went and visited the other carriages, just to do something but feeling very self-conscious. In one compartment, I had the fright of my life, there was a man almost without a face, swollen features, eyes and nose sunk, sitting with another passenger.

I hastened back to report.

'There's a man, hydrocephalic, gassed ...' They were not listening at all, more excited than before, hiccuping, laughing with new inventions.

'Passa-a, petta-a, co-coot ...'

The more I tried stopping them, the more they laughed and banded together. I was homesick for solitude. I would have fallen asleep but I could not rely on those two to wake me up when it was time.

This riding school was called 'the Grange'. Our first school had been near London, in Guildford. Elsa and I went there once on our own, then once again with Vanna, deemed old enough to come with us. And now, the Grange Riding School, Mitford, Shropshire.

It did not look quite like much, in a sort of collapsed look, with a thatched roof and wooden slabs across the white exterior walls, but Elsa said, 'It's the horses that count.' First we had to say hello to Mrs Olmstead and bring our things upstairs. Vanna and Elsa chose the room with two beds and I had the one with the large bed. Glad to be rid of Vanna and of the large bed. A little annoyed about Elsa and Vanna.

Then sit down for tea. The proprietress was a cheerful woman in rather shabby clothes and impeccable hairdo. We were told that Major Olmstead was on a mission abroad or something and was merely visiting. Lower on the totem pole was Jenna, in charge of the stables. Other characters: Miranda O. – the daughter, and a man of uncertain status by the name of Beckwith.

We met some of the other guests, about a dozen, two or three transparent girls, a Belgian boy, another one, Indian perhaps, two Danish girls and a Cornelia from Germany; two French boys, one medium and one small, who instantly looked to us as their saviours and interpreters.

Walking over to the stables, finally! Elsa was saying 'Beckwith, Beckwith,' wrinkling her nose and vacuum-cleaning all vowels. Even if things were not painted and varnished and geranium-ed, the horses were well kept, with a lot of good straw in their boxes, and we soon found that they were not jaded or dull. The main source of atmosphere, the *spring*, was Jenna, our instructor, who spared no effort to keep us moving. A great horsewoman – smooth, supple, unfussy. I wouldn't have been surprised if she was some champion in disguise. We were given two cobs and a pony that actually moved, ran and jumped, and the prospect of cordial relationships with our mount (instead of a war) put us in a good mood.

Mornings were to be spent mucking, riding and jumping in the paddock. Just as Jenna needed a few hours to find out what we were capable of (literally), in the beginning, we established alliances with the riders who seemed to be safe or had horses that were not demons.

Vanna still relied on me to communicate in English.

Vanna (frowning): 'Eugenia, tell the bread stick to stick closer to the fence or I will trample her after the jump.'

'My sister says she cannot control *hers* – she says she once had a terrible accident with *yours*.'

Vanna (annoyed): 'Can you tell her she does not need to excite her horse so, she is going to make us all carnival,' which is our word for horse madness. It was funny to see Vanna so competent.

Initial adjustments took place. Vanna, for instance, made the mistake of thinking that her grey pony Gilbert would automatically be friends with the other little grey pony – oh, I never saw such a rapid climb-down on four legs, ending in the Gilbert sitting on its rear end and Vanna hastily dismounting. The Order of Precedence and the Irreconcilable Differences were clarified: you do not want the wrong set of teeth to be in proximity of the wrong tail (defended by hind legs). Tarek, in his Persian innocence, had not understood Ringo's trick of bloating before the girth was pulled and found himself twice rolling to the side by 45 degrees. I managed a rodeo round of heel-kicking by my cob Pepper, who was very surprised at my tenacity. Jenna walked up to him and scolded him. 'Bloody horse!' she said, and immediately went red as a tomato. It could not have been worse if she had used a megaphone. It was the most juicy insult we had ever heard. To general consternation, it became our leitmotiv.

Lessons in the paddock are meant to teach you how to hold your hands, legs, posture, how to communicate with the horse, how all those things are called, how to jump. How to pick up some courage and try again. 'Keep it short, legs, LEGS!' and you've jumped awkwardly outside the saddle, half on the bars (hurting your leg), half on the horse (hitting your lips). Climbing up again has a flavour of the guillotine. You always have to climb up again, it's the one rule. The horse manages to appear taller than before, prehistoric and malevolent, busy revising his book of vengeances and piques. Your friends and enemies are watching, and on the treetops, the demon crows take an interest, handclapping and sniggering.

My bed was loaded with a collection of blankets and quilts, and felt damp. Unbelievably broken and listing. On the first night, I fell asleep thinking of the new horses, hoping our instructor would be nice, that my back would not act up, and menstruations would not begin.

It began as a nightmare. There was something tormenting, droning, that repeated itself in a circular motion, a problem, something I had not done, like homework, or a chore, something I was guilty of, a stone grinding my breast on and on. I sat up, oppressed. I drank water that felt dusty, and went down like sand. My breath was not coming, it came with a hiss. My throat felt tight, the oxygen barely went in and barely went out. I had a cruel little cough. My back was hurting. I tried to do the motions of breathing, but there was a malfunction, a clogging. My muscles, or membranes, could not perform. I thought there was something I was not doing right. I sat up on the bed as much as possible. I tried opening the guillotine window, and my arms were just shaking, which had never happened. Those few steps I took reeling, I felt swollen, feverish. I tried a little water, sitting up, going to the bathroom, falling asleep, coughing, thinking of other things, but everything turned into torment. The black hunting jacket, I thought it cost too much, and I thought of Elsa and how she was going to be Vanna's friend for the rest of the holiday, and I thought that if I did not ride Soledad often enough, Daddy would sell her. Maybe I had consumption. I tried to go through the next minute, the next ten minutes, for hours. I fell asleep when a pale light appeared outside, and something got better inside.

Elsa woke me up and I went downstairs with the others. I did not know quite what to tell her. I only felt a bit weak. I wheezed and tried to go unnoticed.

We all liked the afternoon hacks. The countryside was paradise. We had a different circuit every day, then every five days, we would start the cycle again. You kept hoping it would be the Castle, or Rat's Bridge. Or the Sands, where one had the impression of being close to some river or in the bed of a forgotten river, with ferns and little bushes, and passages of very light earth, sandy, and mostly quiet trotting and not much else. Everyone was quiet and relaxed then.

I precisely remember one enormous willow where I let the others go by, and said aloud (in Italian): 'It is impossible to be happier.' The landscape would open up at the bend of a road, and it was glorious. Three years before, when I had been told I would go to England, I had had trouble falling asleep for days. I read feverishly 'Angleterre, Irlande et Écosse', where engravings crept inside the text and could be felt with one's fingers. The book had been almost larger than me, and now I was inside the book again. There was a path in a forest, and a hill made for cantering, wind in your ears and your horse all movement. His massive heart is beating for you too, he accepts you and even loves you. You and the horse are on top of the world. There is a girl, velvet cap, ponytail going in five directions, who does those hills like a centaur. The centaur inhabited that place, and will be there forever. Like the Etruscan back home. You can laugh. If you had done it your heart would almost burst. The memory of it. You are flying above the hill, you say 'innumerable heart innumerable heart' without remembering where it's from. All sadness has been scrubbed, scratched. The wind has cleaned your face, your lungs. Armies of your globules walk over all the atoms of earth and grass and conquer and fall asleep watching the clouds running in the sky.

This is also called having a good seat. Never heard anyone speak about 'feeling for the horse'. Unmentionable and covered, like piano feet. Mr Audibert told us about Oscar Wilde and the Victorians. (I swear, in Mrs O.'s den, everything is wrapped in chintz, even the telephone cord has a little chintz accordion dust-cover!) It's a secret, the excitement of riding. Though at a certain point, you and Fourposter will be dead tired, and just long for tea and fodder.

After a few days, we went on a hack called 'the Sullivans'. There were a lot of fences to be opened and closed and much open country. We had some cantering, and some natural obstacles, a joy to jump. The horses were behaving more and more like children after school. We arrived at a great big open space with hills, and it became clear that this was going to be one colossal carnival. Those green hills are just the thing for horse mutinies. There is a sort of shivering and neighing and secret coding and they are just straining at the bit to go, forget all manners, gallop, rear, kick up their heels, be free, forget they have masters and someone on their back. The message is tapped into snorting and drumming of the hoofs of the leaders, the most malicious, and a show of teeth, showing the white of the eyes and lowering of ears – hideous, bouah, whipping of tails. Soon it's bang bang, great explosions of tremendous farts – quite terrifying for the rider, if it's his first time – and a sense that nothing could ever stop the brutes. I was all braking, rigid calves and hands of steel, controlling systems, and so was Elsa, while Vanna did get carried away by the villains – or was she actually egging her gnome on? The rest of the pack, all of them, went like bullets up the hills, and down, assuaging private revenges, biting each other's rumps, and kicking, and the poor Lucys and Melindas thought, understandably, that they were going to be trampled to death. Elsa and I stayed close to Major O. who eyed the scene coldly, not at all thinking about composing telegrams to the families with a variety of broken collarbones and legs – the others yelping and yelling, which of course spurred on the delinquent equines, same as in the cartoon, with those fattish innocent-looking ponies, always up to some trick. You think you are going to die, but the delinquent equines do end up stopping somewhere, especially after they've thrown you – they lose their zest. They are tearing away at the grass, pretending nothing happened, looking at you by stealth, the infernal quadruped returned to normal. But now you know what it is capable of.

'Everybody made a disgrace of themselves, except those two. Kept their cool,' the Major was telling Mrs O. in the kitchen. Referred to – with soundtrack – as our Lawrence of Arabia moment for ever after.

It reconciled me with Elsa, but she had not noticed we were un-conciled, she is never tormented the way I am.

Tarek was Persian. He explained it was not Iranian with a small crinkling of his eyes, a lesson he gives kindly and knows by heart, as is natural in an intelligent and good-looking boy. I would tell this to Daddy, who would be interested. Or – who knows? He has become unpredictable and unstable as dynamite.

I: 'They feed them 'cubes', it's compressed food. Dry. Same concept as corn flakes, but they do not wet them. Ghastly, I think, but British horses, no? There was a horse called Clotilde! But we mustn't tell her, of course. I met a Persian. He was the best at jumps.'

One, two, three: explosion.

'Can you tell me how in the world you go from one thing to the other like that? Is there any way you can speak with some of the fine Cartesian spirit?'

His words excoriate. I have come to expect it. He is right. I am now always prepared with explanations, I rehearse what I will say and the explanation. 'I thought of *Destiny is called Clotilde*, when Filimario is hired as an extra for a party, because he's starving – you know, and he must 'be a French count', which he is, so he is in his frac, and he's just standing there in his frac, and the hostess is displeased, because he is not playing the part. He says, Madam, I *am* a French count, but she wants more for her money, so he starts telling her compliments in French, and she falls in his arms because he is so irresistible. Then for the Persian boy, I thought of *Les Lettres persanes*, the French (the Parisians) are amazed by the way the Persians look and speak, they say to themselves, "How can one *be* Persian?"'

– And I would keep going. Would Daddy go back to Filimario whom he likes so much. ('And do you remember the one when he is starving...?') No, it's been a long time since we have joked like that.

Tarek listened. I wanted to boast enough to be interesting but not to boast meanly.

'They are unpredictable, the older mare keeps her ears lowered or flicking, or fixatedly forward – very tense, a foreigner, can't speak the language. The stallion, I will not ride again, he's always trotting ahead as for battle, shaking his head, then stops to capture all the smells and the signals in the world. He is another *style*. What goes on in his beautiful head. He likes to play, too, he'll come to the window of his deluxe box and greet you so nicely, murmuring, just barely grazing your coat, pretending he'll snip off a button.' So mighty, so delicate. Feminine.

Tarek knew about Arabians. He spoke of his great-uncle who had been an important breeder, and lineage. But he cut the story short.

You could not see very well into his eyes, very dark eyes, but 'looking-pieces', not messengers. He knew the difficulty of explaining – who were his people, and what they represented in his part of the world. *The way they were*. How this state of things, this family, had been broken, dissipated – and the stud. But couldn't his family...? Couldn't their friends...?

'You see, it ends up looking like my uncle did not see things coming, that he was not as able as his father. But there has to be a winner and a loser. There were jealousies and other things, stories I am not told. Now my father wears occidental clothes and has made himself British, and my mother is just as elegant and sweet here as she was in Persia. And we do not speak of the past. But we did lose, a lot.'

So I kept a lid on some very interesting things I wanted to say about our Arabians, and for days afterwards I felt I had been indelicate. The word *gaffe* kept slapping me, I am like that.

I walked into Elsa's room and we went through her prized possessions, the way we used to. She showed me her bottle of Fidji – her father buys it duty-free. I bought mine with my Christmas money from Canada, I needed it, I was upset when my sample bottle was finished and kept shaking it to capture last molecules. It is funny to think that the same ad mesmerized the two of us, she in London, I in Rome. On a desert sand beach, the light of dawn is coming from behind a curve, and a woman is lying, prostrate but with her arms at her sides, you see her face. She is content, in that pose her body is round and polished as a pebble. The text is:

'La femme est une île. Fidji est son parfum.'
Mothers in all major capitals were not pleased by this leap from colognes and Ma Griffe de Carven. *Perfume*, the secret weapon, was on our bedside table and no rational argument could have been used. I mean, we are *fifteen* and soon sixteen. I have another one in my drawer, even I recognize it's a bit much, called Vent Vert. We say it's 'the warm breeze of a Caribbean evening', where we've never been yet.

'What do I say if my mother catches me with Vent Vert?'

'You say: Bloody hell, Mother, you *know* perfume is not spoken of. Just like *they* say.'

We laugh but we would hate to have to defend ourselves. Fidji. Maybe it does not quite smell of the island in the picture, radiating 'good sun', 'body perfect', 'healed skin'. Fidji the perfume is not exactly the island in the picture, but so Eugenia is not Fidji. Elsa is not Fidji, I think. To wear it is to push oneself in that direction. A Eugenia-to-be.

I now had Rowan, Elsa had Pepper, Vanna had Madeline, a dun

cob, very good and clever. There were fifteen of us. The brothers were called Hervé (who was twelve) and Étienne (fourteen) ('the é'), and the Belgian boy, Philippe, not shy about complaining, his bed too short, the food lamentable. He spoke English with a colossal French accent, not embarrassed at all and kept complaining. This was a holiday he had been asking his parents for for a long time, and he thought it was not up to standard. Cornelia spoke with a nasal voice and called me 'my friend'. She wrote to her mother in Düsseldorf about me visiting and I felt helpless. The English girls, beige and transparent, disapproved of us, jointly and severally.

Mrs Olmstead ran the school with her daughter Miranda (I wondered whether she got a salary or something), while Major O. worked in the Middle East (mysteriously), but spent his holidays at home. Beckwith increased his oddity by never coming close to a horse. As far as we knew, he could not ride, could not drive, could not swim. Nothing. We *refused* to believe the way he was called, the way he walked, talked with Mrs O., the way he drank tea, the way he dressed, he was unbelievable and a great source of fun – at a safe distance, because we were very polite.

Philippe wrote long letters to his parents. Actually, he let it be known he also wrote 'some poems'. We would check with the corner of the eye whether he was joining us, wherever we went, but would not ask him. He did not like that. He looked like Caligula in blond, Elsa said. We had found a nearby tea room, and gorged ourselves with muffins and cakes – we were not even sitting down for the school's meagre afternoon tea. The tea-room china had charming pastel colours, and every day, combinations would change – all yellow, or pink and pale blue, or pale green. We got the warmest welcome from the owner, who baked and glazed and fondly thought of us all day. Just to tell you: at breakfast one day Mrs O. had come in from the garden with a handful of redcurrants and announced enthusiastically that she was going to make jam! She shuffled a few things on the stove and produced a saucer of perhaps five spoonfuls of jam. Philippe took bitter notice. Tarek was polite and passed the dish. I decided that in my house I would make all sorts of jam for the breakfast of my guests, by the bucketful.

I became a tea lover. It was nuanced, variable and it had an affinity with the sky, the clouds, time. It was good for dreaming. At the same time, it was just the thing to bestow sustenance. Warm water with a few dark leaves and a little milk, and you felt invested with vigour and daring. Little Hervé liked to pretend he was a circus dog, with the front paws up, begging, 'A little more, please. No, a pink one, *mer-ci!*' (You say it with a fake-happy lilt when you are talking to a Frenchman. A French Frenchman.)

I would sometimes meet B'ck'w'th on the stairs, carrying a book to the drawing room. We had vaguely been introduced. Unfortunately, I am always nice and respectful when introduced, Daddy makes it so momentous and you-can't-live-without-knowing-how. He had a beaky nose, chubby cheeks and lips. No age or any normal characteristic. As soon as we spotted him, we would start our little clockwork circus.

'He's gone on his little walk.'

'To visit the cemetery.'

'The cemetery of dead canaries.'

'The collection of old muffins.'

'Bloody old muffins!'

'Beckwith is gone to the cemetery of old Beckwiths.' This one Vanna's and it became famous.

One day I was waiting outside for the rest of the gang to change to normal clothes after the hack. I saw Beckwith with his cap on take the road to our tea room. It was horrible to think that he would be there as we ate and chatted. I followed him to be sure. He was walking at a good clip. After about five hundred metres, we passed the lane to Mrs Hollins' tea room. He was mumbling to himself and I wondered whether he had overheard some mockery and was cursing us. I was certainly not up to apologizing for ten days' worth of jokes, and slowed down. He kept walking for a minute or two, then he turned into an hedge and presently walked towards an old stone house, where he knocked and pushed the door open immediately. I returned to the tea room to find my friends in an orgy of teapots, iced cakes and scones.

'Who can he go visit? Who can he know?'

'Who would know a Beckwith?'

'Some deceased worm-eaten mummy.'

'A fabricant of abandoned jam jars.'

'A hermit salamander.'

I went to have a look: Beckwith had returned and sat with Mrs O. I went to the tack room to borrow an old pair of binoculars I'd noticed on a shelf and went back to the mystery house.

There was a small stone wall. If anyone came by, I would pretend I was a bird-watcher or a bat-watcher (since evening was coming), who had just stepped up, absent-mindedly, carried away by her observations. I tried to focus, and could manage not much, and almost lost my balance. Oh well. I could see a gleam in the side room that was closest to the front. If I concentrated, I could distinguish it was a sort of study, with bookcases and display cabinets like those naturalists use. A row of small, convex boxes, side by side, dark, monotonous, mournful. Those must be coffins! Whatever he kept in there, dead owls or dogs, or skulls, those were coffins! I jumped from my wall, landing on my weak ankle. I was rather shaken. I had walked into something sinister and repulsive, I was sure. That Beckwith! He was not as innocent as he looked! What was he up to! And who could I confide in? Could I tell Elsa without her telling Vanna? Hatboxes my foot, those were coffins. I just knew.

Miranda showed Elsa and me her father's studio, with his guns, and all sorts of military souvenirs and photos. She gave us a little packet of military rations, and we immediately decided – how do we ever think things like that, I don't know – to play a trick on Philippe. We took a little dish and created a dish: first a layer of some biscuits, then an awful pink potted meat, which we decorated with swags of plum jam provided in a mini-tube. We brought this ceremoniously to Philippe (a little snack we had taken from behind Mrs O.'s back), and stayed to watch him eat and roll on the floor. He took a small forkful, then ate the rest calmly. He ate it all! We *told* him he had just eaten the most revolting, disgusting pap – he said it was not that bad. He offered us a cigarette and Elsa, who doesn't smoke, almost choked on it.

The Major left, but the dog Bracken kept following us on the hack. Adroitly jumping above the ferns, and staying at a good pace, very good about the horses, not teasing, nor going for their legs – a perfect gentleman.

It was Bracken who gave the alarm, on our return. He had been worried, sniffing, stopping. He started running towards the farm as we were still at a good distance. I noticed a smell of smoke, and pulled my jersey's collar up to my nose. Oh my goodness, there was smoke coming from the haystack, and flickers of flame coming from parts of the muck heap. In the yard, Tim, mounted on the Major's mare, was leading away two horses by the bridle, trotting fast. There was some commotion, very organized, English-style, with a chain of villagers throwing pails of water on the hay, and a fire engine dousing the pile. Our horses were very nervous and were backing down, turning away. 'Eugenia, take the others down the lane, far away, and ask Mrs Hollins for the use of her paddock.' We trotted away from the fun and in due course our horses, unsaddled, were munching away at Mrs Hollins' grass. I thought I heard a rattling noise on the path to Munchards and stood up on the paddock's railing. There was Beckwith of the Funerals pushing one of the large wheelbarrows, piled high with things.

I started running. I walked. 'Oh hello, sir, the fire is almost finished, I think,' and looked at the wheelbarrow: it was covered in a carpet. 'Oh, I do think it's *much* too dangerous to leave valuable artefacts there, smoke, you know ... It was a *dreadful* scene.' I kept walking, and held out a hand to keep the pile from collapsing. 'I believe you are a collector,' I said prudently. He laughed. 'You could say that ... I simply take an interest ... in certain historical aspects....' He had a stammer that made words – the ones which did not want to get out, almost explode in your face. I did not need to ask: 'And you are taking this ... to a friend's house perhaps?' 'My aunt – she lives by the vicarage. I hope she will not be too upset, I could not pack the *gullands* properly, you see, she – she is quite a *curator*.' Had he said garlands? Garnians? In English, I become so deaf. There we were at the gate I knew well, and it looked like I was part of the visit now. I gave my ponytail a tug and straightened the velvet bow.

We unloaded the cardboard boxes, and odds and ends wrapped in bits of cloth, even a burgundy smoking jacket hugging some stones, and a couple of hatboxes. A housekeeper gave the whole sad pile a few symbolic strokes with a duster and went. A ginger cat came sniffing. Without removing his cap, Beckwith walked straight into a sitting room, and said, 'Aunt Clara, there has been quite a commotion at the farm, Miss Ceccomori here has helped me with the *rescue*,' and there was the aunt, an ancient lady with very young eyes and the frame of a young sailor boy, half swallowed by a an armchair.

'Well, Beckie, I daresay you'll be wanting tea, do sit down and you can tell me all.'

And that, of course, changed everything. There were some very good cookies, which the aunt, Clara, said were cardamom shortbreads and shenkélé. 'Clara has lived in Turkey, in Egypt, in Morocco and Spain,' said Beckwith. 'My sister Emma was an oceanographer, and I spent many happy years with her, abroad. I helped her with her notes, and I would indulge my own interests – tribal funerary customs.' We went to the study, where on a sort of operating table with overhead lights the aunt bent over bits and pieces of ruffles of paper that Beckwith set down before her. She would say, 'Ah,' and 'Yes, I see,' and turn them about with pointy little instruments.

'Eugenia, these are fragments of maiden's garlands,' he said with emotion. 'They were made to accompany the coffin of a maiden who died, sometimes she would have been engaged to be married. It's a ... *mostly* English tradition dating back to the seventeenth century, garlands and wreaths always having been associated with the celebration of young girls, and then ... ah, a more durable remembrance, the mortuary garland. There is a reference in Hamlet ... ah, a variation in the old quarto, "Allow'd her virgin crantz", that is, garlands in German ... he's referring to Ophelia, suspected of having taken her own life. Just a fascinating field. Aunt Clara has moved heaven and earth to alert the churches and museums to the neglect the garlands had fallen in all over England.'

'I will show you some of our best specimens,' said the aunt. She opened one of the little caskets. It was lined in yellow sateen, and fitted with a sort of knob, from which hung a paper bonnet, stitched with colourful cloth and paper decorations, not unlike my mother's most flowery bathing caps – the dernier cri in Capri. 'You see, the colours are faded. But they used to be rather bright. Look here, and here – this celadon green, isn't it extraordinary?' It was a small piece of paper, but so vivid. I had never heard of such a thing. So bizarre that it became fascinating.

'The paper crown or garland would be placed, initially, on the coffin; then, it would be hung on the church door for three weeks. You can imagine how sad for the fiancé. It was a sort of very terrible last adornment and memento mori. Her last vanity, you could say. Of course, people had a very different attitude to death then.'

'One of the churches where we made our best finds, isn't it, Aunt Clara, is called St. Brigit, a Catholic church by the way' (he bowed to me). 'It is extremely interesting that the church itself has carved stone permanent decorations, above the main entrance, of bones and skulls and smiling sniggering skeletons. So one must have inspired the other ...'

'You wouldn't believe how obtuse people are. In the village of St. Mary in the East Hallen, in Derbyshire – just two years ago, isn't it? As a new minister was expected, some committee decided on a huge clean-up of the church, and an army of well-intentioned parishioners zealously hunting down all dust-catchers, and the garlands, would you believe it, the most exquisite, were thrown in the dustbin like vulgar crumpled newspapers. We were alerted by the *greatest* of chances.'

We walked back to the farm.

'In some rare cases we have the name of the young girl, and the dates, inscribed on the inside or on a little scroll. To think that such fragile messages, have endured, hung from the rafters of the church for centuries, sometimes with a few naïve verses ... You know what the Queen says to Ophelia, now dead' – thankfully, he did not wait for me to say it – ' "Sweets to the sweet, farewell ..." ' and Beckwith half-closed his eyes, carried away by divine music.

Of course I had to tell the others, and that B. had mitigating circumstances. Somehow the story lost its lustre for being told, but I got so carried away and recited some rather mistaken Ophelia verses with such flame that they relented. Vanna, who has been cultivating a British style of humour, burst out with one word she had been practising: 'PP-preposterous!'

I regret to say that Beckwith acquired another nickname.

Sand in my windpipe. Muscle going clonk below the ribcage. I woke up in the morning, almost late, lungs burning and weak legs.

Jenna was overseeing our saddling. 'My, Yougeenia, you have a touch of asthma!' She knew what it was! Asthma. It sounded rather grand. I was so happy someone had noticed. I hoped this asthma would stay in England when I returned to Rome.

We were caught in the rain and I had a great big imbroglio of cough and sneezing. Philippe passed me his sweater, blue and mauve. I had thoughts of not giving it back, as we sometimes do in Rome. But you could not do that with him.

One afternoon, we rode horses to pasture. Jenna and Major O. actually keep an eye on the tired ones, and rest periods are meted out. Poor little beasts! To carry us all day long and such perfect artichokes we can be. I suspected the need for rest is also mental, as there is a limit to how much idiocy or oddity (Philippe) a horse can endure.

These transfers had to be done without saddles (because on the way back, the van sent to pick us up had not enough room for riders and saddles). We rode cautiously on the asphalt, clippety-clop, trotting at times. English drivers do slow down when they see you, unlike Italians, a horse is not an object of stupor, does not trigger savage honking, as an accompaniment to the military band – what military band!? I hate riding bareback, spines are hard and protruding, but it's supposed to teach you a good seating. I can't imagine galloping, it's amazing the number of people who claim they used to do it when they went to their grandparents' farm in the year 1850.

We rode nonchalantly. The ponies were tired but the thought of all that nice green grass.... England has this haze, and vapour, the sun through the clouds that makes you pink but not bronzed – it was one static suspended afternoon. We left the horses in vacationland and heaped the bridles in the mini-van. Elsa, having briefly checked with us ('Let's do something!'), told Tim that we'd go home across fields. She was infernally self-assured, as if we actually had received permission for it. We started off, with Philippe and Tarek, in our riding breeches sticky with horse sweat and hair, rather stiff, and we felt quite adventurous for not following the program. We calculated we might perhaps arrive late for dinner – 'Hardly a tragedy', said Philippe. You should see the victuals we keep in our suitcases, Rolos, Milky Ways and chocolate digestives.

We came up to a fantastic alley, with trees of legend, and although I was nervous about trespassing, I did want to walk there and look – Elsa, Tarek and Philippe, unconcerned, joked about being invited for dinner, and to the county ball. I rehearsed what I would say, 'lost our way', as Elsa would naturally be our spokesman if we got caught.

We walked under the canopy. Feeling we might get too close to the main house, we walked sideways, cutting through the woods, as from the folds of a theatre curtain, left stage, to the stage. We came to the most colossal park, a very long, but also emphatically broad esplanade, leading up, in the distance, to a façade of the main building. Or you could say that from the main entrance, very far away, a bolt of green grass had been thrown towards where we stood, and beyond, and it had unfolded in long sinuous ripples. This was done with magnificence, in the sense of large, beautiful, and generous. A statue stood roughly in the centre of the width, and in the first third of the length of this space, to give a sense of the distance, if possible. It was the figure of a woman in flight, intent, not frightened. It all said: we have preserved an immense expanse of nature for the use of a few, it's outrageous maybe but not to us, our fortunes may come and go but this will be forever. It was very beautiful.

We were like ants in the middle of this green, rather like worms, if you consider our status as non-guests, smelly gypsies – only redeemed by our horsy clothes and our foreignness.

'Yeah, they will serve us tea.'

'They will invite us for dinner, there will be evening clothes laid on our beds.'

'And you mustn't complain about the size of the bed, Philippe, it would be an insult to the noble house of the Untiltea-Pinkinson-

Baldertons and you will have a duel on your hands.'

'And when *you* return to your room, careful you don't get into the wrong one, the Lost Pale Damsel of the year 1234 will keep you eternally.'

Philippe was funny. He knew a poem about King Arthur, and a magic sword rising from a lake. I felt my inferiority because I speak much better English than him and I only know 'To be or not to be'. One always feels inferior. To Italians who know huge pieces of Dante, and Ariosto, also to the lycée types who study more than us, I always suspected. Is it possible I am *always* inferior? How can I appear as I am, that is, once in a while, on top of things, even, superior? Some day, I will rip myself out of this amoebic state.

So we sat down on the warm dampish grass, and kept conversing, hungry, stealing the park, the view, the now yellow late afternoon haze, pretending it was ours, really enjoying ourselves.

When we got up, stiff all over, Philippe started a sort of clumsy canter. That's how we left, stage right, cantering, pretending we were holding reins very high, toddling like kings on wooden horses, like idiots.

Asthma is when everything that worries you surfaces, although you should try for quiet things, like the time I was smallish and made myself think of green pastures with colts, and I had a wonderful dream just like that. You try to breathe, you try to sleep because you are exhausted and if you sleep it means you have no asthma; and sometimes you fall into a horrid half-sleep where everything is obsessive, the homework you did not do did not do did not do; a sin, a fault, a gaffe, will drone on and on, like the wheezing that can't be relieved.

Before we left, two weeks ago, I was looking for a scarf in my mother's closet, but they had changed place. So I looked everywhere, and there was an odd bag at the bottom of a drawer, where she keeps her facial massage kits. In the bag, the watch I couldn't find! *My lost silver coins*, a medal, Piero's chronometer, a pair of gold cufflinks, five coffee- and eight teaspoons, the diamond earrings that we all thought had been stolen ... I was so shocked I sat on the floor. All those things we have been missing ... strangely bundled up in this plastic bag. Is something awful coming and she is preparing? Like a war? Why? What is going on?

Daddy had instructed me to contact John and Sybil Devine, a phone call at least, they might invite me over. Always this thing of knowing more and more people. I asked permission to make a long-distance phone call, and within hearing distance of Mrs O., who was neurotic about the expense, called Sybil Devine.

She was an automatic inviter.

'You simply must come over this weekend, and bring your riding gear. We are going to have a point-to-point, fundraising for the hunt, and Golly is organizing a little historical show, do come, it's going to be great fun,' and she explained the trains. I really did not have a chance to say I was with Elsa and Vanna and all the rest. To avoid distressing Mrs Olmstead any further, I walked to the village to send a telegram. 'Invited Devine weekend confirm permission.' Daddy telegraphed back: 'English telephones disastrous as always enjoy yourself,' which I read in an edited version to Mrs O.

So I left for my grand weekend at Larendon Hall, having mumbled to the others about someone Daddy wanted me to meet. I had promised Beckwith to help him making notes but – they said nothing, luckily.

It was a day of scorching sun and clouds. John Devine walked down the steps of the house wearing boots and an open-necked shirt which conveyed both 'county' and frequenting 'the Mediterranean'. Two servants followed and got hold of my bags. 'John' (because they want to be young, and they are in a position to dictate) had florid terracotta cheeks and the air of being spoiled – but who spoils you when you are my parents' age, master of a castle (practically), miles of countryside and cheque book? Liking to be spoiled then. And here was Sybil, graceful movements, flowery muslin and ribbons in her straw hat, and finely cut brown eyes – I remembered those, again eyes that do not transmit – only promise to.

'We are preparing for Sunday night's rehearsal, the second dedication, there is so much to do, Golly is driving us all to distraction – he is a veritable tyrant, and then of course the point-to-point tomorrow, you will enjoy that.'

She said John, dear, would show me around, and wasn't it
wonderful to have me. I cut down on the thank-yous. It was not
the place for ordinary things.

I am so used to not understanding things right away –
doubtless because I never do my homework. What did she say? –
Secondation? Dedication?

Larendon Hall had an asymmetrical face. A powerful boxer
with a bruised eyebrow and a moue. A large self-assured toad,
famous for its toad beauty among toads. The mighty square tower
on the right had certainly rained arrows and boiling oil on its foes,
and stood the test of time and God knows what wicked clever
enemies – and what a lot of work it must have been to ram-head it.
Historical battles had raged, but it was now a pleasant summer
afternoon of 1970, when hot pants and purple miniskirts were
strolling on Carnaby Street. I was wearing a Liberty shirt in pink
flowers, and orange jeans, walking the orderly, floribund grounds
and exchanging pleasantries with the host.

Elizabethan, Georgian? Tudor? I trotted alongside John
Devine, whose suntan was overheating, keeping a pious veil on the
depth of my ignorance about the kings, the queens, the periods and
the botany. Oh, they were more or less familiar, and I did have my
little gallery of portraits, it's just I did not put them in the right
order. My host, in the detached tone of heavyweight name-
droppers, discoursed of Capability Brown, Inigo Jones and
Palladio.

If I just turned John's travelogue down, and merely *looked*, I
would have been exhilarated. But how sophisticated was I? Should
I exclaim Wonderful! or murmur, Very nice? John's breeches had a
little rip, Piero and Guillaume would find unique ways to exploit
that. We walked on delicious caramel-coloured gravel. Near the
house, the grounds were tailored with great precision, then gave
way to a park, the park had a pond, a little of this, a little of that. I
glared in spirit at the sombre idiot who wrote my first book of
history. It said that there were two *opposed* types of gardens, *à la
française et à l'anglaise* – French meant geometric, and English,
inspired by nature. They were antithetic. Each, a national
expression necessitating opposition. Not true. In this garden,
designed by someone, built by someone else, with help from a third

character, and subsequent later additions, Symmetry and Nature had come to a happy marriage, both breathing the warm afternoon air. We were walking through the geometry of well-behaved low-growing red rosebushes hedged into boxwood frames, and, in controlled, pleasant asymmetry, clouds of flowers, lilac, cream and yellow here. Further, lawns sloped gently for trees that seemed to have chosen the perfect spot by absolute luck. On the west side of the Hall, lush topiary yews – Vanna would love those – benches and little huts.

The minuetting rose garden gave you a view of the south aspect of the Hall, the private, softer side, with large French windows and a marvellous terrace basking in the four o'clock sun.

'This is the realm of Georgina. She keeps the garden staff like a regiment, they would do anything for her. Constantly winning agricultural prizes. Oh, hullo George, this is Eugenia Ceccomori, my friend Enrico's daughter.'

'Very Japanese, those –'

'*Cimicifuga racemosa*, and a frightful nuisance they've been to establish.'

We were, I was informed, in the midst of *Belamcanda chinensis*, *Baptisia australis*, *Begonia grandis*, and *Kniphofia*. Most, it seemed, were moody stars who did not always like their hotel room. Georgina was their manager, nurturing and coaxing with special loam, chalk, sand and bone meal – something like crushed bones from canard à la presse I wondered?

'I know that one ... violacciocca? Matthiole?'

Georgina's turquoise eyes sparkled under her canvas cloche painted with blue poppies. She answered with benevolence, 'Polianthes, actually.' Perhaps I had not been very far off.

We reached the shore of a smallish artificial lake, with a similarly artificial island, decorated with what looked like the exact copy of the temple of Vesta. Lonely, excluded from the company of other ruins and the familiar noises of Rome's traffic jungle, the temple felt deliberate and cold, the caprice of someone who had stopped caring a long time ago.

'You get to the Temple of Fortune from behind, there is a bridge actually' (I squinted, indignant at my eyesight deceiving me) 'or by punt. There' – he pointed to an arch under which water cascaded gently, 'there used to be the statue of a naked woman, but some prudish Victorian had it taken down – might have put it in his secret romping room, ha ha. Oh here come some of our valorous – Michael, my stepson, Golly, you know Golly, and Selenia.' A flat-bottomed boat was approaching, and the only thing I could see – and with difficulty avoided looking at, was the possessor of a pink shirt, with the eyes and the cheekbones of a Saxon warrior. My idea of a Saxon warrior, if you like. I also took a look at the girl, blond and composed, an unknown entity. Golly, whom it would have been offensive *not* to have met before, as I understood it, was a gentleman of perhaps sixty, hair combed back, crumpled white trousers and a gold signet-ring that drew the eye to spatulate fingers – although, after all, those were not his fault. He put his arm around my shoulders.

'Eugenia, this is Golly of course, and Selenia Sutherland, and Michael.'

'I adore Italy. I spend all the time I can on the Costa Smeralda,' and I expected he was going to go on to the Aga Khan. 'I say, John, old man, we are going to need *masses* of greenery, if we want to pull this off ...'

'Porter shall see to it, Golly, I'll tell him. Michael, would you show Eugenia the horses? And tea's on the terrace.'

'So you've heard all about the dedication?'

'The dedication of the temple.'

'It's supposed to be the great event of the summer, mid-August, it is driving everyone to distraction. There is a director – Amalia, a relative of my mother's, and Golly is doing the historical accuracy thing, and they argue night and day. Selenia you just saw is Amalia's daughter.'

We were walking to the stables, he with the imperceptibly dragging step of a son who's been told to show the visitor around. I know the feeling.

There had been, he said, a Viscount DeVere, who, returning from his Grand Tour with a mass of antiquities and an Italian architect, had started a series of modifications to the ancestral home, including the southern wing, an atrium to replace the old hall and the building of the Temple of Fortune. This was the year 1770. Golly, who was a sort of permanent guest, while rummaging in the library, had found accounts of the original dedication and had put it into John's head that it would be just the thing to do to reproduce it.

'So the temple has been scrubbed, and a script drafted, with side dishes of chanting and invocations – not to mention props, a litter, goatskins, costumes …'

It dawned on me that John was not a DeVere, and not a nobleman, for that matter, and what was Michael? And Golly?

'Sir Gandolphin Hornwill, Marquess of Twinninghurst. Came into it after his brother. More or less wiped out by the death duties. The National Trust took over the ancestral seat as only they know how. Seeks refuge among his adoring friends etcetera, all over England, France, Italy and under the Caribbean sun.' I wondered how wiped out. No money to go visit friends abroad? No money for cigarettes and food? Very poor? Just a basic flat and cartloads of antiques and old books, and a bohemian life?

'I have a good mind to be away sailing in the Pacific when this whole madness actually happens,' said Michael.

I stole little glances at him. Corner of the eyes. Hands. Looking for signs – love for Selenia? But you never can tell with Englishmen. At first sight, I had been sandbagged. Bowled over – a backwards somersault and POW! written in the sky, as in Linus. Now I felt little gnawing bites. Every word he said made me blush, the ancients would have said symbolic of a fire inside. Yes, I know – ridiculous, blush and blush. As all blushers know, it cannot be stopped. But it was a very warm day – effect of the heat? (The Voice of Reason: what in the world does he have? What do you answer??? Maybe it was the pink shirt.) I looked away. I did not like the idea he was going to Tahiti.

'And here is Arabella. Out of Nutria by Engelbert. She's to be yours tomorrow. She is well-mannered, a rather small hack as you can see, perhaps a little high-strung.'

I walked around Arabella and did not say a thing, just in case. Outside my usual circle of horses, I don't know much. He must have thought I was completely stupid. Arabella was a pretty bay, almost thoroughbred, a bony head, forehead and neck irked with a tightly braided mane. She quivered a little when I came near. I too would not be in a good mood with my hair pulled like that. I was shown some of the local glories, who were munching away in their stalls and counting their blessings. We came out into the heat again.

From a pen, young beagles were yapping madly. I walked over and yes, they said, whoever I was, I was most welcome. Soon I was sitting on the ground feted to death by a gang of ferocious licking and chewing puppies. Four of the little things thought Eugenia a good address for a spot of siesta and conquered comfortable positions. I relaxed. Stepsons may not be captivated, but those adorable little beagles knew a simpatica, delightful girl when they saw one. And that was not insignificant.

The dinner table was enormous. There were no flowers but terrific buissons of candelabra flooded the crystal and china with light. Our group of twelve or so loosely filled about a third of the table. Conversation could only be with the left- and right-neighbour. Phenomenal hearing required to catch the rest. I strained to understand the sequence of events.

'The point-to-point meet is here at the Hall.'

'Keep the huntsmen and horses' weight down during the summer.'

'Foxes must be given a chance.'

'In order to be hunted at a later date.'

'Pave the way for an actual hunt meet, who knows.'

'Michael has been working with Captain Kendall to create a nice course, you will see, it would be about five-mile, Michael?'

'The Relley Marsh has merged with the Appledore Hunt last fall, and the ripples are still being felt. There are now two joint masters and John would very much like them to use the kennels – to be discussed at their next committee meeting ...'

'On Sunday, we have the first costume rehearsal of the dedication, with a small dîner champêtre on the isle for neighbours.'

Oh Social Intensity! Saint Proust! 'Tu l'as voulu, Georges Dandin.' I had wanted it, but did I want it? I barely looked at the food, and drank little sips, containing those blessed goosebumps that make me feel like a baby. The wine was poured from glittering decanters, which I always thought ridiculous, but not here. The butler, the footmen, the decanters, it was not at all ridiculous.

'I assure you, it was part of the propaganda, John, you must support me here – no, you're too young – Eugenia won't believe me, the Special Operations Executive were constantly clamouring for some printed pornography to discredit the Germans. Why, you must have heard of the – *modified* photograph of Hitler on the balcony? I remember distinctly there was much discussion about the caption.'

'... worked with Ann Bolland, the costume historian, who is making tremendous efforts to preserve a full array of eighteenth-century clothes, from the maid to the duchess ... She has written about what dress, underwear, stockings, what shoes a Jane Austen character would be wearing, how they were made, how comfortable you could expect to be as you walked ...' And the shape of their feet, how they cut your nails then. I was enthralled.

Between bites, some morsels did come through to my tastebuds: we had been served some terrific vol-au-vents with – lobster – the day had finally come! And, joy of joys, sole in a voluptuous mushroom sauce. Oh to be eating all alone, in peace, reading *The Hound of the Baskervilles.*

'The fifth viscount, Sir Francis DeVere, had a resident hermit on the grounds, not far from where the Heather House is. An underground apartment was excavated, very comfortable – my goodness, it must have been awful, and a fellow was paid to stay there, and behave like a hermit, not go out, nor cut his hair, and presumably be displayed to guests as a curiosity. Books would be sent in, and meals. He had to commit to a – residency of at least five years. And someone did manage, I believe, three years, then gave up. And that was called an ornamental hermit.'

Michael, on my left, whispered, 'Well, then Golly is our ornamental nobleman,' and we laughed, which made my heart beat.

A satiny lemony meringue ice was served, soft and crackling. I was wondering what were the chances to have some more, when Sybil stood up and left the room, followed by all the women. I thought for half a second, oh, they are going but I want to stay.

The men rose in a body and sat down again. Ah, they were being left to commune, as stated in innumerable novels, memoirs, films etc. Time-honoured, still honoured. The dining room now strange territory like men's toilets. All right, I wasn't staying.

'We'll leave the men to their port,' said Sybil.

'As long as we have our own. Let's go to the yellow drawing room, for a change,' said Amalia, 'but no talk about the Temple of Folly at least for five minutes, I beg you. Eugenia, do tell us, what do you *do* in Rome?' lighting a cigarette.

To be completely Italian, I only need to be in England.

'Well, I go to school' – I said with a grimace – 'and I ride, and I go to parties' – I added to enhance it a bit. It's hard to say what you do. 'Anyway, my parents are crazy,' I added, to make things a little more interesting. That went well with Selenia, who unexpectedly made a face at her mother's back.

She was leafing through a huge magazine. 'Oh, here is Celia, she did manage to get in. Rather frozen, don't you think? "Miss Celia Elly-Armstrong, a younger daughter of Captain Ronald Elly-Armstrong, and of the late Mrs Elly-Armstrong, is to be married to Mr Richard Armour ..."' She showed us the photograph of a good-looking blond girl in a quiet sweater, a full page, black and white, very tasteful, dreamy eyes gazing at her future – and coincidentally at a colour advertisement of Boucheron, on the left-hand side, depicting 'gold and diamond feather clip £1,850' and assorted ear-clips, some very flat wrist-watches and gold and diamond bracelets. Would noticing something vulgar make one vulgar? I did not say anything.

Georgina called me to the record player and a huge stack of records. I picked *Segovia Plays Bach*. We went out on the terrace.

'It is a very fine house.'

'It used to be my uncle Charles's. I'd come here for holidays. When John and Sybil married, he bought it from William – my nephew, he lives at Marlin House now – which is wonderful for me as I adore the gardens. He gives me a free rein – except for fritillaries, which he hates, so I plant them in hidden spots – I had black ones out in June, just stunning. John's a darling, you wouldn't think, for such a brilliant businessman. It is a blood sport, I mean, social climbing on a huge scale. Being the integral snob. Poor lamb, Sybil thought that Golly would be a mentor for him! Well *that* did not work out. Golly has rather sharp teeth.'

'But if you are married to someone like Sybil, does it not change everything?'

Georgina paused. 'It *does* give you a leg up, but for instance, it took Sybil the longest time to persuade him to give up on *buying* a title, you see? He had not quite understood that being Lord of the Manor of Ballantyne, or Lullamoor, does not get you in Debrett's. Drawbridges will go up. Even the smallest earl will smell you miles away. I don't know how you say it in Italy, "not one of us"? Then you must grovel and smile all the time for that matter, and do a lot of favours, do horsy things, and give great big parties, hoping they will come – which they usually do, if only to see whether you will pull it off.'

The others joined us on the garden chairs.

'Eugenia, do you know Contessa Mariani?' said Amalia, 'and' – a chuckle – 'the beautiful Dora? Her villa outside Carigneto. Fabulous Renaissance garden. They really like gypsy little girls …'

I wanted to set fire to her. Not that I believed her. The others were laughing and going on. I wanted only to listen to the crickets. I wanted to become a Hermit. Things that creep inside and poison. They would laugh. 'That Eugenia. Pompous, serious as a pope, not fun, not Good Company.'

I slept not so well. The pillows were dusty, I mean, dusty for people like me. I felt chalk in my mouth, throat and bronchia swollen, irritated. My belly would hit something hard, below the ribs. The lungs were inert slabs. Atrocious ideas of pink *mortadella*, the huge pink roll of ground ham with little pockets of fat. The awful smell of pulp and paper factories, in Canada. My mouth and throat invaded, swelling, nothing to breathe on.

You don't really wake up when you haven't been sleeping properly, but I suddenly stood up, dressing ultra-fast with the certainty that things were already underway outside. I rushed out of my room, and found Michael going up the stairs. He stopped and said, 'Not quite so formal, a polo shirt perhaps?' I mean, he saved my life.

A sea of horses and riders were gathering. A girl groom was

holding both Arabella and a sort of Irish steeplechaser. A footman was offering stirrup cups which I adroitly avoided. I rushed back inside to pick up hat, gloves and stick.

The course had been explained to me, it was to be a friendly type of race, with twenty-five fences. Not knowing the area, I would have to follow whoever was going at my speed. And I was nervous about the fences, since the English call fences things like picnic tables, fifteen-foot ponds and stone walls.

We were off at intervals. I started Arabella at a cautious canter. I would have liked to tell someone how wonderful it was to be there. What lovely countryside you have here. But the riders were all business and fervour, this was as close as it gets to a hunt, a treat to be savoured and no time to be lost. There were serious little girls, coriaceous middle-aged women, men and youngsters, either well-matched with their mount, or riding the first one they had managed to catch and saddle. A red-haired Woody Allen rode a farm horse that made the earth quake. There was a rather large man whose legs were too long for his grey cob. All cantered merrily. Arabella made a side-jump at a stray piece of paper and snorted, but kept going. Fair warning that she was a sensitive creature. I tried to pick out Michael's burgundy polo shirt and his Irish chestnut.

'Down a dale, up a hill, round a copse, one more hill, over pastureland.' This I remembered. Fences were on flat, John had assured me, which was good since I had no idea how to jump uphill. I started scheming ways to take shortcuts in case of need.

Fences came soon enough. There were smallish, steeple-like hedge ones. Arabella jumped lightly, better than I did. Little girls went hell-bent, ponytails flying, passing fences with concentration, as doing all operations on a page. Red-haired men were having the time of their life. Miss Gartner (whipper-in of the Joint Hunt of Relley Marsh and Appledore, John had told me) slowed down to look at a fine willow in the distance, perhaps making a note to sketch it some time.

I jumped a huge tree-trunk in a sort of coppice. More intimidating than really tall. My companions were more and more scattered, and I was not sure I was following the right ones. I heard a huge splashing, and harsh cries at my right and assumed I had just missed a water jump. Arabella pointed her ears in fear and I did not hesitate to spur her on, away, that is, from that cold, and noisy, frightful water. We were in open country now, going down, and then up again.

Now for a stone fence. It was slightly uphill. I was not sure how to take it. Arabella caracoled, when we approached. She was uncertain, I was very far from certain. I suppose I was left a little behind when Arabella sprang up, pushing well off her hocks, and my unbalance made her twist up over the fence.

I fell, that's all. Arabella just stumbled a little on landing. My hat flew and my head hit the ground, echoing like a loud bell, which I thought happened only in cartoons. 'Climb up again,' but everything went grey, which scared me. I resisted, then I thought, This is as bad as being seasick, and gave in.

'Eugenia has come to grief at the Great Oak fence.'

A kind gentleman was propping me up against the Great Oak. I was not dead. And here came Michael, who must have been patrolling the course, checking on the guests. Arabella's reins were fastened to a small branch.

'There have been all sorts of falls, you know. Miss Gartner was ducked – what a sight. She survived though. Are you all right?'

I rose slowly, a bit shaky on my legs. I did not want to jump again. 'I would try it one more time,' he said. 'Tell you what, exchange horses, I'll do it first.'

He went a little distance and turned Arabella to face the obstacle. She took five strides of canter, hoofs lightly clattering, drumming, and took the jump with ease, two sets of springs combined, with the flicker that is the sound of the decision to begin the run up, and the soft hiss of the saddle where the knees are squeezing in.

His horse had this wonderful chest, round, broad, warm, a cradle for that huge heart inside. I wanted to hug the horse, I wanted to hug Michael and roll on the incline with him, forget the jump. 'Keep with the horse, Eugenia, all the way, and your weight forward as you jump.' So I took again the Great Oak fence and would have gone on jumping fences all the way to Moscow, giddy, euphoric, shaken and light as a feather.

* * *

At the Hall, the riders walked their horses a little to let them cool down, holding a sandwich in their free hand, keeping an eye on the award-giving. Horses were given a little water, waiting with resignation for the next part in the program. The huge spread was decimated, I never got to the strawberry shortcakes. The participants left on horseback, distinctly more dissipated and loose-corseted. The horses lolled their heads and let their ears relax like a herd of tall and distinguished donkeys. My right elbow was hurting and I went to my room to have a siesta.

I was in the bathtub.

My bathroom was grandiose. There was a coiffeuse with a ton of accessories and make-up things, and an upholstered chair and matching toile de Jouy drapes. It was a *room* that happened to contain a bath. The centrepiece was a bathtub encased in Delft tiles with 'fish boats at harbour', extraordinarily deep. I was holding with my good hand one of those *Country Life* magazines. There were fantastic bits about show jumping events. I marvelled at the economy of the writer: 'Unfortunately, Miss Rachel Margison-Ronaldsway died from heart failure when negotiating the simple 12-ft water jump.' That must be the English way, I thought. I reread, and marvelled again. I read again: 'Miss Rachel Margison's Ronaldsway died from heart failure ...' A little better, but very restrained, I mean, *a horse!* It's because the water jump was simple, I thought. Otherwise, it might have been 'gallant Ronaldsway, an amazing little horse, etc.' Requiescat.

There was a rap. 'I say, Eugenia, are you in there?'

It was Michael, still in his horse things.

I sank a little deeper in the bath. A deep tub, I said, but not as deep as a lake or a pool.

'I'm not looking, all right?' He played with the stuff on the coiffeuse, picked up a lipstick. Made a few streaks on the back of his hand.

'Isn't this bath heaven? They found the tiles stacked in the stables.'

He sat on a little stool.

Could an 'impartial observer' hidden for instance behind the oval mirror on a stand (psyché in French) think: look at that terrible girl making advances? No, I was not.

'You all right? Any headache?'

'I am fine, I think. The elbow is getting green and blue.' I showed.

'That was a good speech Major Reeds made. I think they all enjoyed the day.'

I wish I knew how to make advances! Oh to be a proper – gourgandine. Femme fatale. To be forward. To have paid attention to the wiles of Mae West perhaps, of the feathery, the light, the fluffy ones. Those with marabou powder puffs on their slippers.

Because I would have liked to kiss him. Just get out of the water a little, rather like a siren, and kiss him, and he would kiss me. And I would get back in the water. And then we'd see.

I turned the hot water knob with my right foot, fortunately painted in Everglades Sunset.

'Eugenia, no monkey business!'

He got up and went further, to the window.

I was letting my hair get wet, water inside my ears. 'I am very serious,' I said, but what did I mean? It was like talking under water. I was feeling a perfect Madame de Pompadour.

'I am in a terrible jam. Will you listen? I have been having an affair with Amalia, you see.'

'Your aunt.'

'My mother's cousin. My mother would not be very happy. But it's not that. What's happening – Selenia and I, we have this thing – and Amalia will find out. And Selenia does not know, you see.'

Window shutters slammed by wind before a storm. Stabbed. Marat. I was hurting fiercely. I did not mind that those two would suffer too. Greek tragedy, I thought. Wonderful on the page. I always thought they make us read them to fortify us. Amalia would know all about it, she is in the theatre. Ay-ay-ay. I thought that if you were beautiful like Michael, and worldly and all that, *if* you did crazy things, you *adored* doing that. If you went to a forbidden rendezvous, you thrived on it. I mean, he could make *anyone* fall in love – fall for him. He could jump fences, feel no fear. Instead, a *panier de crabes*, a basket of crabs, people who will soon hate each other. It was a garble of wrong everything. What would the hero do, kill himself, kill, or go to war – there needed to be blood. Michael?

'I don't know what to do. Selenia wants to join me in Australia, if I go, I told you – but my stepfather is not likely to fork out any money, nor will her father, for that matter.'

Her father would not. What about Michael's father – not John? Where was he? What was he thinking? Where was everybody? From coup de foudre to being struck by real lightning, the one that explodes and blackens. They were not nice here, they were not – clean. The water was getting cold. Nonetheless I felt sad for him.

'You must tell Amalia – you must. Then you leave a letter for Selenia. But you do it cleverly,' I hastened to add, 'more or less at the same time. You call a friend, or someone, and say you accept that invitation, and go and spend two weeks with him. You study or you write your school, or you look for a job – maybe abroad. And then September comes, and you have to concentrate on working and you won't be thinking about all this as much.'

He was continuing.

'– she has this absurd idea I can teach horseback riding. "Mr Sands Riding Academy"! and he hid his face behind his hands, and laughed like someone who wants to cry.

I said that things would turn out all right.

He said, 'I must do some big thinking.' And went.

I slept a little. When I woke up, everything had become Real. And pathetic, even a five-year old could see that. I had hoped sleep would have put everything in the proper perspective, cleaned the slate as it sometimes does. I wondered if I could go to a sleep clinic. Santabarbara would know. Good old Santabarbara. And all the others. And the others. I called the Grange Riding School. My elbow hurt, my head. I got Vanna on the line, who said that Beckwith had taken her and Elsa to his aunt's for tea, and he was teaching her backgammon. I told her about the beagles. I rang off.

They all came to say goodbye, as they were dining at Sir Malcolm's, 'hoping to relieve the existential tedium', said Golly rolling his eyes, and I saw Michael wince. I wore a dressing-gown as a sort of invalid's outfit. A maid brought me a platter, and went off, I thought, to an evening at the disco. After eating, I felt in the mood for a cigar, if you can be in the mood for something you never did before. I assumed cigars would be found in the smoking room.

It was a splendidly cluttered kind of studio, a relief from the very studied reconstructions and redecorations elsewhere. Someone had stood firm, or maybe John had become impatient with the lengthy repairs. There were books that had escaped being bound in morocco and gold; there was a clock; two or three desks; two deep seated sofas, with armrests like walls, and a sweetish smell of old perfume, old tobacco and dust. I tried to breathe the people who had sat, and talked, but nothing came. They were gone and nobody cared.

I saw two decanters on a sideboard, forgotten.

I sneezed.

It had been at the back of my mind that my incapacity to drink was ridiculous. Those shivers, those goosebumps. I was clearly missing something. The person who is handed a cocktail is always smiling. It's elegant, it's pleasant. The colour, the texture. My mother's Negroni, the quintessence of all that is summer and Pucci and Capri. The aroma. See my father. Swallowing with visible relief. A healing seems to come from it. Surely you can acquire the taste. Practice. I winced at vague things I'd read about virginity. Selecting a glass, twisting the cap of the Scotch whisky, pouring two fingers. It is time. It might heal me, divert my asthma, turn the tide.

The first glass was hard. I *think* it was whisky. I held my breath and gurgled it down. In no time at all I was drunk. A flash of surprise that it was so effective. Yes, words did stumble and sound drunk. I fell prey to a peculiar melancholy. I cried. It kept getting worse. I started a sort of testament. I drank another one, for good measure. Crimes confessed in the shadow of the guillotine. 'Vanna, your new slippers, they were not lost, Carletto found them and chewed them up, so I hid them …' And on and on. All sorts of important thoughts swirled, and I found myself at the bottom of the vortex, not drowning yet – a strange ancestral wisdom told me I had just enough legs to stagger upstairs and through the passages, and reach my bed. I sank, drunk asleep.

Any drunkard in the world would have slept until midday. I woke up at a quarter to one in the morning, I saw with despair. I had almost killed myself with drink and I had not even got to sleep three hours. I felt unwell, I thought of Michael, and I had asthma. It had not worked. Getting drunk would not cure asthma, not cure love. It wasn't meant that I would become a horrible habitual drinker, a frightful scandal at fifteen, I would have had to live in the tack room. I would not have cirrhosis. But I would have grinding bits in my lungs. My shoulders were hurting. I wanted to be like everyone else. I had not succeeded. I was sad. The worst thing is the loneliness. Nobody really knows how bad it is because people sleep at night. I fell into a semi-sleep, exhausted, lonely, mouth and lungs irked, propped up by three pillows, sitting up like the Inca mummy in *Tintin et le Temple du Soleil*.

The next morning, the weather had held, luckily for the rehearsal of the dedication and the alfresco dinner.

I went looking at the roses, vivid and vain in the morning light. Petit Prince roses. A rose, then what.

Walking towards me, Georgina was chatting with someone who looked just like Beckwith. What was he doing there? He was looking strangely modern in some rust-coloured corduroys, and he carried a basket.

'Eugenia, you know Mr Russell, he heard about the beagles and he's just purchased a nice one.' This select beaglette already wore a shining collar and seemed earmarked to be a spoiled child. I gave her a tickle.

'I used to have one. No time like the present!' said B. 'I think Melusina is eager to settle down. I'll see you at the school, day after tomorrow, is it?' and *he gave me a great big wink*. He must have been to a James Bond movie. Beckwith's wild weekend. Preposterous! But I cannot say it like Vanna.

AT THE TEMPLE

Chatting died down among the spectators, sitting on canvas chairs by a side of the temple. Some were festooned in laurel and oak, others, more reluctant to play, wore light summer clothes. I was wearing my last clean shirt, my batik trousers and my first pair of earrings, pressed on me by Georgina.

'Ladies and gentlemen,' rang Golly's voice, 'we have tonight the privilege of rehearsing for you the New Dedication of the Temple of Fortune at Langdon Hall.'

Presently a procession came from the bridge. There were Silenus, Fauns, Satyrs, even two Bacchanals (one was Georgina, much enjoying herself). A very grand lady – ('I'll be – Violet, you naughty girl!' exclaimed sotto voce my neighbour) was being carried on a litter. A goat was being dragged on a leash. A Pan played a fife, rather nicely. John was recognizable as a Satyr, and there was Selenia, marmoreal as a High Priestess, holding a torch and chanting invocations. Lesser characters followed, draped in white and red, wreathed in ivy, some masked, some carrying baskets or skins. I was beginning to enjoy myself. The chanting sounded like 'O Fortune, O Hera, always remain Formentera,' but of course it was Latin in English and I did not understand.

Golly, resplendent in a toga, read aloud, '… Ye Priests and Priestesses of Fortune, call the benign attention of the Gods on the Temple …'

The spectators, herded by the Narrator, followed the procession inside the temple.

Narrator: 'Commanded by Venus and Cupid, the Rosy Goddess of Universal Love is enthroned on the Celestial Bed.'

At the temple's door, the Cleopatra, made up to defy any competition, descended from her perch and majestically walked towards the middle of the temple, where a sort of triclinium had been set up. There, engulfed in gauzes and oriental pillows, the Cleopatra slithered in a snake-like way.

Narrator: 'The Goddess requests that her subjects show their obedience and pay tribute to the god Bacchus.'

A sort of dance of the grape harvest was performed by what we were informed were Bacchanals, Sylphs, Dryads and Naiads.

Finally the Goddess stood up and clapped her hands. 'The Goddess presides over the Feast of Very Fat Things.'

Preceded by two torch-bearers, a group of lesser supernumeraries appeared carrying a large board. In a few minutes, to the sounds of tambourines and fifes, a meal of the medieval-Roman type was displayed, with all manner of roasts, plates of fried things and groaning baskets of fruit and sweets. The spectators and the actors were mingling, applauding, complimenting ... Sybil and John were being the amiable hosts without a minute to drink champagne in peace, wondering perhaps how long was the climb to supreme snobocracy. Outside, dusk had fallen, and torches everywhere were reflecting on the lake. The punts had been fitted with lamps. Little tables had been scattered. It was a perfect night.

For me, all the more lonely.

The goat was feeding on garlands torn from the decorations.

Philippe was punting.

'Where to, mademoiselle?'

Laughter at something Elsa was saying. We came alongside the other punts and held the boats side to side.

'How did you come?'

'Mrs Romilly mentioned the party at the temple tonight, and that nothing stopped me and friends from, ah, a little boating and enjoying the – Sight and Sound.' Beckwith was rather pleased with himself.

'We have the van, and a tent, but I drove my Mini – must return tonight,' said Jenna. 'All right, everybody, let's meet again at base camp,' and the boats scattered.

The temple seemed a warm and happy place, lights flickering and scattered surges of women's laughter. Philippe stood at the back with the punting pole, giving a small push once in a while. By the light of the lamp, he looked different. He was punting away, enjoying himself. Imagine being a carp or catfish or monster below, beatifically dozing in between eating or being eaten, and being speared! It felt good to be dry on the boat's cushions, to be taken, transported, rowed by someone. Oh the glory of being out so late, and nobody caring.

We were drifting into some reeds.

'It's funny, I have one warm foot and a cold one.'

'Let me see,' he said.

I put the cold foot above the gunwale.

'You know, it could be very bad.'

I was getting worried.

'My uncle is a specialist. I think … he'd say – cut it off!' and he burst out laughing.

I went for him as when you want to silence a sibling, meaning to push him or tickle him. I didn't know, I just moved towards him. He was holding the pole with both hands and leaned forward to put it down. But I was already grabbing him hard below the ribs and he could not do anything, except perhaps throw me overboard. But we were not fighting any more. He let go of the pole and just grabbed me who had grabbed him. And. We stood. We were in some sort of love. By degrees, we were kissing. Our hearts were galloping. There was nothing to do but be together. I had half-thoughts of currents pushing us to Spain, but we were in a pond. We were in a magic circle. Is it necessary to explain how it is to be kissed by the boy you want? You see it in comedy sketches, the Germanic-looking, myopic scientific lady-professor pointing her stick to a board giving instruction about elementary facts. It supposes an inept audience. You are not inept. You remember, you know romance and kissing. Majuscule kissing. We were just madly happy.

Beckwith had thought of bringing a radio. And a jar of Nutella. I had a basket of odd bits from the temple. Melusina was chewing Elsa's toes. Radios were sending their signals. '… and half an hour later in Newfoundland.' A lovely guitar piece – a voice, reading, 'in the heart of the heart of all my hearts …' Who? Where? Would I ever go there?

The others were scattered like old tires in a gipsy camp and just as dilapidated. Tim said he was going to sleep in the van, and there were muffled noises. Philippe had taken my hand, and we were going somewhere. He was walking, but I was the one who knew where to. Something repulsive came biting for a moment, the uninvited image of Golly. I pushed it in the pond, dark and malodorous, and kicked it away.

We were walking through the shrubbery. We walked through the French doors to the smoking room.

No more can be said. He was looking for me with his hands,

and I thought he could never find me enough. End. I liked his mouth and it was not quite enough any more, there was something more difficult to come that was important. With a sigh we went into assault. End. It had been another thing to kiss and play with our hands. End. You have seen how boxers embrace. End. To kiss was to be waltzing lovers to the end of the span of the life of the world. This was different. End. We just destroyed each other. We ground ourselves. Sanded, rough and smooth. Match striking a surface. Burning. End. It is how things go when you don't know but no one is teasing. End. Or I did not move he did not move. I did not care about being beautiful because there was no more distance, there was only skin, and you were crushed anyway. End. You stay close no more distance than your arms.

We did not sleep. We spoke about everything. We went through some famous Belgians. Hergé, Jacques Brel, Simenon – ?, and Brassens – no, I am mistaken.

Philippe: 'You know the names of Paracelsus – Theophrastus Bombastus?' Paracelsus, paranormal, it makes me nervous. 'Why, he was Belgian?' 'No no, Swiss.' Pause. We laugh.

He spoke about university, and how studying this and that was going to lead to other things. It felt as if I was gaping at everything, and he was thinking of what he would do with all the things he gaped at. A shadow of disquiet flapped by, and went away.

We had found a treasure and were swimming among the precious stones. What could ever happen?

I had drunk you up. I slept.

I woke up coughing. I tried not to. Philippe in his trousers went to look for water. He brought me a banana. We went to the terrace wrapped in a gargantuan plaid, and snuck, smuggled, snug into a garden bed, a little damp. I was better, a little. He said, 'My uncle is a specialist.' I pushed him in the ribs. 'No, no,' he said, 'seriously. He is a specialist of allergies.'

I said, Je t'aime.

He said when was I going to Bruxelles. I said when was he coming to Rome.

His birthday is September 20th. I gave him my Victorian charm. I said, Italian boys wear those, on a chain.

Acknowledgments: I want to thank John Metcalf for his generosity, his audacity, and for the pleasure of his company. I thank Christina Whyte-Earnshaw, Marie-Christine Ceruti-Cendrier, Marg Hammond, Valerio Cugia and Petra Rudolf, Mariella Pandolfi, Giuliano Vittori, Juli Aubin, Claire Aubin, Monique Charpentier, Doris Cowan, Ken Armstrong and Ewa M. Zebrowski – for a mix of memorable conversations and tangible help. My thanks go to my publishers, Tim and Elke Inkster of the Porcupine's Quill. Thank you, my dear family of families.

Samir, Sam, Isa, Tony and Sheila were so very kind.

EWA MONIKA ZEBROWSKI

Francesca Piredda grew up in Rome, of Italian and French-Canadian parents. In school, she followed both the French and the Italian curricula. At eighteen, she had her first job in film production, a career she pursued in Canada and Europe. She now works in communications, and lives in Ottawa. *Bambina* is her first novel, written in her third language.

francescapiredda.com